# About Dani Kristoff

Dani Kristoff is a Canberra-based author, who delights in reading and writing paranormal romance. She's been writing since late 2000, which means some 16 years, although she's been concentrating her efforts on science fiction, fantasy and horror. Published both traditionally and independently, she's currently undertaking a PhD in creative writing at the University of Canberra. Her research area is feminism and romance. Her partner is also a writer and they get up to geekery whenever possible.

You can connect with Dani through her Newsletter, Spellcaster!

Or visit her on her blog http://danikristoff.wordpress.com
Twitter @dani_kristoff

Other paranormal romance books by Dani Kristoff
Follow this link to Escape Publishing to choose your title from your favourite ebook store. Escape Publishing

### *Spellbound in Sydney series*
*Spiritbound – A necromancer has trouble getting a man.*
*Bespelled –A love spell gone wrong*
*Invoked-A ghost of a man will do anything to save an innocent girl*

# The Sorcerer's Spell

*The Cursed Ones Book One*

**by**

**Dani Kristoff**

# Chapter One

In his basement sanctum, Dane completed the incantation. The delicate gold bracelet focused his summoning spell, the personal jewellery vaporising in a flash of light as it was consumed. She was wily this Nira, this sorceress, but her resistance crumbled as the spell clawed at her spirit and began to drag her to his den. Her anger pushed like a bow wave before her and, as the force of it washed over him, he grinned. He could sense her now, the essence of her, as she struggled against him. There was power there and something more. It was hard to place. Yet he smiled confidently, certain of victory.

Nira had hexed him with a powerful spell, one that turned him into a werewolf at the moon's turning and he was desperate to have it removed. Each time he succumbed to it he lost a little of himself and the beast gained more control. Soon it would claim him completely—body and soul.

Nira materialised. Dane kept his face bland, kept his jaw tight; she was not what he was expecting. He thought she would be older, more experienced. Instead, she appeared younger than him.

Her green eyes were wide as she took in her surroundings then narrowed when she saw him. There was no flash of recognition. She frowned and curled her hands into fists. 'I demand you release me,' she said, voice surprisingly deep. Hidden in her words was the spell of compulsion, which Dane deflected with a lift of an eyebrow.

The strength of her magic surprised him. Where had that power come from? He had not detected her accessing it. He sharpened his perception, seeing into her. The poles of her power were not immediately apparent and he was unable to gauge her strength.

Yet his summoning still bound her. Her efforts to fight against his hold made her essence slippery and insubstantial. Impatient, Dane inserted mental claws, anchoring her tight so she could not dematerialise.

Nira eased up her struggles, although by the lift of her chin, she had not given up. The muscles of her jaw bunched and her eyes narrowed to slits as power rippled off her. 'Who are you? What do you want?' Her expression was blank, giving no sign that there was a silent, magic duel going on between them.

The sorceress circled him. Dane's gaze lingered on her long, tanned legs; her thighs teasing the edge of her short skirt. Lifting his eyes to study her, he was tempted by her tawny skin and luscious breasts. Her blonde hair was striking against her darker skin tones. Then there were those eyes, that startling green. His breath caught when their gazes locked.

Perhaps ridding himself of this terrible curse would be more pleasurable than he had first thought. He hid what he was thinking behind a frown. 'My name is Dane Archwright and you cursed me.'

There was a hitch in her stride, and she averted her face momentarily. 'I don't know what you're talking about,' she said, turning to face him. 'Release me.' The accompanying thrust against his hold was anticipated. He squeezed her essence in his mental grip.

'I've tracked the curse to you. There's no point in denying it.' His voice was rough with anger.

Unable to hold his gaze, she lowered her eyelids.

He breathed, letting some of his ire slide. 'I don't even know you. Why did you curse me?' he asked, his voice softer, better modulated, now that his anger was under control.

Her lips drew into a straight line and she did not speak. Defiance brightened her eyes.

*So*, he thought, *she will not explain*. 'Remove this curse.' His voice came out hard, almost a growl, a remnant of the beast that lurked inside.

She froze and then angled her chin to the side. 'I cannot.'

A growl left his throat, despite his restraint. 'I'll give you one last chance. Lift this damned curse.'

She laughed and turned away. 'Never.' She gave a mighty mental heave as she thrust against his spell. Dane grinned when his hold didn't budge.

'Then you will face the consequences.' Dane began the ritual of binding, sending threads of power to surround and penetrate her. Bound to him she would have no choice but to obey. When she realised what he was doing, a deep groan of despair rose up from her.

'No! You can't possibly do this.' Her mouth opened as if to scream.

He relished the taste of her fear. 'You're not meant to have such power…such knowledge,' she said through clenched teeth. Bringing her power to bear, she tried to shake him off, to push and tear into him.

'Ahh…so you underestimated me. A good thing to know. I can and will bind you to me. I will force your compliance unless you remove the curse now.'

She shook her head, frantic jerks. 'I can't release you from the curse. It would be my life if I did. That is all I can say.'

'Do you think I give a damn about your life? You would condemn me to live as an animal forever. Why?'

He waited for her to answer. Defiance locked her face and lips tight. Reluctantly, Dane spoke the final words, sending the last heavy chain of binding to wrap around her throat. He had hoped the threat would have been enough to make her lift the curse. No one went willingly into a binding.

Her eyes rounded with alarm as the spell tightened further. Power smouldered in her eyes as she probed the boundaries of his spell.

As her struggle increased he let a small smile of satisfaction creep onto his face. She was secured.

A surge of sexual desire hardened him so rapidly pain snaked down into his legs. He gasped and doubled over, eyes watering from the intensity. So that's where she hid her power— in her sexual pole. It was the first time he'd encountered such a phenomenon.

When Nira saw that her sexual lance had had the desired effect she ceased struggling, her smile exultant. 'To bind me you will have to master me sexually. I doubt you have it in you.'

'You think?' He could not hide his incredulity. He shook his head and narrowed his gaze. Two could fight at that game. 'Not a chore at all. I will dig so deeply inside of you there will be no secrets between us.'

The fact that she had so much power in her sexual pole gave him pause. He did not know what it meant. Collegiate teachings in sorcery did not encompass such things. Sorcery required the emotional, intellectual and sexual poles to be in balance. Hers were skewed to her sex.

Taking a step toward her he groaned as desire punched up into his gut. Painful, yet exhilarating. He would beat her at her own game. Her brand of power might be different but he was confident he had the means to master her.

A continuous wave of sexual desire assaulted him, clawed at him from without and within as he approached. Yet he knew it for what it was and did not let it penetrate.

This close, he had a greater sense of her power even though, physically, he was bigger and taller. He could smell her scent, taste her before he had even touched her—a gift from the beast that was now part of him.

As he towered over her, he placed his hand on her lower back and she tilted her head. With a brush of his lips against the column of her throat, sexual want flooded into him, set his blood raging through his veins. There was no way to stop the deluge. Her skin was hot, so hot. The thrill of skin-on-skin contact dominated his senses.

Her response was encouraging. Her scent reeked of desire, her pulse beating like a tattoo. He angled his body behind as she fell backwards into his embrace. Gazing up at him she opened her mouth, tempting him with her full lips. He scooped her up and carried her through the door and up the stairs. Once in his bedroom, he placed her on the bed.

With her eyes bright with power Nira lay languid and loose as he unbuttoned her blouse. She moaned as the material parted, uncovering dark-nippled breasts. While admiring her flawless skin and the smooth contours of her body he detected her attempts to unravel a thread of his magic. He reinforced the thread and gave her a mental tweak, letting her know that there were greater reserves in him. She growled in response, her eyes widening with something akin to excitement.

'There's no point in fighting it,' he whispered in her ear before biting softly at the juncture of her neck. She had challenged him to a sexual contest, and he had every intention of winning so that he could seal the spell of binding, end the curse she had placed on him and return his life to some semblance of normalcy.

A low moan escaped her. 'No, you mustn't bind me,' she whispered hoarsely, her breath teasing the skin of his chest. Her eyes rolled back and then her eyelids closed. 'Has to be a way out,' she said, groaning in frustration. Was it desire or something else that overcame her? 'Come on,' she whispered, 'where are you?' She mumbled some more. Her eyes snapped open. 'Found you,' she said under her breath.

Dane watched her as she lay apparently helpless against the sheets. Her skirt slid easily over her hips, revealing black lace panties. These he tugged lower, down over her knees and then tossed them on the floor. It was hard to control his arousal, artificially enhanced by her power. Desire was a two-edged sword if he gave into it.

He ran his hands up her thighs and over her stomach. Nira began to chant. He raised an eyebrow, wondering what the recitation could mean. Reaching in with his other sense, he detected no tampering with his bindings. Deciding to test his hold on her, he said, 'Open yourself to me.'

Her right leg shifted an inch or two, giving him access to her dark, moist centre. He slid two fingers inside her. She was wet and ready. This gave him pause. Why would she be ready for him if she was fighting his hold on her? Was it the battle itself that excited her? Or was it the thought of a sexual encounter?

He captured her lips in his, and she moaned low in her throat. Her hands caressed his chest, her nails lightly scoring his skin. Dane disengaged from the kiss to nuzzle her breasts. Nira arched her back beneath him. Dane's own binding began to draw him in.

*Ah, so this is the down side, to bind her I have given too much of myself. I am as bound as she is. If I do not control this, I will not win.*

The thought that she was faking her reaction to him made him wary, allowing him to control how far he let his own sexual power entwine with hers.

Now actively engaged in enjoying her body, the silken feel of her breasts against his hands, the tangy taste of her nipple on his tongue, he found it difficult to keep his mind on maintaining the magic of his binding spell. He paused for breath. Her eyes were bright and full with arousal. Her body undulated with each caress, her breasts seeking more stimulation. Dane's own arousal was potent. He wanted to be inside her, riding her, hearing her hoarse cries of pleasure in his ears.

Realising he'd been distracted he snapped all his power tight, making sure that her will and her essence were tied down. Testing the bindings, he found them secure.

Her nails raked his back, her hips thrusting into his palms as he continued to probe her heat. His skin came alive. Drawn into her texture, the consummate pleasure of her scent surrounded him. He couldn't hold back.

Moving over her, he placed himself carefully to enter her. She met him, guiding him inside. Dane gasped at the first squeeze of her against his erection. Able to control her muscles, she had him gasping. He tried to win back control over this sexual encounter. Gripping her hips, he ground himself inside her sex, groaning with the pure pleasure of her. The abandoned way she opened herself to him was exciting. A glimpse of her face, her blissful expression, drew him deeper.

He was in her. Her scent surrounded him. He was there, moving with her. The suspicion that she was exerting her power over him, despite his best efforts to block her, allowed him to draw back from the heady arousal he'd almost surrendered to. He shook his head, fighting against the tendrils of the binding that were seeking to anchor in him as well as in her.

His research into binding had hinted at such traps, and he thought himself above such mere physical desires. Yet there was something inexplicable in his reaction to her. He hated and admired her. How could he feel this strong an attachment, this powerful a link? Surely there was hidden magic at work. How powerful was she? He had to win this. There was no other choice for him. He needed to be free of the curse.

The friction of their skin as he slid in and out drew him out of his mind again. It was as if all his nerve endings centred on his cock. He reached down and cupped her buttocks, lifting her to meet his eager thrusts. She was calling out now, 'Let me in. Let me in.'

He did not understand what she was saying, didn't care. He was in the moment. As he moved within her she clung to him, her lips searching for his, her tongue teasing his own. Breaking the kiss, she began to call out, to scream her pleasure. Dane took this as a signal that the binding was complete and lost himself in his ecstasy.

Then a sudden cry from her and she went limp in his arms.

'Nira?'

# Chapter Two

Annwyn Flaydin climbed from the bubble bath. The soap suds slid from her body to puddle on the cool blue floor tiles. Wiping the condensation from the mirror, she pushed her damp dark hair away from her face. Smudged pale skin and brown eyes loomed in the foggy glass. She wiped it again with her forearm. A forlorn figure gazed back at her. This was who she was—a lonely widow with the memory of her husband's hands on her skin, with his love and the joy of his protection a distant echo. Even after three years she was flailing about in life, looking for a purpose, a reason to keep on going.

Yet she kept on living. She took joy in the little things. The children in the day-care centre where she worked filled her with love. The occasional night out with her workmates lifted her spirits. Her garden, too, soothed her soul. The grief had to end soon. She'd move on with her life.

Thomas would not like the life she had led since his passing. He had wanted her to go on and live a full, rich life, marry again, have children, laugh…

After dressing in her pyjamas she wandered aimlessly through the house. A small tea light candle burned on the dining room table, sending flickering golden light around the room. The tips of her fingers brushed against the small ornaments on the display shelf. These held so many memories: of their first kiss, their wedding vows, making love on a stormy night on the carpet in front of the fire. The gentle caress of long ago-spoken words lingered in the corners of the room.

The tears began to build up and she scrubbed her eyes with the back of her hand, sniffing loudly.

'That's about enough from you,' she said to the darkness, puffing out her breath with a heave of self-disgust. 'Time for bed. No point in thinking about things you can't have or moments that will never come again.'

Snuggled in her bed with the covers tucked under her chin, her mind returned to Thomas. Bunching her fists together, she tried to stop herself going back there. Every night it was the same: she dreamed of him and was left pining for him more than the night before. It made no sense. It wasn't natural. He should have sunk into memory by now. Why did her grief still feel so fresh, her longing so potent? But as sleep took hold of her, she found herself there in his arms with his lips savouring hers as she surrendered.

It seemed to Annwyn as she tossed and turned that the dream was becoming more and more real. The texture of fantasy and patched-together moments, which had been the flavour of her previous dreams, was absent. This one was more coherent and directed. Thomas's hands were running up her thighs, cupping her buttocks, moving her sinuously up against his body. There was a scent, so male, surrounding her. She responded to it instinctively, groaning her pleasure. As her arousal grew to a peak and her breathing grew hoarse she could hear Thomas calling her, calling her name and asking to be let in. She began to respond, seeking him in her dream. 'Thomas?'

Then his presence grew, strong, spicy and overpowering. 'Annwyn?' Was that his voice? It didn't sound familiar.

She could not conjure the image of his face, though his presence was there in her mind. Why was he hiding from her? 'Thomas? Is that you? Why can't I see you?'

The voice echoed again, loudly in her mind. 'Listen, Annwyn, you need to let me in. Let me in. Then you can see me, see all of me again. Let me in. Say you will let me in.' Again his voice sounded strange to her ears. It had an urgent, pleading note that she had never heard before. Thomas had always spoken to her gently, caressingly.

His hands on her skin distracted her. He was slipping inside, hot and eager. *God*, she thought, *this is intense*. She let out a moan.

Her dreams had never felt so alive, so real. She was moving with him as he pushed inside her then eased away, only to thrust harder. She found it hard to concentrate. It had been so long since she had been intimate with anyone.

'Let you in?' she panted, feeling her body press against the mattress with the weight of her phantom lover. 'Where? Let you in where?'

His kisses were hard and urgent, kindling a fire deep within her belly. 'Let me into you. It's the only way we can be together again.'

Annwyn thought *he was already inside her. How much deeper could he go?* But he needed her, needed her to open to him on every level.

In the haze of her dream she caved in, surrendered so deeply as she reached out to him that her body shook from the force of it. 'Come to me. Come in to me.'

The face materialised as the haze of dream lifted, the smile vicious and victorious. In her confusion, Annwyn did not realise until it was too late that it was a woman's face, with piercing green eyes, alive with a power she could not fathom.

It was not Thomas at all.

Annwyn was ripped away. Her consciousness spun into darkness, all the while the man in her dream was making love to her, thrusting into her as her body responded.

Annwyn was tied to this action, linked inexorably to each thrust, each caress, each tantalising kiss. It was as if she was caught and held by a spell and there was no way she could break out of it. Her body was owned by that man, that touch. She had no will to stop him. She was being taken high in the sky where the clouds flowed and drifted, leaving her with barely a sense of the world she inhabited.

For what seemed like a long time she floated, tumbling free with no bed, no room, no house around her. Burning in her ears, stomach heaving, and skin screaming, the sensations overwhelmed her. The only constant was those large strong hands, lifting her hips, angling them for the next thrust, hot mouth on her throat, biting without wounding.

Down, down to earth Annwyn plunged. She cried out with the force of the movement, the abrupt arrival. The crease of the sheets stuck into her back. An orange-tinged hue haloed the bed and beyond light and dark waltzed in the corner of the room.

Screwing her eyes shut, she avoided looking. There was

something very wrong in what was happening to her. This was not Thomas's body on her, in her.

She jerked once, sucking in a breath. Then, opening her eyes, she screamed.

Screamed like the devil.

'What the—' said a deep voice beside her.

Annwyn heard him but kept on screaming. He disengaged from her, moved away from her yet remained on the bed. The mattress shifted beneath her as the springs adjusted to the change in weight. She screamed again.

'Stop that,' the man said, without a hint of sympathy. 'You knew the consequences of your actions. You knew where this would lead. You will lift the curse now.'

He grabbed her foot. Annwyn kicked out at him, then curled her body into a ball. Through her light blonde hair, she scanned the room. The sound of paws scratching on wood drew her attention to dogs entering from further down the hall to pace around the bed. Some of them moved to huddle together in the corner. All with yellow eyes, watching her. Maybe not dogs. They were too large for dogs.

A sob escaped her, a terrified, visceral sob. Then her eyes flicked from one shadow to another. She could not look at the man sitting next to her on the bed. Her gaze leapt to the wall-sized mirror and to the image there. On a king-size bed, with pure white sheets sagging to the ground on one side, was the man, a sheen of sweat glistening between the shoulder blades and down the vee of his spine, his chest rising and falling noticeably after his exertions. Tall, with short-cut blond hair and wide shoulders tapering to a shapely behind, he sat staring at a woman with light-brown skin.

Annwyn stared at the reflection of the woman huddled near the bed head. It was her, and it was the woman in her dream— she had the same green eyes. She saw blonde hair, generous breasts and the soft flare of hips. Her skin was tawny, not pale and wan like Annwyn's.

Annwyn sat forward and so too did the reflection. She held out a shaking hand and began trembling all over. That woman in the mirror was her. When she had let the woman in, she had taken over her body and thrust Annwyn here, into the arms of this man—a man the woman was obviously desperate to escape.

The man grabbed Annwyn's legs and pulled her toward him.

Annwyn cried out, 'No, stop!'

The man hesitated. 'What is wrong with you? Nira? You have not broken the curse. It is still there, waiting to fall one final time. Do it now. I command it.'

Annwyn sat back from him, her arms folded, trying to rub the goose flesh from her skin. 'Nira? I'm not Nira.'

The man leaned over her, supporting himself on his elbow, tracing a finger from her collar bone to her left nipple. 'You look and smell like Nira. You respond to my touch like Nira.'

'I am not Nira,' she said, slapping his hand away. 'This is not my body. I am Annwyn. I don't know what's going on or who you are or why you are touching me so…'

The man's blue eyes widened and then narrowed. 'Nira. I never took you for a fool so I don't expect to be treated like one. This is not a game we are playing here.'

'I'm not joking.' Annwyn shivered, shielding her breasts with her hands. The man's gaze travelled down her body, then his hand ran up her inner thigh, lightly touching the moistness there.

Annwyn opened her mouth to protest but found herself gasping instead. He eased two fingers inside her, and she arched her body to receive him. *What the hell? This couldn't be happening.* She could not be in this situation with some stranger probing her body intimately and her body enjoying it on some instinctive level.

The man's triumphant smile angered her. Did he think this was funny? 'See, you are Nira. No point in pretending otherwise. I have bound you successfully.'

This shouldn't be happening. She went to bed as Annwyn and now she was in someone else's body. But it was no dream. She knew enough about dreams to know that this was too potent to be anything but reality. The thought should drive her crazy, but she was calm. What was left of her was intact, even though this new body made her experience alien responses to the man's touch.

'I'm not Nira, I tell you. I don't know what's going on but for God's sake stop touching me.' She bit down on the groan threatening to spill out of her throat. Her stomach was churning with desire and fear.

The breath eased out of him as he took his hand away. His blue eyes glinted with sexual arousal. 'You respond to my touch and cannot resist me, that's how it's meant to be. There's no point in pretending otherwise. Release me from this curse, before it is too late to reverse.'

A howl filled the room. His gaze shifted to one of the beasts who neared the bed, keeping its citrine-coloured eyes focused on her. 'Later, Rolf.'

It was then Annwyn realised it was a wolf, and a rather large one at that. The animal's gaze was too knowing, too clear and it made Annwyn shudder. Wolves were not native to Australia. They were kept in zoos, not in people's houses.

The man squeezed her calf and she shifted her legs, drawing them up beneath her, hiding her body from his lingering gaze. 'I don't know anything about curses. I'm Annwyn Flaydin, a childcare teacher from Red Hill. Last night I went to bed and had a dream. A dream…' She swallowed before continuing, ashamed to admit that her nights were filled with phantom lovemaking. 'A dream about making love with my husband. A voice I thought was his asked me to let him in. I did and then I found myself here.'

His gaze bored into hers. She detected a flicker of something around her head and shoulders, like the wings of a butterfly. The gaze shifted and focused inward. Rolf moved closer and the man scratched him between the ears. Some silent communication seemed to pass between them. Once again he was staring at her, a knot of anger between his brows and drawing down the sides of his mouth.

'I don't like this game. You will make things worse for yourself and will suffer for it.'

Annwyn kept her gaze steady and didn't flinch. It was too

important. It was too unreal, and she wanted things to be familiar. She wanted her house and her things and her memories and her pale skin and dark eyes. She wanted her life back, miserable as it was. Being naked in a strange man's arms in another woman's body was not what she had bargained for.

He lunged for her, grabbing her easily around the waist and easing her under him. His lips left hot trails down her neck to her breasts. Her fists hit against his chest, once and then twice, before her body reacted to the friction of his skin against hers. It was as if her will was undone, unravelled, ready to be rewound into whatever shape he chose.

Those hands probed and the mouth nuzzled. His firm body surrounded her, overwhelming her senses. She was crying out with joy and ecstasy with no thought of being in someone else's body or in a strange man's bed. It was all for that moment and those exhilarating feelings. She responded in kind, kissing and biting wherever her mouth met his flesh. She matched his desire equally and then he stilled suddenly. Gently, he disengaged from her and left her there, hanging, frustration taking the place of arousal.

The man sat back, removing his hands from her body as he retreated. The air chilled as he withdrew his warmth. There was calculation and speculation in his face as if he was still unconvinced, even though, over and over again, he said, 'No, no…not possible, not…'

Annwyn sat up and tried to pull the sheet back onto the bed to cover herself. 'Now you choose to believe me?' she said haltingly, trying to recover her breath, her equilibrium. How dare he excite her like that, make her want him and then just stop. How could he do that? How could he have so much control?

It was not her own body yet she could sense his eyes on her breasts, her stomach and the autumn-coloured hair between her legs. The body she was in was healthy and somewhat sated. She moved slightly and grimaced. She was raw where the sex had been deep and penetrating. Now her blood was up, and she was left wanting. *No*, she thought. *I have to use my head*. She pushed the desire aside. 'Who are you anyway? Where is this place?'

The intense blue eyes returned to look at her face. The speculation was still there but there was something else; shock. 'You really don't know who I am?'

She shook her head, smiled slightly. What a situation to find yourself in—naked in another woman's body, in bed with an equally naked stranger with whom you have just had very vigorous sex.

# Chapter Three

'I am Dane Archwright. This is my place,' he said quietly, his deep voice making her shiver in delight. How was it that his voice resonated within her, caressing her in places she didn't know existed?

'Dane,' she repeated, savouring the sound of his name on those strange lips. The voice that came out of her mouth was deeper than her own. She rather liked the sound of it. Taking a moment to let her gaze linger on his thoughtful face, she considered that his name was unknown to her, just as his person was.

While he was distracted in reverie she let her eyes track the smooth skin of his torso down to where his erection still lingered. His body stiffened. He'd noticed her less than casual appraisal so she shifted her gaze to take in the room. It was large, more like a hall than a room. There were five windows, long and narrow, which revealed fields and paddocks, a farm perhaps, and what seemed to be a hallway leading to other rooms.

The wolves began to stir. Three of them began to tumble together playfully, biting and clawing at each other, but not in a serious way. *They were so big they could be men in costumes*, she thought.

Quite unexpectedly he reached out and tilted her chin to study her expression. 'You look like her, hell, you are her, what am I saying? Of course you're her. I find it hard to accept what you're saying and yet there's something not right about this…the energy is different. You're different.'

His gaze bored into hers. Again there was something light, like the brush of ethereal wings in her mind, and then the presence was gone.

She returned his regard, studying the shape of his brow and the cut of his chin. There was something in his face that warmed her. Even though her current situation was extremely unsettling she did not fear him. It was as if this body was programmed to trust this man, to respond to him, to yield to him, to want him.

'Yes,' he said. 'The eyes are different. They glitter in quite a different way. Do you see that candle over there on the sideboard?' He pointed and her gaze followed.

'Yes.' There was a thick, round candle with a pearly white sheen.

'Light it for me.' His voice was light and curled around her insides.

When his meaning sunk in she frowned, shifting her gaze to and from the candle. 'I don't have a lighter.'

He stroked her hair carefully, letting his hand rest on her back. 'You don't need a lighter. Just relax and reach out with your power. Imagine the candle aflame.' His breath caressed her skin. He touched her with gentle fingertips, placing his other hand on her solar plexus.

She sensed he was serious so she tried to do as asked. She concentrated on the candle and imagined it alight. Nothing happened, of course. She would have been surprised if it had suddenly burst into flame.

A frown drew his brows closer. 'Again,' he said.

She tried it again until the sixth time when he let out a breath. 'Nothing. There's nothing there.'

'What do you mean?' Annwyn asked, finding being close to him pleasant and comforting.

'It means that you could be telling the truth, or…'

'Or what?' She studied his face, looking for signs that he was playing with her, trying to deceive her. He was all sharp edges and forcefulness, nothing like her gentle Thomas.

'Or you are a very clever sorceress and you have found a way to thwart me.'

The harsh tone in his voice jolted her. When she looked up at the well-honed biceps and chest muscles and considered the aura of power surrounding him, she had reason to fear him, but she didn't.

'Sorceress? This Nira is a sorceress? Is that how she stole my body and put me in hers?'

Dane rubbed his chin, the blond regrowth of his beard scratching against his thumb. This sent a shiver of desire through her as she flashed back to the memory of him nuzzling her neck as he made love to Nira's body.

'It could have happened that way, but not while she was bound to me and my power. Yet you have raised the possibility that she may have slipped out of my grasp. You appear innocent, and I can detect no power in you. You could be telling the truth and that means Nira has made a fool out of me. It's a deadly game, one with terrible consequences for me if I do not find her.'

'Your power? Does that mean you are some kind of sorcerer too?' Annwyn's eyes widened. Magic, sorcery, the stuff of popular myth, not something one stumbles across every day. Not in her limited experience, at least. She knew Thomas's family dabbled in that sort of thing, but her own roots were far too conservative. What could not be explained or objectively verified did not exist—until now.

'Yes, though one bound in a curse he cannot break.'

'I don't understand. Can't you use your own power to break this curse?'

He shrugged expressively. 'I have tried. For many months now I have sought the one who had laid this curse on me. I planned well for tonight, for when this Nira would release me. I don't even know why she cursed me. Maybe there is no reason, only that she could. And now she has apparently reached out to you, drawn you into this mess and stolen your life.'

'Then you believe me?' Her lips parted in surprise.

His gaze lingered on her mouth, and warmth gathered between her thighs. *Lord*, she thought, *he can excite me with a look.*

'I consider it a possibility.' He stood up. 'First, where do you live?'

'Canberra.'

'Really? Which suburb?'

'Mawson.'

'That's close. My place is not far from there.'

'Where are we?'

'Due south near Michelago, up in the Tinderry ranges.' He held out his hand, palm up. 'Come on. We'll go to your so-called house and pick up her trail.'

Annwyn frowned, slightly angry that he didn't completely believe her, but still able to understand his mistrust. She found it hard to believe herself, and she had objective proof that a woman had stolen her body. She took his hand and slid off the bed, holding the sheet to the front of her body.

'Then she won't be in my bed asleep, waiting to give me back my body and my life?'

Dane shook his head and smiled fleetingly. 'If Nira stole your body from you without you knowing then she will not be giving it back so easily. She will be long gone. But there will be traces of her, things you will notice. Come on, I will gather up your...I mean, her clothes. Maybe you should take a shower. Come, I'll show you where it is.'

He helped her walk with the sheet trailing behind her and led her to a large bathroom, finished in black enamel and matching black tiles. The chrome of the taps gleamed in contrast to the dark gloss of the walls and the bath and shower screen. In a built-in cupboard was an array of clean towels and toiletries. After showing her these Dane went away and came back with a set of clothes. Annwyn touched them lightly, inhaled the scent of them, the scent of Nira, which was now her scent. She thought it strange to be wearing another woman's clothes, but 'wearing' another woman's body was even stranger.

Under the hot, powerful spray of water, it was an alien sensation washing a body that was not hers. It was like being caressed, but it was her own hands running along her skin, with runnels of water invigorating her as she showered. Tentatively, she touched her clitoris, curious to see what it felt like. It was so sensitive after Dane's touch that she gasped with the intensity. Straight away she was assaulted with the memory of his touch, his mouth on her neck, on her breasts. She stopped and placed her forehead against the tiles, letting the wave of passion wash over her before it receded to a dull ache. *Would she even be able to walk with this much lust in her?*

Over the spray of the shower she heard banging. Quickly, she shut off the water and the door opened. 'Are you okay?' Dane asked, his voice full of concern. 'I thought I heard you cry out.'

Annwyn swallowed her embarrassment. 'No, I'm fine. I...er...this is a bit difficult, you know, being in someone else's body. Feels...you know...strange...'

He nodded as if he didn't quite believe her. He must still consider this whole situation a trick to be listening so closely at the door. She supposed that he expected her to make a break for it.

His gaze lingered on her body. A wave of heat flowed from her head to her toes. 'It will be dawn soon. We can investigate your story straightaway.'

Annwyn grabbed a towel, finding it quite odd to be conversing with this man while naked and dripping wet. Part of her wanted him to grab her and start all over again. Distracting as that thought was, she kept a wary eye on him.

Dane was very businesslike and this annoyed Annwyn, especially considering the man was naked and still aroused. Her hormones raced around her system, making it hard to think or breathe. She nodded at the door. 'Do you mind? I would like to get dressed.'

He blinked once, then grinned. 'I'll be waiting.' He drew the door closed behind him.

Annwyn found that the prospect of going home inspired her to dry off quickly and hurry in dressing. She took a moment for a look at her reflection, but found it so disconcerting she turned away and whipped open the door.

There, surrounded by wolves, was Dane, naked and powerful, just standing there. Her body reacted, sending her skin tingling. He was a beautiful man and so well made. He grinned when she stood there gaping and then stepped past her. 'Rolf, keep an eye on her.' Then the door shut behind him and, not long after, she heard the water running.

The wolves encircled her. Rolf's citrine-coloured eyes continued to regard her. He nuzzled close to her leg, getting a good whiff of her. She wanted to push his muzzle away but dared not to in case the creature bit her hand. She had a healthy respect for the beast, for all of them as they circled her. Dane seemed to be taking his time in the bathroom so Annwyn sidled toward the bed and sat on the edge. She took in the room and the scent of sex that lingered in the air and inhaled deeply.

'Well, doggy,' she said to Rolf. 'This is a funny situation to be in, isn't it? Bet you never thought you'd wake up in a different body like I have?'

Rolf howled at her. Startled, she leaned back. Rolf jumped up, placing his forepaws on either side of her and leaned into her face. Again, there was a strange sense of 'knowing' coming from the beast.

'Rolf!' It was Dane. He stood there in the centre of the room, dark blue shirt clinging tightly to his form, denim jeans hugging his thighs, making him look even more buff than he did naked. Rolf backed down. Dane strode forward and crinkled Rolf's brow with a scratch between the ears.

'Sorry about that. Rolf can be zealous at times.'

She took his proffered hand. 'Really? Just zealous?' Annwyn sensed there had been more to it than that. Dominance and warning came to mind.

# Chapter Four

The exterior of the house was as she had left it. With the grey garage door shut, she didn't know if her car was still in there. The lilac tree hung mauve flowers over the porch and leaf litter fluttered on the morning breeze. Dane had to duck his head under a branch to enter the house. He had brought Rolf and signalled him to stay outside. Rolf trod off toward the back of the house.

With a quick look at Dane's midnight-coloured Lexus in the driveway, Annwyn turned to the front door, noticing that it was slightly ajar. Annwyn had left it bolted from the inside. This meant that either she had been burgled or someone had left the house in a hurry. She checked the lock as they stepped over the threshold and there was no sign of forced entry.

It was strange entering her home in another woman's body. She caught sight of her reflection in the hall mirror and her heart skipped a beat. She was out of place in her own home. It was like a stranger's house. She wanted to feel at home, feel the memories of her life there, but they seemed like stale echoes, fleeting and untraceable.

Dane's presence, too, dominated the surroundings, making her home seem even more alien. Her gaze moved away from him, and she hoped she could pretend he wasn't there. Yet, when they accidentally touched, her heart juddered. There was no ignoring him.

She ran her fingers along the back of the leather couch, liking the cool touch of it. On the dining room table was a half-full cup of cold coffee. Dane went over to it and sniffed it.

'Traces of magic,' he said, putting the cup back on the table.

'Did she use magic to make the coffee?'

He shook his head. 'No, to heat it. Check your bedroom. Look for missing items, clothing, etcetera.'

Annwyn nodded and went into her room. The bed covers were thrown off and the pillow still showed the indent from her head. She saw her underwear littering the hall to the ensuite bathroom. She followed the trail, careful not to touch the clothing in case Dane wanted to check it for signs of magic.

In the ensuite the mirror was still fogged. Nira had not used the exhaust fan. *Lazy cow*, Annwyn thought to herself as she wiped the mirror with a tissue. That woman's face stared out at her, a frown creasing the forehead. Turning away from her reflection, Annwyn found the scene quite disturbing—a damp towel on the floor, water everywhere, and drawers open with her personal items strewn about. That woman had been there invading her space, touching her things, touching her body in the same way that Annwyn did. She trembled.

Dane called out. 'In here,' she responded. About to leave the small room she paused when she saw the hair on the floor. Stepping closer and kneeling down, she saw hanks of dark hair in the bin, with some lying on the tiles beside it. Then she caught sight of her dressmaking scissors. Nira must have ransacked the spare room to find those.

'What is it?' Dane asked from close behind her. She straightened and was suddenly overly warm. Dane's body heat radiated around her and his light scent floated around her head, making her lose focus.

She swallowed once. 'She has cut off my hair.'

His gaze narrowed. 'I'm sorry. Does it mean a lot to you? It will grow back.'

The room started spinning and her vision went dark. Next thing, with her eyes fluttering open to adjust to the light, she lay on her own bed. Dane's body weighed down the edge of the mattress. He was stroking her forehead, looking at her with a searching expression. 'Are you feeling better now?'

Annwyn nodded. 'What happened?'

'You blacked out for a minute or two. Must have been the heat.'

Her gaze took in the room. 'I'm not sure what it was. It feels so strange to be home. It's like I'm a stranger in my own home as well as in this body. That bitch has violated me in every possible way. I can't really express it.' Annwyn was surprised at the vehemence in her voice. *Was this really her talking like that?*

Dane smiled slightly and nodded. 'You seem to be doing a good job of expressing yourself. Wait here a minute. I have to gather up the hair and then, when you're ready, we need to check the rest of the house to see what else she has taken.'

Rubbing her forehead and waiting for the dizziness to clear, she asked, 'What does it matter? It's only things.'

Dane spoke over his shoulder. 'You can vest a lot of yourself in things. That is how I managed to summon Nira to me. Rolf found something personal of hers, a bracelet, something that she was fond of and had a connection to. However, once she discovered we were on to her, she decamped never to return and left little trace for us to follow. I used the bracelet to summon her.'

'Can you use it again?'

Dane shook his head. 'The bracelet was consumed by the spell. It was against her will so it took more power. Now she is in your body it will be harder to work through. To tell the truth, I'm not sure how I could summon her now that she's changed places with you. It blurs her "signature", for want of a better word.'

'So she has escaped?'

Dane stroked her forehead. Annwyn felt that he wasn't really aware he was doing so.

'I'd wager she has taken something of yours, something that has high emotional value. That way she can stay connected to you, know what you are thinking and what I am doing.'

'And the hair? Why did she cut it?'

'Perhaps she wanted to disguise herself. That reminds me; we must get a photo of you so I can get the word out. However, leaving the hair behind may have been a mistake.'

'Mistake? What do you mean?'

'It is a physical connection to your body and it could come in useful.'

'To summon her?'

Dane stroked his chin and stared into the middle distance. 'Not to summon her, but tracking could be possible.'

Annwyn thought about this. It was her hair, part of her body and it shared the same genetic material. Was this a strong enough link? She knew too little of magic, too little of the occult to fully understand. Thankfully, Dane had a good knowledge of his sorcerer's world and could handle himself. Then she remembered the curse that hung over his head and frowned. She didn't like the thought of him being hurt, being damaged in some way. She found she liked him as he was.

While Dane was in the ensuite gathering up the discarded hanks of hair Annwyn lay on the bed, trying to put some order to her thoughts. The wardrobe was open so she gathered that some of her clothes would be gone. She supposed that she should get up to see which clothes were missing in case it could help them track Nira down. She doubted there was a strong enough emotional connection to her clothes to provide some kind of magical link, though.

Sitting up, she looked about the room that was once so familiar, trying to rationalise how weird it was to be in her own bed but in another woman's body. Would Nira's experience be the same? Was she groping around uncoordinated and gauche, or was she well prepared and well adjusted to stealing bodies and all that it entailed?

Tears threatened when Dane called from the ensuite to remind her to start looking for missing items and a photo. There were many things in her home that had sentimental value, little things that held memories of Thomas, of their life together, before he became ill and died. Hadn't she been wrapped in memories before this whole episode began? With a heavy heart she swung her legs over the side of the bed to begin her search.

The lounge and dining room appeared to be in order. She found a photo of herself and left it on the dining room table for Dane. Her ornaments were where she left them. The stuffed rabbit Thomas had won at the local fete was in the corner gathering dust. The old dart board that Thomas used to practise on was still in the kitchen. On top of the fridge was his favourite mug. She remembered the dressmaking shears that Nira used to cut her hair. They had been in the spare room where she had all kinds of things packed away.

On the threshold of the spare room, she could see that Nira had been in a hurry. Carefully packed containers were lying on their sides, their contents spilled out on the carpet like tempest-tossed foam. At first, Annwyn found it hard to see what in particular had been disturbed.

There were swathes of material, hoarded for quilt-making, family photos, old letters, all strewn in the corner. There was sheet music, journals full of her life from before her marriage.

'God, no!' she said and fell to her knees. There was one very special journal in which she had chronicled her romance with Thomas, their first date, their first kiss, the time when she lost her virginity to him. She was eighteen and so very young, now that she thought about it. Yet it was a special journal for in it were Thomas's views, too. He had commented on her thoughts, her feelings of love, and had added his own. Sharing it with him had been the most intimate thing she'd done. She remembered the look in his eyes when she'd been brave enough to show it. The gut churning had ceased, the moment he said he remembered this moment or that and asked if he could add his perspective. It was her most treasured possession and something she never wanted anyone else to see.

The chocolate tin where she had tucked away the journal was gone. Annwyn could hardly speak. It was her heart. Her life was etched in there. Sobs rose in her throat but she stifled them. Still her eyes burned with unshed tears.

Dane's heavy step sounded behind her. He paused for a moment. 'Something is missing? Tell me.'

Still kneeling, Annwyn kept very still, her face averted. She couldn't answer. Kneeling beside her, he scanned the room. He touched her shoulder gently. That soft touch undid her, and she fell onto his shoulder, sobbing. Patiently, Dane waited for her to talk, stroking her along her back and running his fingers through her hair.

When she calmed she managed to speak through loud

intakes of breath. 'Mmm…my journal.'

'I take it this was a special book,' he said quietly in her ear.

'Yes. It had a lot of intimate moments recorded in there. My husband's, too.'

'You're married?'

'I was.'

She lifted her face away from his shoulder and knuckled the tears from her eyes. He held her head between his hands and his gaze fell softly on her. She noticed the pale grey tones in his blue irises. 'Then that is our link.'

'Her link to me?' She sniffed and wiped her nose on the back of her hand.

Dane let her go. 'Yes, and if we are clever we can use it against her. You might be able to link to her as well.'

Annwyn groped around for a tissue, found a box and pulled one out. 'So you believe me?' she said after wiping her nose.

Dane moved closer to her and gently brushed the hair from her eyes. 'Yes. I think I have to believe. I don't know how she did it, particularly without me being aware.'

'Why me? It's so unfair.'

Dane lifted one shoulder and dropped it, then rubbed his chin. 'There must be some link between you. It's hard to believe it was a random occurrence. Some preparation was required for it to go so smoothly.'

Annwyn visualised the body she inhabited, and she could find no memory of ever having seen this woman. There was no intimacy between them. 'I honestly don't know her.'

'Has there been anything unusual, cars following you, the feeling of being watched, your house being invaded while you were out?'

'I can't recall having any incidents like that.'

'What about magic…er…occult? Have you ever dabbled?'

Annwyn let her mouth fall open before exclaiming. 'No! Well, unless…'

'What?' he asked, brows furrowed.

Annwyn let her gaze slide away from him to her past, to her life with Thomas. 'My husband's family, they were interested in new-age philosophies and the occult, too. Some of them were plain weird—you know, wands, knives…'

'Athames.'

'Yes, that's them, and spell books and strange gatherings in the night around bonfires…Not that I recall going to any of them. Although, we did socialise with some of them on occasion, and the family talked about the gatherings.'

'And have you been mixing with the family recently?'

'No, not much at all. Once Thomas was gone so was their connection to me. No children, you see.'

Dane nodded. 'It could be the connection, but it does seem to be, by your account, a little cold. What about your husband? Where is he?' he asked, his blue eyes wide.

Annwyn hung her head, scooping up some photographs and placing them back into the container. 'He died about three years ago.' Her voice was barely a whisper. She'd been unfaithful to his memory. Even though the choice had not been hers, she was guilty.

Dane's lips compressed in a sombre expression. 'Oh, I'm sorry. I didn't realise.' He stood up, bringing her to her feet. 'Yet you said she used his memory to unlock you. Nira must have studied you, collected items from you: hair, skin, photos, your habits, even your grief.'

Annwyn shivered, feeling a cold hand of fear sweep up her spine. Someone had got close to her without her knowing, had invaded her privacy, her mind, her body. 'Are you sure she needed those things?'

With his fingertips under her chin he lifted her face to look her in the eyes. 'The way she accessed you was too smooth. I did not detect it when I should have.'

After he released her Annwyn stood up and moved to the door. 'I don't recognise her or her name.' Annwyn's nerves were on edge. Her hands were shaky, and she clenched them tight to hide her agitation. Having him close was making things worse, unsettling her in ways she had forgotten were possible. He was so damn attractive, it was difficult to stand near him without reaching out and touching him.

'That is going to make things difficult. Her study and preparation must have been from a distance. Somehow she has a connection to you.'

Annwyn threw up her hands. 'How do we follow her if we have no idea where to start?'

Following her down the hallway, Dane put his hand gently on the small of her back and leaned down to whisper in her ear. 'I'll send Rolf to track her, I mean your, body's scent.' When she glanced over her shoulder at him he created a space between them. 'You should keep thinking about how someone could have collected things from you without you knowing about it. You might have a breakthrough.'

'Breakthrough?'

Dane cast his gaze around the room again as if checking once more that he hadn't missed anything. Then, touching the cold cup of coffee again, he answered. 'Yes. It's possible that you had an encounter, and she has fudged your memory. If she did that then she is very skilled and powerful indeed and our lives are more complicated than I first thought.'

He picked up the photo and studied it while chewing on his lower lip. 'So this is you, the real you?'

Annwyn lifted her chin. 'Yes.' With her eyes she dared him to say anything derogatory about her looks. He didn't. He traced his finger over her picture and put it in his pocket.

'We should go.'

# Chapter Five

Annwyn hugged herself, feeling a chill prickle her skin. It was time to leave her house and go hunting for her body and the sorceress inhabiting it.

'I'll go and get changed.' She turned toward her bedroom and stopped dead in the middle of the room.

'My clothes aren't going to fit me, are they?' she said, turning back to him and meeting his questioning gaze.

He jerked his head up, suddenly understanding. 'Ah no, they won't. Don't worry, first order of business is to buy you some new clothes, and then we should head back to my house. You'll stay with me until we resolve this situation.'

'Why can't I stay here? This is my home.'

'Yes, it is your home, but you are not Annwyn anymore. It's not only your clothes that don't fit. Your life doesn't fit. Your house. Your job. Your friends and lovers. To everyone else you are Nira, or whatever the name is she went by. What will your neighbours say when they see this body in this house? You can't even use your credit cards or your driver's license. They are hers now. Your life is hers.'

Annwyn's knees buckled at the enormity of what had happened to her. Dane was there in two long strides to catch her and hold her to him. 'I know it's not fair and right. You didn't ask for this, and I'm sorry. I need you to help me now, and I promise to help you too.'

Annwyn wanted to yell and scream and rage at the world, at this Nira and even at Dane, but he held her so close, so gently, that her fear evaporated as she clung to him. What choice did she have but to trust him, to be with him? He was her only hope of getting her life back and, oh God, he felt feel wonderful! Her skin burned with desire just from his touch.

'I feel so helpless. I didn't ask for this. Why would she want my body, my life? It's a miserable existence.'

Dane's mouth drew into a line. 'You were unhappy?'

Annwyn's face flushed when she let the comment slip. Had she been miserable? Yes, but it was mostly her own doing: being unable to let go of the past, unable to find a new life. Now she had no choice. All she was had been ripped away.

'Not overwhelmingly so, but I can't believe anyone would covet my life or my person. Do I really have to leave?'

Dane stroked her hair and rested his hand on her shoulder. 'Yes, we cannot raise suspicion and draw attention to the fact that something strange occurred here. You have been drawn into a world within a world. One that is kept safe by secrecy and discretion.'

Annwyn's gaze swept over the things that she had once held dear. Would she return to this life? Could she get her body back and forget this had happened? It was unlikely her life would resume its normalcy even if she did. 'Wait by the door for a moment. I need to do something,' Dane instructed.

Annwyn stood on the step and saw Dane disappear down the hallway. Not long after she heard a deep-toned chant and tried to get a better view. Was he leaving some kind of spell?

Before her curiosity could get the better of her, he trod back up the hall. 'What was that?' she asked.

With a light touch to her lower back, Dane ushered her into his car. 'I left a warding. I will know if anyone enters.' He signalled to his pet. 'Rolf!'

He took the wolf to the road and knelt down to hold something under his muzzle. Rolf lifted his head as if taking in a scent and then bounded off down the road.

When Dane returned to the car Annwyn asked, 'So you think she will come back?'

He shook his head before opening the car door for her. 'No, it is a precaution only. I think she is way too clever to make that mistake. There is nothing for her here.'

While she let her gaze linger on her home, a knot of sadness formed in her stomach. Maybe there was nothing for her either. How was she going to cope? How would she live? Fear grew.

What if all possible futures from this point in time led to heartbreak?

Dane climbed in the car, interrupting her thoughts. One glance at him and her body sang with arousal. She was drawn to him. It felt natural to be with him, to want him. This was a significant event in her life, one she wasn't going to get over easily. With a shake of her head she reminded herself that she had only met the man a few hours before. What was she thinking?

He climbed into the driver's seat, brushing her leg when he put the car into reverse. Annwyn converted the shiver of pleasure from his touch into an overblown sigh, and kept her gaze locked out the passenger window.

The sight of her home as they left etched itself into her mind. It felt so final.

***

Nira shuddered as she gazed in the mirror, the toilet block's hard light sharpening the planes of her pale face. What an insipid creature she looked. Bile filled her mouth and a light sweat dotted her forehead. The blasted spell had nearly ended her. Leaning over the basin she retched silently before once again taking in the stranger's face she now wore. How was she going to bear looking like this, being this woman? She had to get her body back.

Overhead, a voice announced that the bus to Sydney was boarding. She quickly checked the overnight bag she had packed at Annywn's and headed out of the ladies' room. A blinding pain speared into her head as a powerful mind touched hers. Knees nearly collapsing, she grabbed onto the wall for support, hunched over.

*What's happening? Why haven't you reported in?* The words filleted her mind, their power taking away her power to breathe. It was him. Threads of dark power threatened to spill out of her skin. She tried to fight them, contain them, but they wormed out of her ears, eyes and mouth, making her gag.

Someone came through the door and it thunked back into place. Nira straightened, pretending a calm she didn't feel as the other woman passed her with unseeing eyes. Brows drawn together, she struggled to form an answer.

*Complications.* She thought back. *Why didn't you tell me he had such power?* She took a breath and thought the last at her master. *Nearly caught me in a binding spell.*

She sensed anger and surprise from her aged master. *So he bested you? Interesting.*

*Not quite bested me. I am incapacitated. Had to switch bodies. Temporarily weak.*

A flume of anger delivered straight into her mind made her piss herself. She would have to change her panties now. *Deal with it*, came the harsh thought. *I want him out of the picture. He is a threat to us.*

As fast as it had arrived the presence vanished and the black coils of the connection fled. How she wished she could do that, reach out over such a vast distance and thwack into someone's mind and pour evil essence into it. She'd been his for so long now she couldn't remember life before it. A visitation always left a bad taste in her mouth, like drinking petroleum. He'd promised her equality, he'd promised her glory in the collegium, and she knew that she was no closer to obtaining it. Still, a bargain was a bargain and she was his.

After a quick change of underwear she raced for the bus and made it right before the doors folded shut behind her. She had to retreat now, but she had other ways of getting what she wanted. That bastard Dane would pay for what he had done, and she would get her body back and then some. Piss-weak Annwyn Flaydin was going to suffer. All that goodness and longsuffering made her want to puke. Reaching into the bag she picked up Annwyn's credit cards and licked them. Oh yes, she would have some fun.

# Chapter Six

Before heading out to Dane's place, which was situated on a rural property about one hour south of Canberra, they drove to the civic centre, the main shopping district, and spent several hours buying a large store of clothes, underwear and other essentials in the Canberra Centre. The local shopping mall near her home didn't suit Dane's taste.

Annwyn found the shopping experience completely disconcerting. Her customary choice in clothes looked out of place on Nira's body. The colouring of her usual choices was all wrong, too. She found she had to rely on Dane and the shop assistants to advise her.

Nira was taller as well so that meant different shoe sizes. After selecting a range of casual clothes: jeans, T-shirts, jackets, Dane purchased some tailored suits for her, as well as a couple of formal dresses and accessories. She supposed such an outlay was necessary. Her own clothes didn't fit her, and they didn't know where Nira lived so they couldn't use hers.

The wardrobe Dane purchased made her wonder. It looked like permanence, but that couldn't be right. Surely, once he found Nira, he could reverse the spell and send her back to her own life and things would go back to normal. A trickle of doubt eased into her mind. *What if things never went back to the way they were?*

Letting him pay wounded her pride, not that she could afford such an outlay in any case, but he had spent double her credit card limit. Yet what choice did she have? She had no means of identification, no idea where this body lived and what its real name was. She was a penniless non-person. As the realisation hit she grew quiet. Total dependence, through no fault of her own, on top of losing her life—that was going to take some adjusting to.

They had a late lunch in one of the outdoor cafés. Sitting in the spring sunshine, Annwyn tried to sort through the whirlwind of her life. She was wearing strange clothes as well as a strange body. Her future was a void. She couldn't think ahead, couldn't even think what she would be doing tomorrow or next week. Even with the turmoil in her mind, she found her gaze repeatedly drawn to Dane. He was the only solid thing in her life. Dane sipped his coffee and took a taste of his curry. How was it that she was so aware of him physically, and how was she to control it? Lunch in the civic centre had always been a regular activity. Now it was out of the ordinary and filled with weirdness. Her life was never going to be the same, no matter what the outcome, that's for sure.

'Can you tell me more about this binding spell?' she asked quietly, leaning forward so he could catch her words.

He shook his head and talked directly in her ear, his warm breath tickling her neck.

'Not out in public. I'll tell you more on the way home. It's not the only problem we have. This kind of body-switching is new to me so I'll need to research further to see if I can find out how she managed it and whether anything can be done. Perhaps you can enjoy an afternoon by the pool while I'm busy in my library.'

'Pool?' She drew back, not quite expecting the suggestion. There were hundreds of reasons why she couldn't be swimming.

'Yes, pool.'

Her eyes narrowed. 'It's too cold to swim.'

'It's heated.' There was a twinkle in his eye that was overly familiar.

'But we didn't buy a swimsuit.'

His smile was rather sexy. 'It's private,' he said. 'You won't need one. You can use a robe to cover up away from the water.'

'Oh?'

Annwyn lowered her gaze and pushed the remains of her salad around on the plate. Dane finished his coffee. Why did the thought of skinny-dipping sound so exciting? She had never dared such a thing before, but now the prospect was, well, tantalising. *This Nira had been very adventurous,* she thought, and some of it had rubbed off on her. It couldn't be her true self that was acting in such a way.

***

Dane gripped the steering wheel as he drove them back to his property near Michelago. His two thousand acres had seemed expansive but, now, with a new person sharing it with him, it would be small, closed in. A mortal human, too. He would have to deal with the differences, the morals, the questions and, he guessed, even the hysteria. Dane liked his privacy for a good reason.

As he drove he caught a glimpse of his reflection in the rear vision mirror and frowned. The vestiges of his previous transformation lingered in his hairline, in the curve of his ears and the arch of his brow. It made him ill just looking at it. Vain he might be, but he hated the physical changes—they constantly reminded him of what happened when the moon turned. The curse was not normal—it was slowly eating into the essence of him. He chewed the inside of his cheeks. The blasted curse was still there and it grated. What was he going to do? He had no idea how Nira had escaped him, nor any real idea of how to shake off the curse.

He had set so much hope on being rid of it. Yesterday. Now he was in an even worse position because he was physically bound to Nira's body with some poor human woman's spirit inside it. What could be more complicated? That he was bound in an attraction because his spell worked both ways? That he had been out-manoeuvred and had inadvertently stepped too far into his own power? That the sorceress cow had goosed him good and proper.

He glanced sideways and took in the woman beside him. To be near Nira's body was a pleasure. He corrected the thought. To be near Annwyn was a pleasure. There was a softness to Annwyn that could not be disguised—a certain something in her eyes. He noticed it, too, when he looked at the photo of the real her. Her spirit could not be denied. The ramifications of this were not lost on him, that someone had a definable spirit that exists separately from their body. It made sense to his mind, but to see the evidence was confronting to say the least.

Sitting this close, it took all of his resolve not to touch her, caress her. It took mental stamina to keep his mind on the road and on the traffic around him. The way Annwyn looked at him, responded to him, drove him to the edge of control. She was the flame and he the moth. It was an attraction that could lead to insanity or commitment, which was even worse because he could never be certain if it was a true love and attraction, or the spell. What was he thinking? Of course, it was the spell of binding.

Annwyn sat quietly as they cleared the traffic and headed down the Monaro highway. He knew she was waiting for him to tell her more about the spell that had backfired and snared her too, for she was twice-cursed. Not only had her body been stolen, but the current one was bound to him. She deserved an explanation, even if it wasn't his doing or design which had caught her up in it.

Because Dane lived in Australia it was easy to keep his distance from the Collegium of Sorcerers. Not many of them ventured this far unless, like him, they had a reason. However, there was a downside as he didn't know all the sorcerers or their particular leanings. This ignorance could only be addressed by fronting up in person and he'd like to do that forearmed, after a bit of research.

Tord, his father, had been well placed in the hierarchy. Only at his untimely death had Dane turned his back on the collegium. He had suspected that one or a number of its members were involved in his father's death. With the collegium's hierarchy blocking his investigations he'd had nothing but his suspicions to go on. Already an outsider by choice, there was no way he was going to join them, even though he'd been invited to.

Annwyn coughed and fidgeted, disturbing his train of thought. Their gazes met briefly and then Dane returned his attention to the road, his pulse thumping in his neck. God, he wanted her. Damn this bloody curse.

'You were going to explain about the spell.' She spoke quietly in a way that curled around his insides. *Curses, even her voice was turning him on!* Was she having a similar reaction? If so, she was good at hiding it. The thought just made him grind his teeth. She had no right being so controlled, particularly more controlled than he was.

Dane cleared his throat. Why did he feel so damn guilty? Why did his skin turn red so suddenly? He blew out a breath through his teeth. Because he'd fucked up. Annwyn was in this predicament because of him. Partly, at least. 'I used a spell of binding that was meant to ensure that Nira bent to my will and released me from the curse she placed on me.'

'So she cursed you first? Why?'

'I don't know. I had never met the woman. But I really wanted to know why or who had put her up to it. I took a risk. The binding spell was a terrible threat, a last resort. I was desperate, you understand? The mention alone should have been enough to encourage her to release me. No one would willingly let themselves be bound, at least I thought so.'

Her face turned toward him. 'The threat didn't work on her so you went ahead?'

'Not an inch.' He swallowed once. 'She had her power hidden, the quantum of it at least. We call the powers poles: intellectual, emotional and sexual. It's not common to have so much power hidden in the sexual pole. I was not expecting it.'

'So you don't usually…er…have sex when making spells of binding?'

He grinned lopsidedly. 'Ah, no, not normally. Well, this particular spell can involve sex, if that is the nature of the binding. In that case, it is similar to a love spell. However, she used her sexual power to fight me, and I had no choice but to engage in the same way.'

'So she had you thinking with your penis?'

Dane glanced at her sideways, wondering if she was making some kind of feminist dig. She was right. Hadn't he been admiring the physical Nira as soon as she materialised in his den? Perhaps he was more to blame than he first thought.

'Yes. You could say that. Once I engaged on that level it was difficult. The more I gave of myself to her and the spell, the more ensnared I became.'

'Ensnared? You?'

He ground his teeth, not liking that he portrayed himself as some kind of sexual weakling or that he lacked in skill. 'Yes, me.'

'I don't understand.' Her skin grew pink, and he thought she did have an inkling.

Their eyes met briefly. 'I'm as attracted to you as you are to me. That is the nature of the binding.' The words sparked between them.

'I see,' she answered quietly. He glanced to her lap and saw her clenching and unclenching her hands.

'Do you? Do you really?'

Annwyn turned her head away and stared out the window. 'I'm attracted to you sexually.'

'Is that so bad?'

The hint of a smile touched her lips. 'Embarrassing…disconcerting, but bad? No. I don't mind that the attraction is equal. What is disconcerting is that I trust you without good reason. That is odd and I—'

'I will try not to let you down. I want you to trust me, and I want that trust to be well-placed. There are other emotions bound up with the binding too. Attraction isn't all about the sexual act.'

'What do you mean? Sounds like there is a catch.'

'The more we have sex, the deeper the binding becomes, the more difficult to lift the spell.'

She jolted when he spoke and she gaped at him. 'God! Do you mean the attraction can get even stronger?'

He nodded sombrely. 'I'll try to divert the energy elsewhere to minimise it.'

Sweeping her hair behind her ear Annwyn nodded, then turned her head to peer out the passenger window again.

There was nothing but grey-green fields dotted with alpacas and sheep to keep her engrossed. She needed time to think it through. Dane slowed to take the turn-off to his place. *This was going to be difficult*, he thought. He wanted to pull over and take her. Every movement, every nuance of her expression burned across his skin. His arousal was intense. He did not know how long he could cope without sating himself. He needed all the concentration he could muster to analyse the spell and find a way to track Nira down. One minute he was talking of diverting the energy and the next he was thinking of sinking into her and gorging himself with sex.

When she stepped out of the car and took some of the shopping bags from him he knew it was going to be more difficult than he imagined. With the spell growing more powerful, the longer he was with her, the more entangled they would become.

His thoughts spiralled out of his control, driven by raging hormones, the spell and the attraction growing in him. He could picture her naked. He could imagine her moans as he made love to her. These things were going to distract him from his research. Perhaps they could just…

He shook his head. Control. He needed more control.

After the bags were inside the front door, he grabbed one of his bathrobes and handed it to her with instructions on how to find the pool. Without speaking another word he left her to herself.

***

In his basement sanctum, Dane commenced searching through his collection of arcane texts, trying to find reference to a body swapping curse, the name given to what Nira had done. He did not have a large collection of texts on sorcery, only those he had managed to slip out of his father's home before members of the collegium had arrived to prevent unauthorised removal of magic-related property. The rest remained in his father's library, sealed by the collegium's securitas, their clandestine security officers.

If he couldn't find what he wanted with the references he had, he would have to seek permission to examine the rest of his father's library or try to access someone else's. As he leafed through the pages the more likely it seemed that he would need to seek assistance elsewhere. The spells were not referenced using terms that made them easily searchable. He tried looking under soul-switching, body-stealing, but could find nothing that related to what had happened to Annwyn.

It was necessary for him to understand how Nira had tricked

him because it was something he did not want repeated. Not only because Nira had been able to thwart his spell of binding but also because of Annwyn, who had been deliberately or otherwise caught in the aftermath. Human or not, it had been callous how Annwyn had had her body hijacked.

The thought of Nira led him to picture her body, and then the image of Annwyn as she headed for the pool wrapped in his black bathrobe came to mind. He remembered how she inhaled deeply when she held his robe close to her. His scent. How could he not respond to someone that found even the smell of him arousing?

The attraction was a curse. She couldn't help reacting to him that way. It was a spell. He had to remind himself that it was magic and not something born of love. Even knowing that his own response was also the result of the spell, he could not help but want her.

Intellect could not win out over these seething passions. Even now, sifting through these texts, he wondered what she looked like naked in his pool. Surely, he could find a spot upstairs to watch her from without her knowing. It would torture him, but what exquisite torture.

After closing the book he was reading he caressed the carved symbol on the front while endeavouring to fight off thoughts of Annwyn. He would need to consult with Rafael from the collegium. The only reference he found to a similar spell made reference to Rafael d'Armac. Apparently Rafael had shifted himself into the consciousness of a Scottish wild cat for a short period.

Memories stirred. Rafael had been a close family friend and confidant until his father's death. Dane hoped that he could consult the old sorcerer—without getting caught up in collegium politics. He sent a mental signal to his father's old friend requesting an interview.

After that he quietly climbed the stairs. It wouldn't hurt to take a break while waiting for a response. It was night on the other side of the globe after all.

He glanced out the tinted window. He could see out. She

could not see in. Just then, she hauled herself out of the pool, wetting the pavement with spray. The water on her body glistened in the afternoon sun, beading on her tanned back and legs. Her blonde hair was dark when wet and hung straight down her back. She turned slightly, and he saw that she was watching a pair of rosellas nibble on one of the fruit trees.

A pert breast came into profile and, when she picked up her towel, her luscious brown thatch too. He was achingly hard.

Behind him the click of claws on the wooden floor let him know his wolf friends had come to join him, drawn perhaps to the vibrations and to the scent of his arousal. One of them howled quietly.

'Yes, I know. I have to bed her before it kills me. The deities have mercy on me.'

***

Annwyn stepped inside, slightly dazed from the sunlight outside. The hallway looked dark and hazy so she stood there waiting for her eyes to adjust. Her skin was cool and damp after the swim. She needed to shower and dress. She guessed she could find a book to read to amuse her until Dane showed up. Maybe then they could discuss their options together like rational human beings. Surely there was something she could do to fix her predicament. She didn't need to rely on him.

The thought of Dane mesmerised her—the way his body moved, the way his muscles flexed, the way the light reflected on his irises and the shape of his lips. Just thinking of him had her moist and ready. Her nipples tingled and her clitoris throbbed. How she ached to have him pleasure her, ride her.

Drawing in a shuddering breath, she rubbed her upper arms, appalled at the train of her thoughts. She was out of control. Even her love for Thomas had not led to such lust, such wanton desire.

Stepping along the hallway, she searched for the bedroom and the bathroom and then remembered it was at the end of the long hall.

On the threshold she hesitated. Should she be using this room, his room? Light spilled in through the five tall windows, making the white sheets on the unmade bed glow. This was where she had found herself in the early hours. In that bed. In a different body. Up close and personal with Dane.

Just as she dropped the robe to the floor, large hands encircled her waist from behind. The scent of him washed over her and she moaned as his touch pushed her arousal over the edge. His hands crept up, cupping her breasts, then his fingers teased her nipples. His mouth nuzzled the back of her neck. Her knees went weak but, before she could fall, his other hand caught her gently between the legs, fingers pressing against her clitoris. The position was so vulnerable and fulfilling. She wanted to surrender to him, wanted him inside her, spreading her, fucking her.

Lifting her arm, she grabbed the back of his head, pulled his hair gently. His fingers delved into her moist folds. Her back arched as she cried out. Her body was held up against his. His erection pressed against her back. He moved against her, mock-fucking, making her swoon with excitement.

Her imagination went wild. Her legs shook. Unbidden she was begging to be taken.

If this is what a spell of binding was, she liked it. His fingers slick inside her moistness probed more urgently. She spread herself wider, giving him greater access. A sudden climax had her legs buckling. Dane held her as the tremors of pleasure faded. Then he lifted her, carrying her to bed. Guiding her gently so she lay face down with her lower body hanging off the edge of the bed. The vulnerability of the position released feelings of surrender. Her pulse throbbed in her sex again.

Shaking with anticipation, she wanted him to take her from behind. She wanted him so deep, so hard, that thoughts fled. The moment had to dominate. She knelt there, hands grabbing the bedcovers as he thrust inside. Her passage was so moist she could accommodate him easily. Another thrust and she could hardly breathe, the pressure building was so intense. She wanted, no, needed more.

She spread her legs as he drove into her again and again. Her hands clung to the sheets, to the mattress beneath. His hands tugged at her hips with an ever increasing pace. Guttural, incoherent sounds came out of her mouth. She didn't care. She was being fucked so exquisitely she thought she would die from it.

This had to be heaven.

He withdrew suddenly and she cried out at the loss. But he was not done. He pushed her forward and then flipped her face-up. His large body covered her. The skin on skin contact titillated her fingers, her thighs, her breasts.

Silken lips teased hers. He had the power to keep her in the moment. It was all Dane, his maleness, his sex, his power. She couldn't get enough.

His hot mouth suckled on her nipples, then bit gently on her belly, and then his eager tongue moved lower down. The first taste was a long lap along her labia, the next he found her clitoris. Her eyes closed, this was spinning her out of control. She gripped his head and cried out.

Already high on endorphins, she went further, to a place she didn't know existed as he sucked and licked her.

His name was on her lips when he lifted her hips and entered her once again. Her rapturous screams added to her excitement—never before so had she lost control like this during sex.

Thomas had made sweet love to her. Dane overpowered her senses, made her body sing and tingle in ways she hadn't experienced before. Was this part of Nira inside of her? Was there a remnant of that woman still there, still calling the shots, making her hot and sex-crazy?

Dane changed positions again, turning her on her side. He held her leg over his shoulder as he entered her. Her body moved in time with his. Her breasts wobbled. He reached down and cupped one, squeezing gently. Annwyn's mind began to fracture, her sense of self drifting away.

Was this the power of the spell or was it the presence of Nira? She grabbed hold of that thin thread and followed it while Dane's flesh met hers. She was beyond climax now, her sense of self, returning. The thread led her to a hotel room.

Nira was there. Rough cropped hair made her—Annwyn's—dark eyes appear large. She was in Nira, looking out. Nira was naked on the bed, her body tense as she pleasured herself, gasping as a climax threatened to spill. With Nira's eyes, Annwyn saw her own body in a mirror: legs splayed, fingers exploring inside. Through the window, she saw a sign that said Coogee Bay Hotel. So Nira was in Sydney, near Coogee Beach.

Dane climaxed with a roar, slamming himself against her. His hands on her hips gripped her firmly but gently. She heard his hoarse breathing slow. Annwyn slid back into herself, leaving Nira and the hotel room behind.

Then she was back with Dane, tender from their lovemaking. Dane fell to the bed and cradled her in his arms. The wolves traipsed in through the open door, sniffed around the bed and then went to curl up in the corner. Rolf was not with them. He was still tracking the sorceress.

Annwyn loved the feeling of Dane surrounding her, the gentle sound of his breathing and the touch of his skin on hers. Deep inside she acknowledged that these feelings must be the spell, but right then she didn't care. It was good. Nothing had been this good before.

'Dane?'

'Mmmphf?'

'Dane, I had a connection to Nira when we were…I think I saw her.'

He sat up, spilling her from his arms. 'What? Tell me everything exactly as you saw it.'

Annwyn rearranged herself on the bed, hugging her knees as she explained. She tried not to blush but her face heated anyway, particularly when he asked her to repeat the view from the mirror. His left eyebrow lifted.

'And this was when we were at it?'

Annwyn nodded. 'Yes.'

'Did she sense you, do you think?'

Annwyn shrugged. 'I can't tell.'

'It's too late to organise to go now. There are some arrangements I have to make beforehand. Be ready to drive to Sydney early tomorrow morning. We'll check out this hotel room you saw. If she sensed you, she'll be gone, but we may pick up a trace. Rolf should be back soon. He can come with us.'

'Your wolf will come with us in the car all the way to Sydney?'

'Yes, of course. How else will I put Rolf on her trail?'

Obviously, Dane was very attached to his pets. Not willing to challenge the certainty glittering in his eyes, she did her best to hide her surprise by picking up a pillow and burying her face in it. After such intense love making, her body was ready for sleep. It had been a long day.

# Chapter Seven

The smell of fresh coffee woke her early next morning. Alone in the bed she realised that Dane had left her during the night. Probably a good thing, she thought, when she moved and detected the rawness. How many times? Four or five? She'd lost count sometime early in the morning. He had so much stamina and she had so much lust. It was not a combination for restful sleep. She slipped from the bed with a groan and made her way to the shower. It was time to get herself some of that coffee.

The hot water helped soothe her hurt but she couldn't find a salve to help her feel comfortable, particularly on the long drive to Sydney. A peek out the window and she could see it was going to be a sunny day. From the wardrobe she chose a linen dress that hugged the lines of her body. Not her body, Nira's body. She shivered, remembering how she had connected to the sorceress and had seen what that woman was doing with her own body. She shrugged her shoulders. Annwyn had been madly screwing in Nira's body so fair was fair, she supposed.

The sound of male voices reached her. Dane obviously had company. Annwyn wasn't sure she should show her face. A tap on the door startled her. 'Breakfast,' Dane called from the other side.

'Coming!' she responded quietly as she slipped on some gold painted sandals and left the room.

Early morning sun bathed the veranda where Dane had set up breakfast. A tall man wearing jeans and a checked shirt was standing by the table. He was taller than Dane, with dark hair and broad shoulders. He had a goatee with fine ginger flecks through it and his hazel eyes had remarkable slivers of yellow in them. Her greeting was met with a grunt. Before she had time to more than blink in surprise Dane came out with a plate of bacon and eggs and slid it down in front of the other man. 'This is Rolf. He will be joining us on the trip to Sydney. We can't leave until he is fed. Being hungry makes him irritable.'

'But I thought Rolf was your dog…I mean, wolf.'

Rolf pulled out a chair and got stuck into his breakfast. Dane grinned at her before heading back to the kitchen for the rest of the plates. Annwyn spied a large pot of coffee and sat down to pour herself one. She eyed Rolf over the rim of her mug.

There was something familiar about him, though she'd never met him before. He effectively ignored her until Dane sat down with his breakfast. 'Thanks…did you name your pet after your friend?'

Dane glanced at her and then he looked at Rolf whose head had shot up. 'Something like that,' Rolf replied. His voice was deep and gravelly and contained no hint of amusement. Dane chuckled.

Annwyn gaped at them both, slightly annoyed at missing the 'in' joke. When they didn't offer any further explanations she turned her attention to breakfast. The coffee had done wonders to restore her. Breakfast was a quick affair as they needed to be on the road. Chances were that Nira was long gone, but at least they'd pick up some sort of trail.

When it was time for her to climb into the car Dane noticed the hitch in her stride and her wincing as she sat down.

'You're in pain,' he said.

She blushed. Rolf loomed behind Dane, interest glittering in his dark gaze. 'I'm a bit tender, that's all. Nothing to worry about.'

Dane leaned into the car, urging her out again by tugging gently on her hand. 'Come back inside and I'll deal with your discomfort. I should have realised. My fault.'

She climbed out of the car and faced Dane who gazed at her with a soft expression. 'Really, it's nothing and it's equally my fault.' Dane harrumphed before standing aside to allow her to precede him. 'You think so? You're the innocent one here. You don't control anything—your emotions or your desires.'

'To some extent I do. I could have said no, could have pushed you away. I didn't want to.'

They were near the front step, with Dane putting the key in

the door. 'You think so? I'd like to see you try saying no. For your sake, I had better keep away from you.' He had his back to her.

'But I don't want you to.'

Dane's response was a growl, low in his throat. He glanced at her over his shoulder with an intense look in his eyes that went deep into her gut. Throwing the door wide, he gestured for her to enter. Inside, he guided her to sit on one of the leather lounge chairs. 'Now, open your legs for me so I can apply some healing.'

Annwyn looked askance at him. Rolf had followed them in and stood leaning on the doorjamb watching with those strange eyes of his. 'After what you just said to me, no.'

'So it's going to be like that, is it?' Dane ran his hand along her thigh. 'Open,' he said, and her legs parted of their own accord. With a brief chant he touched his fingers to her moist centre through the layer of her panties. There was a flush of excitement and then a mild burning sensation. All her tenderness vanished, and he removed his hand. She sat there rather puzzled by what had just happened. Considering what else he could do it was not surprising that he could heal, too. What perturbed her more was her own lack of volition. Her body had responded to his command. How far did his command of her go? Could he instruct her to do things? Things she would not normally do, like kill, or maim?

'So do you feel better now?' he asked, grinning at her.

'Yes, thank you,' she replied, tugging her hem over her knees and trying not to blush. 'Handy skill you have there.'

'Yes, very handy. Sorcerers are naturally immune to many human diseases and with the ability to heal we are pretty resilient.'

'So no condoms required?'

'No, fortunately.'

Dane offered her a hand and helped her to stand. She noticed Rolf standing there and his gaze made her feel uncomfortable. What was the relationship between the men that Dane was so relaxed that he could touch her intimately in front of him? Her gaze shifted between them. Perhaps Dane was bisexual. Her skin coloured at the thought. That would be an interesting conversation if she chose to question him about it. Not that she had the right.

Rolf headed to the car as they approached.

This time when she climbed into the car she was fully restored. Rolf climbed into the back and popped some earphones into his ears and started listening to music. Once on the highway the time went quickly. They stopped for a break at Exeter, grabbing a quick espresso coffee, before heading onto Sydney. At around lunchtime they were driving along the hilly and narrow streets of Coogee Beach, looking for a place to park. The ocean was a startling blue with soft white caps where the light wind frothed up foam.

Rolf's stomach growled loudly. Dane chuckled. 'Something to eat, I think, will be our first order of business.'

Rolf grunted, and when Annwyn glanced back at him he had a toothy, feral grin on his face. Annwyn turned back to the front. When the car was parked Dane led them to lunch in one of the beachside seafood restaurants. Annwyn was hungry, too, and ordered some fresh grilled fish and Dane ordered the same. To Annywn's surprise, Rolf ordered a rare steak. The waiter did not raise an eyebrow as he took their order.

While they waited for food Dane quizzed her about the angle from which she had seen the Coogee Bay Hotel sign. He drew a little map in his notebook. 'I'll check this out while we're waiting for the food to arrive. Be back in a moment.'

After he left Rolf played with his beer glass, and Annwyn gazed about the room. It was full of holidaymakers and business people—typical for the location and time of day.

'So, Rolf, you been friends with Dane long?' she asked, to break the ice.

He shrugged. 'Long enough.'

'I see…and what do you do exactly?'

'I work for Dane on a freelance basis.'

Annwyn's mouth drew into a straight line. No joy there, trying to get along with her companion of the day. Their food arrived and Dane had still not returned. Rolf dived straight into eating his steak, barely stopping to chew. Out of politeness, Annwyn waited and, before the food went cold, Dane returned. Straightaway, he started eating and so did Annwyn, stopping to take a sip of her drink.

'Found out where she was staying. Registered under your name and charged it to your credit card. We can see the room after we finish up here.'

'That seems a little obvious, doesn't it, using my credit card?' Annwyn commented, finishing off her side salad.

'You think she wants us to find her? That is food for thought. On the other hand, she's in the same boat as you. She is in your body; effectively, she is you. She's gone, though, but we'll see if she's left a clue.'

Annwyn pushed her plate away and finished off her drink. 'So if she is using my bank accounts, I can track her on the Internet. In the short term, at least. I have the account codes until she sees fit to change them.'

Dane nodded before signalling the waiter so he could pay the bill. 'Good thinking. A small window of opportunity. She could have changed the passwords already. The banks are open today.'

Annwyn's stomach dropped. With each step, she felt more and more violated. Nothing was sacred about her life anymore. A sudden desire to have the same access to Nira's home and bank accounts sprung up within her. Two could play at that game. Maybe they would get lucky and someone would recognise her and she could find out Nira's identity. As long as it wasn't the police.

***

The hotel was rather dingy, a cheap beachside hotel, commonly used by backpackers. The room where Nira had stayed was clean enough but basic, having only a bed and a dingy full-length mirror on the far wall. Annwyn shivered when she saw it. The scene matched the one she'd seem when making love with Dane. So it was a connection then, not something conjured up by her imagination. It wasn't until then that she realised she'd had a secret hope that it wasn't sorcery.

Rolf searched the room, getting on his hands and knees to peer under the bed, into the corners and even the small bathroom. It looked bare to Annwyn. Dane frowned as he stood in the corner of the room. Annwyn rested her back against the door.

'Be careful. There's something here. Annwyn, stand by me.'

Annwyn took a step and was then held firm by some unseen force. 'What—' she managed to screech before being cut off.

Dane muttered something and gestured. A wall of blue encircled her to clash with one that was eerie green. 'A circle. She is trying to contain you. Hold on while I try to break it.'

Rolf growled from the other doorway and then rubbed at his chin thoughtfully. 'She is close by, I think. I found this.' He held up a business card. As Dane was concentrating on breaking the circle, Rolf read the card. 'A card advertising a local sex club.'

Dane nodded while chewing his lip as he battled the lurid green energy surrounding Annwyn. As if on cue, the connection to Nira snapped open, making Annwyn cry out. She fell to her knees, letting out a shriek as she was dragged along the connection into another room, into Nira. The sorceress was having sex—lots of sex, with lots of people. Annwyn tried to pull away, tried to get the woman out of her head. Nira chanted while two men penetrated her simultaneously. She could feel the woman's thoughts because the anal penetration hurt. Annwyn's body had not engaged in that type of thing, while Nira's body was well-accustomed to it. Nira let a twinge of pain down through the connection before she took a large black penis into her mouth. Annwyn struggled against the vision. She did not want to experience it. Nira chanted in her head, weaving her magic. Annwyn was afraid that they would change bodies again —not that she didn't want this to happen but not while Nira was engaging in group sex in a swingers club.

Dane called out to her. 'Annwyn. Can you tell where she is? Can you break free?'

'No,' she panted. 'There are a few people there with her. All...er...copulating in various ways.'

Dane's voice wove through the air, his power encircling,

making her hair stand on end. His voice cut in. Nira didn't want her to answer but Annwyn couldn't resist the command. Dane raised his hands, the words of his chant cut into the circle that held her. Annwyn saw the circle shimmer a sickly translucent green. Annwyn could feel Dane's power now and so could Nira. Spitting out the mouthful of man she'd been licking, 'Whip me!' the sorceress called to someone near. 'Quickly, now.'

She was straddled over one man with another behind her, both thrusting into her, when the lash hit across her shoulder blades. Annwyn's shoulder blades. The lash cut into her soft flesh and Annwyn cried out as the pain snaked through her. Nira's hold tightened, her claws cut into Annwyn's mind. Annwyn thought she would die, she was held so tightly, so painfully. Another lash of the whip and Nira's climax was upon her. There was a moment of disconnection and then a black nothing. A great crunch heralded the collapse of the circle. Rolf caught her as she fell, shivering and barely conscious.

When she came to she was sprawled across the bed with Dane lying behind her, stroking her hair, and Rolf positioned on her other side, stroking her arm. It was disconcerting, after what she had witnessed, to find two men beside her. She pushed away from them as she sat up. Her heartbeat was frantic. That was a situation she didn't want to experience again. Would that woman invade her every time she was with Dane? That thought appalled her. Spell or not, she enjoyed Dane, every look and every touch, and having that woman invade her every time was intolerable. She had to find a way to fight her off.

Sitting up, Dane asked, 'Are you okay?' His blue eyes assessed her. Annwyn looked to him and then to Rolf, who propped himself up on his elbow. There was a twinkle in Rolf's eyes as if he knew his closeness rattled her.

'Yes,' she lied. Despite her abhorrence of what Nira was doing, she found herself aroused and nothing but sating herself with Dane was going to alleviate it.

Dane nodded to Rolf. 'Go now. Tell the manager we'll be down in a little while. Pay him for our time.'

Rolf got off the bed and paused at the door with a slight flare of his nostrils. Before heading out the door, he stopped again to give them a last quick look.

Dane stayed on the bed with her, gently stroking her hair. 'Tell me the truth now. All of it.' Despite not wanting to, Annwyn described the whole scene in the sex club, the intensity of the feeling, the pain, the sensation of Nira's claws in her mind.

'And how does this affect you?'

Annwyn stared at the wall, avoiding looking at him, resisting the compulsion to answer, to tell him of her lust, the fierce desire to be fucked senseless by him. His hand trailed down her body, between her breasts, over her navel and, then, as if he was pointing a wand, he touched the nub of her sex through her clothes. She gasped, her gaze boring into his, her arousal washing over her in waves.

'Get up,' he said.

Not needing to be asked twice, she lunged off the bed. He bounded up, towering over her and advancing. Annwyn backed up against the wall. Dane captured her mouth in a searing kiss, tongue dancing against her own. Desire trampled over her will and her knees buckled. Next thing she knew, Dane's hand was in her pants, spreading her juices as he probed inside of her. She panted, excited, dazed and possessed. He ripped off her panties and tossed them to the floor. The sound of his zip descending reached her before he lifted her, hiking her dress up and thrusting into her. Dane was riding her, hot and strong, and Annwyn grunted with pleasure at feeling him so full inside of her, stretching her, pumping her. She came first and he kept on, until he too was spent. She clung to him as he gently untangled her limbs and lowered her to the floor.

Straightaway she collapsed on the bed. He sat on the edge while he rearranged his clothing.

'Well?'

'Well what?' she asked dazedly.

'Nira?'

'Not that time. No.'

'Ahh…then she must be on the move.'

'Is that why you fucked me all of a sudden? So I could

connect with her again?' Annwyn found her anger rising, even though she had no cause to be irritated with him. He didn't love her. He owed her nothing. He was just as caught as she was. Yet she'd never enjoyed a sexual encounter like this before. Each time he took her further, higher. Still, the anger was raw.

He stared at her and then leaned in close. 'Your eyes. They changed for a while when Nira had possession of you. They didn't this time so I wanted to check if my hunch was right.'

Annwyn sucked in a breath. She was sated and it felt fantastic. The scent of him was on her, and she inhaled again. 'My eyes?'

'Yes, I noticed there's a difference. When she held you in that circle, she crawled into you, just for a moment, and your eyes changed, grew very dark. If it continues, I'll be able to tell when it is you and not her.'

Annwyn couldn't help but shiver. She did not want to share that woman's thoughts again, but understood that she probably had to if they were to track her down. 'So you wanted to check it out again and see if she could reinsert those claws?'

He shrugged. 'Maybe. Although I think it had more to do with your description of what Nira was doing when she connected with you, and the proximity of your sexy body and your heady arousal, which I dealt with like a good man should.'

'God, you're an arrogant shit.' Annwyn blinked. Had she really said that? To her surprise, Dane laughed.

'You're a fast learner. Come on. Let's see if we can get you on the Internet. I have a laptop in the car.'

Annwyn used the bathroom and tidied her clothes. She tossed her ruined panties in the bin and hoped there wasn't a strong breeze. She'd rummage through her overnight bag and put on another pair in the car.

While they waited for Rolf to return or ring in with news Annwyn logged onto the Net. She was able to check her accounts. Because of the time lag only the accommodation had been billed to her account, although she could tell that other purchases had been made because they had been taken off the balance of her credit card. She shifted to her savings account, then swore. 'The bitch!'

'What?'

'She's emptied out my savings, about nine thousand dollars. I'd been saving to renovate my kitchen. She can do a lot with that. My Internet access codes are still working but I can't tell where she's going next because of the time delay in the transaction descriptions. Even if I request a stop to the credit card, she's got my cash.'

'Okay. Not much use then. Here comes Rolf. Wait here.' Dane got out of the car and went to talk to Rolf in the street. They pretended to be looking at the sea, but she could see their intent conversation. Rolf had not found her. Nira had gone.

When they climbed back into the car Dane said, 'Dead end.'

Annwyn turned in her seat. 'Had she been in the club?' she asked Rolf.

He nodded, scratching his goatee thoughtfully. 'All morning, apparently. She broke off her session about the same time as Dane pulled you from the circle. They say she leaped into a cab while still pulling on her clothes. She'd used your name and your credit card. Fifteen hundred dollars for a group romp.'

Annwyn turned to the front. Great, she was developing a reputation as a sex fiend. She glanced at Dane's hands, remembering what he had been doing with them not long before and felt warm and gooey inside. Okay, so she was a sex fiend.

'So what now?' she asked Dane.

'I'm going to book us into a hotel suite. Rolf's going to see what he can do to follow our sorceress tonight. I have to catch up with some business. It shouldn't take long. I'll make sure there are some good movies.'

Annwyn pouted as she looked out the window. She was being dumped by herself in a hotel room. What if Nira tried to connect again? No problem. If she did, this time maybe she'd find the woman on her own. In fact, two could play at that game.

# Chapter Eight

Dane handed their bags to the bellboy at the Brighton Novotel and tipped him generously. While driving, he had received a mental message from Rafael confirming their meeting—on collegium ground.

Dane was puzzled that Rafael had chosen one of the Denver conference rooms at the collegium's headquarters instead of the old man's refurbished Scottish castle, complete with roaring fire and home-brewed whisky. Perhaps Rafael had business in progress in Denver that precluded meeting on his home ground. Dane had to admit, entering collegium territory unnerved him slightly.

The hotel suite had two bedrooms, both with locks. This meant he could transport to Denver without outsiders noticing. Normally, he'd use his sanctum but that was not possible at the moment. Annwyn would be safe enough. He could always order her to stay in the suite until he told her otherwise. He was tempted, but considered it an abuse of the spell and not in keeping with his honour as a gentlemen and a sorcerer.

Annwyn sat down on the couch with a sigh, kicked off her shoes and folded her feet under her. Her gaze travelled over the room before resting on him, a slight smile playing about her lips. There was still something different about her and he wasn't sure what it was. He shook his head. *Must be the spell*, he thought, *seeing more than what is there*. God, he had enjoyed having her in that hotel room earlier. It had been intense and extremely satisfying. He tried not to think about her description of Nira's activities at the club, but her words twisted around him, tortured and teased him until his hard-on ached. He could picture Annwyn like that, lips wrapped around his erection, her squeal of delight as he penetrated her in every way. He shook his head again. That blasted Nira was polluting his mind, tainting him.

Rolf waved him over and whispered fiercely. 'You shouldn't leave her alone. Can't you wait till I get back? I'm worried for her. This Nira is playing with her, manipulating her. She could reach out and kill the poor girl if she chose.'

Dane lifted his eyebrows. 'And kill her own body? I don't think so. Look, transform in the stairwell downstairs and then sneak off when it's dark. Go back to the club and see if you can pick up her scent. I'll be back as soon as I can.'

Rolf frowned, his dark brows drawing together to wrinkle his forehead. 'Very well. I'm not happy about it. I don't like any of this.'

'Any of this? What in particular?' Dane could think of a lot of things not to be happy about. A curse that couldn't be broken keen amongst them.

Rolf's gaze rested on Annwyn, then he sighed softly. 'Though I guess I can't blame you. She's very...'

Dane slapped him on the shoulder. 'I'm not sharing this one, okay?' The thrust of jealously rocked him to the core. He didn't want anyone to touch his woman. His woman?

Since when did he get so proprietary? Fucking binding spell. It was really seeping into him. Logic dictated that none of it was permanent. Annwyn wanted and needed her body and her life back. Although the current mix of lovely soul and hot body was a heady combination, it was one bound in magic.

Rolf faced him squarely. 'Somehow I knew you were going to say that. I don't blame you. I wouldn't share her either. She's a keeper.'

Dane's grin tensed. With a knowing nod, Rolf walked off to read a magazine in the corner. Since meeting and befriending Rolf they had shared women, particularly within the pack. The women were either female werewolves themselves or women who liked it rough, tough, and weren't particularly loyal to one man.

It was part of the fun of being a werewolf alpha, he guessed. Although, technically, he'd been Rolf's guest in the pack. If he didn't shift this curse, he was going to get a lot more acquainted with pack ways than he wanted. He had no idea what would happen between him and Rolf if this change became permanent.

Dane was alpha and so was Rolf. His gaze slid to Annwyn who lay with her head back on the sofa. He doubted she would adapt to that life. What was he thinking? He had to get her body and her life back. He could not fall into the trap of loving her, of expecting something sound and lasting to develop from this debacle. Living for someone else was an alien concept, and yet…

Dane had to touch Annwyn one more time. He enjoyed the smooth silkiness of her hair as he stroked her head. She leaned into the caress, almost purring with happiness. He knelt next to her.

'I've got to go now.' He kissed the top of her head. She looked at him with an open and warm expression, slight puzzlement marring her brow. 'I want you to stay here. Don't go out and preferably lock yourself in your room.'

'Okay, but do you mind if I go out on the balcony and look at the view?'

Dane glanced out the window. It was growing dark. He sensed the moon's presence, not quite full yet. The curse had linked him to the moon's thrall. The dusk spread vivid pink and violet across clouds marbling the horizon. He nodded. 'Do it now because once it's night there will be nothing to see—just dark, empty ocean. I'll see you in the morning. I have to head out now.'

He cupped her chin and planted a light kiss on her lips, pleased he'd made the contact non-sexual for a change. She nodded as she went towards the balcony and shut the door behind her.

For a while he watched her there looking out over the dark waters of the bay, then he went to his room and locked the door from the inside. He showered, mentally preparing himself for the meeting, then dressed carefully and initiated the transfer.

Dane materialised in the corridor of the Denver headquarters. It was near dawn, and the building was quiet. Dim lights illuminated only small circles of bland grey carpet, leaving spots of shadows to obscure its pattern. The door in front of him was open, one of the collegium's many magic-insulated conference rooms. Casting a glance left and right, Dane stepped forward and detected the familiar vibrations of his old friend emanating from within.

On entering, he found Rafael already inside waiting, his waist-length grey hair neatly plaited, contrasting with the rich red robes he wore. The older man stood facing a huge stone fireplace, a simulacrum of one from his Scottish home, Dane guessed. A slight movement in the corner of his eye and Dane turned, catching sight of a young, thin man with slicked-down hair and wearing a tailored suit. Dane pulled up short. He was not expecting anyone else to be there.

The old man turned in Dane's direction. 'Ah, Dane. This is Max, my aide.'

Dane noticed that Rafael's beard was well trimmed, but now mostly white. Had it been that long since he'd seen him? Dane couldn't shake the impression that Rafael's dark gaze was rather grim. Something was troubling the old sorcerer.

Dane nodded in Max's direction and received a nod in return. The young man appeared to be doing a good job of pretending not to be there. Yet his presence raised Dane's hackles. There was more to this situation than he had expected.

'Greetings, scholar,' Dane replied as he walked forward to great his old friend with the formality expected. Dane wore a black Armani suit and tie that contrasted with the Rafael's rich crimson garb. The hem of the older man's robes swept the carpet as he surged forward in greeting, his hand automatically going to his ceremonial knife secured in the gold belt at his waist.

'Dane! Welcome, welcome. I hope this urgent summons is because you wish to tender your application to the collegium. Your father would have wanted you to take your proper place amongst us.'

As a second master of the stewards, Rafael always tried to secure Dane's application and even offered to sponsor him. Dane always refused as politely as he could. His father had been a member of the inner circle, the triumvirate that oversaw the running of the collegium, and what good had it done him but cut short his life?

'You'd never catch me wearing those robes,' Dane replied, keeping it light. 'I prefer modern and well cut.' He spread his hands, emphasising his well-tailored lines. He cast a quick glance at Rafael's aide. The man stood still, but his eyes watched and Dane assumed his ears heard.

With a chuckle, Rafael came forward and embraced him, slapping him firmly on the back. The old man had always accepted his refusal with good grace, never voicing resentment for the mentoring he had provided over the years, which had come to naught.

Holding Dane by the shoulders, he gazed into his face. 'Well, despite the urgency of your summons, I see you are looking fit and well, except...there is something...different about you.'

Seeing Rafael brought it all back—the angst, the confusion and his rebellion against the establishment. Dane had only worn traditional sorcerer's robes at his father's funeral eighteen months earlier. He had refused testing by the collegium, not quite convinced that it hadn't been one of its members involved in his father's death. Self-inflicted misuse of magic, they had determined. Dane had never believed it so he had refused to be tested, to restrict them from knowing anything but the barest essentials of the limits of his power or of his life. Hiding away in Australia had helped him stay out of sight and out of mind.

It was better they didn't know the extent of his powers. He did not want to advertise them, or have them measured and calibrated. No need to excite unnecessary envy. Only his father had any inkling of the extent of his powers, although Rafael might have suspected. Somehow, he had come to someone's notice and attracted a powerful curse. He had no standing in the collegium, except as Tord's son. How different things would have been if he had chosen to take his place.

'There is much to discuss.' Dane made the formal sign of greeting, thumbs crossed with hands splayed. Rafael acknowledged the greeting.

'Dane, I'm pleased to see you, whatever the circumstance. We meet so rarely now that your father is gone and that saddens me. We were once so free and relaxed in each other's company.' The old man studied him, his gaze travelling from the top of Dane's head to his feet. 'How like him you are.'

Dane felt a twinge of guilt. 'I apologise for not coming to see you more. Despite how it seems, I am grateful for your friendship and your guidance. Things have been a little interesting of late. I need some advice. Perhaps we could talk alone.'

The old man's gaze narrowed as he caught the gist of Dane's request. 'Ah, yes. Max. Be so good as to rustle up some light refreshments, will you?'

Max bowed slightly to Rafael but, as he left the room, his gaze lingered on Dane. Interesting, Dane thought.

'So Max is your aide? I detect very little power in him.'

'You are correct. He has little gift for magic, but he is useful in other ways. He is a very competent administrator. He came with excellent references and the goings-on around here barely cause him to raise an eyebrow.'

Dane tilted his head to one side, letting the information sink in. 'Administration, you say?' Alarm bells started ringing. He really should have kept in touch with the old man. Something had changed. He struggled with indecision. Should he take his leave now? Walk away before revealing too much? He had known Rafael for most of his life and thought of him as a friend, but could he trust someone so loyal to the collegium? Dane examined all his choices and realised he had none. He had to trust. Had to risk.

Rafael sat down and offered Dane a seat beside him. 'I'll get to that. So you seek advice from the collegium? Or from me?'

Dane laughed softly. 'Depends on the question and the answer, I suppose. You. I come to you as a friend and mentor. I'd like to keep this quiet and out of official circles, if I can.'

His friend frowned at the table top, an expression that that brought back memories, unwanted ones. The pain of when he was told of his father's demise. The guilt he felt because he hadn't been there for him, despite the fact that his father had encouraged him in his choice to settle in a semi-rural region of

Australia and to distance himself from the collegium. Dane's father had wanted him out of harm's way, although Tord's warnings had always been vague. A threat never completely articulated.

The Europeans may call Australia the arse end of the world, and maybe it is, but it is also a very useful place to go unnoticed, particularly in the way of magic. Australia is so off the beaten track it is shunned by members of the collegium and other paranormals generally.

Other members of the inner sanctum, Vollos and Brun, had excluded him from investigations and from decisions about the disposal of his father's magical property. The accusations against his father were unjust and unproven, to his mind, but Vollos and Brun had held a secret inquiry and published a report damning Tord, and bringing disrepute on the family.

Dane had never believed them and yet he had done nothing to disprove them. Secretly, he had worked on it, researching and delving, trying to put together the last weeks of his father's life, his activities, his motivations and his thoughts. A few months earlier, he thought he had stumbled on something, and it was then that the first cycle of the moon's curse had hit him, sending his life spiralling out of control. It made him sweat thinking about it, or was that just the closeness of the imminent full moon?

Rafael squirmed in his chair and avoided looking directly at Dane. 'You were wondering about my need for an administrative assistant. Well, you see, I'm part of the inner circle now.' He stopped to take a breath. 'I replaced your father in the triumvirate.'

Dane's mouth dropped open. 'You have ascended?'

Rafael nodded. 'The collegium and I are one in the same.'

Dane ran his fingers through his hair. He felt so many conflicted feelings which he was trying hard to disguise. Rafael had taken his father's place. This hurt on so many emotional levels that he couldn't digest it. Now was not the time.

'I hope you will forgive me. Your father's place was offered to me six months ago and, as it was such an honour when Vollos and Brun invited me to rule alongside them, I could not refuse it.'

Dane clasped his hands. 'Congratulations. I'm sure you'll be a positive influence on the collegium.' He suppressed a wince, hoping his comments were not seen as criticism. Damn politics.

Rafael folded his hands across his middle and inclined his head. 'I hope to be. There is much work to be done.'

Dane realised at that moment that he was now in fact asking the triumvirate for help. Just the kind of notice he was trying to avoid. Rafael was now a part of the inner circle, the three who made the decisions, controlled the power. He could not expect that Rafael would assist him now without consulting his colleagues. 'This makes things a little more difficult. I had hoped to avoid involving the hierarchy of the collegium in this business, even though I'm certain it involves at least one of its members.'

'What do you mean? You have accusations to make?' Rafael's dark eyes grew larger, his mouth a grim line.

Dane shrugged. He'd come this far; he had to confide in his old friend. To withdraw now would signal a lack of trust and offer grave insult to the new member of the triumvirate. 'Of no one specific. I have been cursed.'

'What?' Rafael stood, then circled around Dane, hand outstretched, hovering above Dane's head. 'Yes, there is something I can feel. That certain something I sensed when you first arrived. Tell me more. What is the nature of the curse?'

Dane let Rafael examine him, using his senses to assess the three poles of power. Keeping himself calm, Dane made sure he hid the full extent of his powers in the way his father had showed him. It was as if there were pockets sewn inside of him, and it was there he squashed down and compacted his power, making it appear less than it was, making it appear normal, unremarkable and ordinary. Luckily, Rafael's examination was not as extensive as a testing would be. He talked so he could keep his mind off what Rafael was doing.

'It is a tight curse, expertly placed. I can see no loose ties to unravel. In fact, it looks as if it has sunk into the very fabric of your being—a truly remarkable conjuring. Tell me more.'

'Three months ago, at the full moon, I transformed into a wolf. Not a fully-fledged, ravenous werewolf, but as close as one can be without being lost forever. For a week I ran wild, eating game and vermin to survive. I was sunk in the most primal of feelings and experiences.'

Rafael continued his examination, pursing his lips before speaking. 'You do not have any tainted blood in your line, as far as I know.'

Rafael knew this because Dane's father's lineage was a matter of public record. His mother, Freja, was Danish, a middling sorceress who ensnared his father, Tord, in what by all accounts was a very passionate affair. It had been too short, though, because his mother died when he was around ten. His father's grief had been bitter and long and seeped in misery. Sorcerers generally live several human lifetimes so her death had been unexpected. It was then that his father directed his energies towards the collegium and to furthering his career. Dane was not exactly neglected but the shine was gone from his father's eyes after his mother died. He still remembered how tall she was and how fair. Both his parents were registered with the collegium and their genealogy was well catalogued. He was descended from a long line of talented sorcerers. Much had been expected of him. There was a lot of anger when he walked away from a brilliant magical career in the collegium.

'Yet the taint was on me. The alpha of the local werewolf pack befriended me in my distress. I had inadvertently taken on a few of his pack mates in a brawl, leaving a couple injured. My land is part of pack territory, something I was not aware of. It was his examination of me that revealed the nature of my curse. Somehow he can tell through my scent that there was magic involved in my transformation. I wasn't a hereditary werewolf.'

'I see. It must have been very difficult for you to find yourself in such low company.' Rafael removed his hands, closing his eyes while sifting through the energy patterns he sensed.

Dane watched, hope surging through him. 'I researched long and hard to find the source, the cure and the instigator of the curse. I had no luck and then the second full moon rose and once again plunged my life into chaos and blood. This time my recovery was slower, the beast harder to shake. Even now I feel it stirring in my blood. The next full moon comes.'

'Intriguing. Why you?' Rafael stood back.

'I have no idea why. I live a low-key life, out of the way. The level of my powers is unremarkable, and I stay out of the collegium's way. Yet for some unknown reason I was targeted and the curse has proved impossible to shift.'

'I sense how it has infiltrated you, altered you. The curse has been made for you, made for the very fabric of you. I fear you're right. One, maybe two more full moons and it will be impossible to reverse. Have you discovered anything at all in these months?'

Dane sat back, crossing his legs at the ankles. 'We found the sorceress who cast the curse on me. I summoned her to me.'

Rafael's eyes widened. 'You summoned the sorceress? Who was she?'

Dane gazed at his shoes for a moment before answering. 'I didn't recognise her. Nira was her name. She was very surprising.'

'In what way?' Rafael was pacing now, and he wiped his hands on his robe as he walked.

'She is rather young when you consider the complexity and the strength of her curse. When I confronted her she masked her power.'

Rafael paused in his pacing. 'Masked?' he stepped closer. 'Did she attack you? Defeat you?'

'No, she did not defeat me. I bound her. Well, sort of…'

Again Rafael's eyes widened, and he sucked in a breath. 'The binding of another sorcerer or sorceress is a difficult thing; it requires much power. I didn't think you had it in you.' He narrowed his gaze as if reassessing him. 'Was it a success?' Rafael stood back and watched him closely, his dark eyes glittering with speculation.

'Partially, but not the kind of result I was expecting. There were complications.'

'Such as?'

'Well, this is the main reason I'm here seeking assistance.'

'Obviously, she did not lift the curse. It is still upon you.'

'Rafael, she is young and a stranger. There was no reason for her to curse me so I'm guessing someone older and wiser put her up to it. She confessed as much to me.'

'So she revealed her master, her teacher?'

Dane shook his head. 'No. She said she couldn't lift the curse because it would mean her life. It was then I found where she hid her power. A lance of sexual energy pierced me as I was making the binding. She fought well and hard, but I was prepared and desperate.'

Rafael walked back over to the window, his thumb and forefinger stroking his chin. 'So you used the binding, but you still bear the curse. What happened?'

'To successfully bind her I had to meet her like for like, except somehow, while I was sealing the binding, she slipped through my fingers.'

Rafael turned to gape at him. 'You tried to seal the binding through sex and still she beat you? You are naturally dominant. She must be a very impressive specimen. Your own admissions raise my admiration for your skill and power. You should be part of the collegium. There was much regret at you not joining us, despite the unfortunate circumstances of your father's passing.'

'If you can in all honour avoid telling all, I would be most grateful.'

'Does this Nira creature still run free?' There was a knock at the door and Max entered, pushing a trolley. Dane tensed. Had Max heard this last question?

'The refreshments you ordered, my lord.' Max lifted the cover of an array of cold meats, cheeses and what appeared to be antipasto vegetables. A crystal decanter filled with red wine and a bottle of *Pol Roget* stood on the tray next to a selection of glasses.

'Yes, but it's complicated.' Dane kept his focus on Max until the man withdrew.

Rafael grinned at Dane, nodding absently to Max as he shut the door. 'So how did she escape you in the end? Slip away during your post-coital nap?'

Dane's brows drew down over his eyes, and he rubbed his forehead. 'No, she stole another woman's body —a human, to be exact —and thrust that woman's consciousness into her own while we were still having intercourse. The woman, Annwyn is her name, is inside Nira's body and bound to me.'

Rafael sat back in surprise. He ran a hand over his hair and shook his head in disbelief. He blinked at Dane a few times before getting to his feet and walking to the window. 'Impossible,' he said, his voice but a whisper.

'You don't know how much I wish it was impossible, but I have confirmed it.'

Rafael walked back toward him, his face haggard with worry. 'Tell me the rest.'

Dane nodded. 'The woman in Nira's body is innocent. As far as I can establish she has no connection to this sorceress and has no power of her own. I need to reverse the body swapping spell to set her free. And I need to undo the binding curse. To do the first, I need help to find Nira.

'But I do not know such a one as you describe. The collegium would not sanction such a perversion of power. To have so much tethered to one pole, such as the sexual one, would require some deviant practices.' He raised his eyebrows and then arrowed them together in a frown. 'I know of no one who has such capacity as you describe.'

'Then if not the collegium, then who?'

Rafael glanced at him and looked away. 'There are other factions.'

'Other?' Dane did not know of these other factions, well, of any that were a threat. 'But surely this body-swapping stunt she pulled has been done before. I read that you had managed to shift into an animal at one stage.'

'Me? 'Rafael gaped at him before snapping his mouth shut. 'How did you know that? Never mind, I can guess.' He stood up and walked the length of the room. 'That was long ago, and it was for a short time only. I did not swap places with the creature, just shared its body for a short period. Not a comfortable trip, I assure you.'

He paused at the trolley laden with food. 'Please, take something. I need to consider matters further. What you have told me has shocked me greatly.'

Rafael resumed his seat and sat there quietly, lost in thought. Dane poured some of the wine and took some meat and cheese. It had been a while since he last ate, and he found his appetite increased before the full moon.

He had to accept the fact that he would not escape the curse before the full moon in two nights' time. His admissions would certainly cost him his privacy and, possibly, his freedom from collegium interference in his life. If he sought the help of Rafael, he was effectively asking the collegium for help. What choice did he have? He would not give up and lose himself to a werewolf curse. He couldn't do it. He was too stubborn by half. Despite wishing that Rafael could help without the bureaucratic procedures, he knew that if he needed the collegium's assistance, it would come at a price. He would have to submit. He would have to follow the rules; he would have to be tested and have his every action open to inspection. Could he also be in danger, like his father had been? If only his father had been more open with him before the end. If only he hadn't died.

Anger rose up, anger at Nira and what she had done to his life and to Annwyn's. She hadn't asked for this trouble—hadn't asked to be something akin to his sex slave. She deserved better: a home, a man who loved her, who desired her without the assistance of a binding spell. This made his anger at Nira, and whoever was pulling her strings, greater. He thumped the table and then strode about the room, wanting action, wanting something, anything, to ease the tension.

Why did someone seek to ruin him? As a result of this curse, even if he could shake it, he could no longer live outside the official world of sorcerers. He could no longer go unnoticed. Did he not also owe it to Annwyn to restore her life? She was cursed to love him and desire him, while existing in the body of another woman. She had lost everything: her body, her life, her chance at real love. It was possible he could find away to undo the spell, but there was a missing element—Nira.

Rafael rose wearily from his chair and stood against the wall, keeping clear of Dane's restless pacing. Dane slowed, conscious that his greater size could intimidate the smaller, older man.

Rafael guided Dane back to his seat and said, 'This is serious indeed. If I help you, we must be careful. At anytime I may have to reveal to the other members of the collegium the state of your affairs. Your audacity in using spells, which are usually the reserve of the highest of the collegium, will not go in your favour, if the truth be known.

'So often you have ignored the advice I have offered you, spurned the offer of embrace from the collegium. While I understand your concerns about your father's end, you ask much of me. This situation is serious. The collegium faces external threats as well as internal at this time. This attack on you and the actions you have taken as a result could be enough to overthrow order in the collegium.'

Dane swallowed, finally seeing the old man's viewpoint. He had tried to mentor him, encourage him to join the collegium, and Dane had spurned him. 'I'm sorry. I see how you must view my behaviour. I haven't been able to speak my heart on the matter. There is grief and there is suspicion. It's not easy to rid myself of them. I apologise for offending you. I have always looked to you with respect and friendship.'

'And I you.' Rafael shook his head, his expression grim.

When Rafael didn't speak again straightaway, Dane asked, 'What are these external factors anyway? Is not the collegium the highest and most respected of all supernaturals?'

Rafael sat down and relaxed his expression. 'We have long thought of ourselves that way, but things change. Other groups want us to join with them, or at the very least participate more.' Rafael noted Dane's look of puzzlement. 'The vampires, for one, grow more daring, and their numbers have been on the increase since a few of the older ones stopped fighting among themselves.

United, they seek more recognition and dominance.'

'And the collegium stands in the way?'

'Yes. Then there are those who do not qualify for the collegium. Those, you understand, that have some talent but lack discipline, the connections and, therefore, sponsorship to join our ranks. They see us as elitist and would gladly see us brought down.'

Dane could tell there was more to the situation than Rafael was letting on. He could not understand why those who wanted to join the collegium were so bent on destroying it. He tried to extract more information from the old man. 'The stance on werewolves?'

Rafael rubbed his chin and inclined his head in acknowledgement. 'Them too. We have not made friends these latter days. For over a thousand years we have reigned supreme among our fellow supernaturals and paranormals. Now change is upon us. I see it clearly, but the remainder of the triumvirate do not.'

Dane could picture Brun and Vollos. The old sorcerers were obstinate and impossible to shift in their views. His father had despaired of them toward the end. Tord had told him once after a particularly bad session that their intransigence would bring the end of the collegium. A week later, he was dead.

'You need to be careful, Raf. My father locked horns with them before he died.'

'You suspect them of murder and treachery?' Rafael bristled with indignation.

'No, no. It's just that what you're saying to me now brought back recollections of what my father said before he died.'

Rafael relaxed. 'You should have come to me months ago and not delved into your father's hoard of rare spell books without proper guidance and supervision.'

'I see that now. Forgive me my pride and my suspicion.'

'Where did you find the sacred texts by the way? They were not recovered during the investigation. A few other rare works are missing as well.'

'He sent them to me before he died.' This was part-truth.

Dane had also secured some of his father's collection before the family home had been sealed by the collegium.

Rafael lifted an eyebrow. 'Really? I would not have suspected Tord. Very well. You must stay tonight so we can run a forensic examination on this spell.'

Dane wished to respond to the slight against his father. Tord had believed in the collegium wholeheartedly. He had thought all sorcerers should be regulated and accountable. He did not want a return to those dark times when sorcerers ran amok, raining down spells on the unsuspecting populace, fighting wars among themselves and tinkering with the destiny of humans. 'What about the human woman? She is alone and unprotected.'

'We will deal with your human in due course.'

'I will consent to the examination, but I must return to Sydney by morning, which is in eight or so hours.'

'If you are open to it, we could use the collegium securitas to aid you in your search. Justice could be yours sooner than you hope.'

Nothing could be further from his mind. He tried to come up with a good excuse to keep others out of his way. 'I am not a member of the collegium.'

'Not yet, but you must be.'

Those words were no comfort to him. They weighed heavily, threatening and inevitable as the moon's thrall. To give in was to lose control of his life.

'Truly? Can you tell me nothing of this body-swapping spell? Have you heard of it? Can it be reversed?'

Rafael sat up in his chair and squared his shoulders. 'While you are not a member of the collegium I cannot answer your questions. All I can tell you is that I will do my best to remedy the situation, if indeed it can be remedied.'

Dane met his mentor's gaze. 'This is the only choice I have? Join the collegium or nothing? What if I hunt down this Nira and force her to reverse the spell?'

Rafael tilted his head, his gaze firmly set on Dane. 'Didn't your efforts to do so already backfire? This Nira has proven wily. She is not likely to assist you willingly, is she?'

'No. However, if I can learn who is behind her, who put her

up to it, then it will open things up.'

"And what if what you find is not one sorcerer, not one known enemy, but a horde of unknowns? What then?'

The air rushed out of Dane's lungs. 'I don't know.'

'She could be a renegade, one of those who were spurned by the collegium when seeking admittance, but one who still chooses to practise. You yourself could be considered one also.'

'Me a renegade? But I do not defy the collegium or work against it. I just don't want to cooperate. There is a difference.'

'In times of war it is often those who are not with us who are against us. It's not a tenet I agree with, but I understand the sentiment.'

Dane sat back, suddenly understanding the depth of feeling Rafael experienced and the issues facing the collegium.

Rafael leaned forward, his hands outstretched, imploring. 'Will you join us? Will you allow yourself to be tested? I assure you that the triumvirate will welcome you as a much cherished son.'

Dane had now reached a point in his life where he must take a stand. His father had tried and failed. If Dane walked away from Rafael's aid, from the collegium's aid, then he too could be doomed to failure, to worse than failure. He could see the logic of Rafael's argument and couldn't turn away. The magnitude of the issues facing the collegium had escaped him. He could no longer be idle. He had to make a stand.

'Yes. I will submit to testing.'

# Chapter Nine

Annwyn stayed on the balcony for some time watching the restless ocean waves silvered by moonlight. Anger lingered, misdirected and futile. Considering what she had been through, she was coping quite well. Watching the dark ocean did nothing to counteract her state of mind. A cold mood crept up on her and deadened her mind. After returning inside she ordered room service. She had no idea what she was ordering. Words just came out of her mouth. The pacing began when she hung up the phone. It was a disconnected type of pacing. It was as if she was observing and not really participating. When the tray arrived she drank the merlot straight from the bottle. If she ate she had no recollection of it.

Much later, Annwyn was aware she was sleeping. There was wine in her system, making her feel sluggish. The sour taste on her tongue was unpleasant. Her head on the pillow did not help the room stop spinning. The hotel was quiet. Very soon her awareness of her surroundings dimmed, and she dreamed.

Her dreaming eyes opened. She was in a house, one that was familiar yet strange. It was Dane's house. She could hear the intermittent sweep of a tree branch against a window, the croak of frogs from the pond outside and the snore of dogs. The sounds comforted her while she rose up through the layers of sleep to wakefulness.

The bed she was in was empty. For some reason she knew Dane was gone. The absence of Dane left a physical ache. Her dream shifted to the cause of that ache, the fantastic sex they had shared that day. Part of her was angry that she was out of control. Nira's presence in her mind had caused her arousal, had artificially amplified it. Even knowing that, she wanted more, wanted his hot body on her, in her.

In her dream he was naked before her, aroused with burning desire in his eyes. He wanted her badly. It made her heart beat faster. She was so safe, so nurtured in his arms and so fulfilled when he touched her sensually, he brought her to easy arousal. Dane had said that it was the binding spell which was a double-edged sword for them both. It went both ways. Annwyn did not have to live with the knowledge that she desired him and that the feeling was not returned. She found it hard to digest that it came from a magic spell. Her emotion and desires were real and natural to her.

With a sigh, Annwyn tried to shift the direction of the dream, tried to stop the natural progression and failed. The image of Dane pumping his seed into her filled her mind as she slept. Her thoughts took a more erotic turn as their positions changed. In the dream she was not shy or careful. Dane was not so restrained. Annwyn was aware that these positions, these postures, were bizarre and outlandish. She fought to change them but then gave up. It was just a dream. Desire swept through her, and she heard herself moan from the power of her arousal.

Images rapid and colourful swamped her. She opened her eyes, and she was in another room. Chanting and smoke filled the air and a feather stroked her naked flesh. She looked down and saw her pale body, and fingers probed her sex. *Nira?*

Again there was a mirror, but this time Nira was not alone. From what Annwyn could see there were other people there, naked men. One was behind Nira. He slid into her from behind. It hurt. Nira inhaled the pain and then channelled it, letting out a sound of pleasure. Annwyn shuddered. This was her body that was being defiled like this. Then, as Annwyn watched, another naked man approached with his long penis fully engorged. As he stood there Nira pleasured him with her mouth, then brought him to his knees, letting them both penetrate her. Nira let her arousal flood their connection. Annwyn had no way to combat the surge of desire that ripped through her, leaving her senseless and with her defences down. The positions changed again. As Annwyn lay there gasping, Nira smiled as she crawled into the man's lap and slowly lowered herself onto his erection. The man stared, his expression blank and trance-like. The chanting hovered in the air, soft wings of words around their heads. As she fully impaled herself Nira let desire rip through her and she slipped into Annwyn. Annwyn could not fight the connection, nor the overpowering assault by Nira. She kicked off the covers, touched her breasts, her own moist heat, in a last-ditched attempt to bring her back to herself. As Nira blanketed her with her presence the light receded, leaving her in a dark space from which she could not escape.

***

Rafael summoned Max. The assistant opened the door quickly. 'Yes, sir?'

'Please set up one of the testing rooms. The rest of the triumvirate will arrive shortly. See to it that all is as it should be.'

Dane lifted an eyebrow. 'The three of you will test me? That seems a little bit of overkill.' There went his plans for keeping things circumspect, and it made the task of hiding his power undetected more difficult.

'I will test you. Brun will witness. Vollos wants to be included. They think highly of you.'

'But is that normal for you all to be involved?'

A sad expression slipped across the older man's features but was dispelled with a quick smile.

'No. It is not normal for the triumvirate to officiate. I'm sponsoring you so it is natural that I be there. The others, I think, come for your father's sake. He was a member of the triumvirate for a long time.'

Dane tried to calm his breathing. How was he going to hide his power from three of the strongest minds in the collegium? It could be done, but he would have to hold his nerve. He hated to deceive Rafael, but he couldn't let the full extent of his powers be known. Tord had taught him from an early age how to hide his powers from others, even before they fully manifested themselves.

Dane nodded, pretending outward calm. He had already begun the mental preparation he required to begin the testing. Surreptitiously, he was channelling his power into pockets within himself, compressing it down so that his power would appear less.

Rafael stared at him for a few moments. 'You do not have to worry, Dane. The testing is not harmful and you will pass if what I suspect is true.'

***

Dane's natural reticence dogged him because he found Rafael's assistant annoying. Max always seemed to be listening, while doing a bad job of pretending not to. Dane did not want news of his testing broadcast to all and sundry, yet he could not think of a polite way to exclude him. Max anticipated Rafael's every need and organised everything for the testing perfectly. It wasn't until Rafael asked him to leave when the testing was about to commence that Dane's tension eased. He could have done without the distraction of the other man's comings and goings.

Vollos materialised first, his expression glowering. Hunched over and ancient, the old sorcerer held out his hand to Dane. Without hesitation, Dane stepped forward to kneel and kiss his hand. The old man reeked of age and power. Dane had only ever heard rumours of Vollos's age.

He had a Slavic accent. 'I welcome you, son of Tord. I welcome you to the collegium. This moment was long in coming.'

'Too long,' another voice said from the shadows. Brun glided forward. He was taller and slightly younger than Vollos. His rich robes hid much. Dane could not tell if he was muscled or had an emaciated frame within the velvet folds. 'It is good to see you, Dane.' Brun had been born in Bavaria several centuries earlier. A slight accent still lingered. Brun did not smile but nodded once to Rafael. 'Commence the testing. We will stand witness.'

Dane sat in a chair set in the centre of the room. Concentrating on his core, he let his power rise, the power he wanted to rise. Rafael examined him, pushing at his magic essence, pulling this way and that and, lastly, gauging the strength of it. Dane performed a few minor spells and was then asked to conjure images, which he did. More intricate tests followed until he judged that he had proved himself worthy, without revealing the true extent of his powers.

'The testing is complete. Congratulations, Dane. You have satisfied the test to enter the collegium. You are a sorcerer of mid-range power, a level five, with potential to grow to a higher rank.'

Dane cast a look about him, catching the disappointed sigh from Vollos and the bright-eyed stare from Brun. Had they been expecting more?

This was surprising to Dane. Only Rafael's revelations had made him aware the triumvirate had any interest in him. Now it seemed certain. They wanted something from him, and they were disappointed. Dane thought he had successfully kept the true measure of his power hidden, but the glint in Rafael's eye made him wonder if the old man suspected what he was doing. He wondered if his old friend had discerned the untapped potential.

Vollos officiated at his swearing in. When the old sorcerers left Dane was a full member of the collegium and bound by his oaths and the collegium's rules. Rafael could then be unrestrained in his agreement to help find the person who had targeted him, and to help unravel the binding spell and the moon bound curse. But that would take time and Dane had just about run out.

'A nightcap before you go, Dane?'

Dane agreed. It was a small sacrifice to take a drink with the old man, and he would still be able to return to Australia and to Annwyn before dawn.

Back in the conference room where they first met, Max had prepared a lace-frilled tray with a bottle of liqueur and two silver goblets. Two comfortable chairs had been arranged facing one another. All that was missing was a roaring fire for the scene to look like one from Rafael's castle. Max left the room as they sat down. Dane eased his shoulders, still not comfortable around the other man.

Once they were alone, Rafael poured a goblet of red liquid and passed it to Dane. The liqueur was sweet and cloying and slid easily down his throat. *A liqueur Muscat*, Dane thought, *and a good one*. Rafael nestled his goblet between hands resting on his stomach. 'So tell me about Annwyn. Is there anything remarkable about this human? Any hint as to why she was chosen to be Nira's vessel?'

Dane took another sip of the liqueur and swallowed. 'Nothing that springs to mind. She was living alone and seems to be a sweet, honest sort of person and kind of lonely. She had no recollection of ever meeting Nira before the transfer. I admit I'm puzzled as there is no obvious link.'

'I would like to examine this human of yours. Will you permit me?'

Dane wasted no time in hesitation. 'Yes, but if it is not too impertinent of me, may I ask you do so at my home? She would find it more comfortable there.'

Rafael finished his drink and placed the goblet on the table. 'That is acceptable to me. Tomorrow evening your time?'

'Yes, that will give me time to drive her back. We are currently in Sydney on the trail of the sorceress.'

Rafael poured some more liqueur and stared at the liquid while deep in thought. 'So you can track this Nira?'

'When Nira is sexually active, she can establish a connection with Annwyn. From that we were able to trace her.' Dane did not mention Rolf. While Rafael was a friend, he was not sure how he would take his close association with werewolves, given the traditional view of them as lowlifes. Although Rafael had been his father's closest friend, Dane had reservations about telling him all the details of his life. Whether this reticence was deserved or not, he did not know. For now, it would have to do.

Rafael nodded. 'I suppose it is natural if one has such an emphasis on the sexual poles, and if that is her practice.' He shuddered visibly, then shook his head. 'I will see you tomorrow. Perhaps I will know more by then.'

***

Rolf slipped quietly into the hotel suite. It looked like the sofa was to be his bed for the night as both the bedrooms were taken. There were worse places to sleep, he supposed. He growled softly, remembering his frustration in losing the sorceress's trail.

He'd lost her in Kings Cross among the prostitutes and sex clubs. Obviously, she knew he was onto her, given the deliberate smearing of scents and misdirection. He admired her skill at evasion.

Dane was going to be angry about it. What good was Rolf's nose if he lost track of important people? Well, Dane could sniff his arse for all he cared. His friend would have to live with being a fully-fledged werewolf if he couldn't rid himself of the curse. Rolf lived with it and so could Dane. So what if in the eyes of his sorcerer kin, he'd be considered as being less than human. Rolf lived with that discrimination daily. He was sure Dane would get used to it.

The biggest problem involved territory. Rolf was an alpha wolf and had his own pack, and Dane looked to be an alpha as well, meaning either Dane or Rolf would have to move out of the pack's territory or fight for leadership. A difficult choice because Dane owned their hunting range as it fell in the boundaries of his property.

Rolf ran his hand through his hair, making it stand up in spikes, and groaned. It was for this reason that Rolf had remained a loyal friend, and he'd happily serve Dane as an employee—freelance, at least. He'd rather keep his friend than fight him or lose him. Yet as an alpha of his own pack, leadership was not something to give up lightly. Death was the only likely way out of the situation. After stripping off his clothes Rolf sprawled on the sofa. There was no use worrying about the situation now, and Dane had to be master of his own destiny. He put the thoughts of pack and Dane out of his mind and tried to sleep.

He'd not been long asleep when he heard the human woman moaning. He sat up and sniffed. There was definitely the scent of sexual arousal in the air. He sniffed again. Dane had not returned so it couldn't be him dallying with her and causing the wonderful bouquet filling his nostrils. That meant either that the woman was masturbating or that the sorceress Nira was back again, reaching out to the poor human and manipulating her. In either case, his cock hardened in the presence of such a wonderful scent.

Rolf pulled on his boxers and padded over to the bedroom door. He tried the handle and it was unlocked. Carefully, he edged the door ajar and peeked in. Annwyn writhed on the bed naked, sheets tangled around her throat, hands twisting, twisting, tightening further. Without thinking, Rolf leaped on the bed and loosened the bed covering from around the woman's throat. After flicking the lamp on, he barely ducked the hand intent on punching him in the side of the head.

Annwyn's eyes were dark and large, filled with something, another presence—*Nira*. He tossed the sheet to the floor. Annwyn sat up and grabbed for his boxers, ripping them from his body. His erection sprung out, growing in size as arousal washed over him. He gaped at the sight between his legs. He'd never been that big or had an erection feel that painful before. It had to be magically enhanced. This Nira could do that? God help him.

Naked, Nira crawled over the bed on all fours, arching her back like a cat, licking her lips and grinning hungrily at him. Dane had said no sharing. Yet he figured that it was Nira in control of the body at this time. A little oral sex wouldn't hurt anyone, would it? And he ached so badly, he needed relief. His cock throbbed in such a way that only a good fuck would do. He recalled that Annwyn only had eyes and lust for Dane. The intent in Nira's eyes was for sex, sex with anyone.

To gauge what she would do, he edged back out of the woman's reach. The woman growled low in her throat, a sound that ripped up his spine as if it was full of 'were' lust.

Shaking her blonde hair like a dog flicking water off its coat, she let her lips pout and then moistened them with a red tongue. Rolf's nostrils flared. She was good. He was well and truly hooked.

'Let me have a taste,' she said in a husky voice. 'Don't be shy.' Her gaze was riveted to his cock, a glint in her eye. Her lips curved into a smile. 'Nice, well-hung wolf like you can't be afraid of a little woman like me now, can you?' He stayed perfectly still as she drew closer, nostrils flaring as he caught the arousal on her scent. She licked her lips as she cautiously approached on all fours, bringing her face closer to him, closer to the tip of his erection.

Rolf was bound to the spot as her warm breath teased the tip. He looked down as she moved her head from side to side and brushed her lips against him. A groan escaped as his erection hardened further. *Not possible*, he thought, as he gasped. Suddenly, her hot mouth enveloped him, sucking so hard and fast that his knees nearly buckled. Relaxing the pressure, she let him glide out of her mouth, flicking the tip with her tongue before sliding it down his shaft, wet with moisture. His growl of pleasure filled the room. He looked on as she lapped at him, keeping the pressure up, teasing him until he could hardly breathe.

Changing pace, she took him deep into her mouth and sucked, hard and strong. This time he fell to his knees, thinking he would erupt with pleasure as she increased the rhythm, leaving his cock wet and throbbing when she released him. An involuntary groan slid from him. She had brought him so close, timed her withdrawal perfectly. Before he could speak or move, she had reversed her position and began rubbing her arse against him.

Rolf took his time admiring the curve of her buttocks, back and shoulder as well as the feel of his cock in the crease of her arse. A frustrated growl erupted from her, a dark, reverberating sound that echoed in his bones.

With a voice of command, she called out. 'Take me! Take me now!'

She reached behind and grabbed a cheek in each hand, opening herself up to him. When he didn't move fast enough, she said. 'Come on, you cur, fuck me, if you have it in you.'

Through the intoxicating haze of arousal, he detected something in the voice. Command and magic laced together. He knew this wasn't Annwyn he was dealing with. The danger should have been apparent from the very beginning. Annwyn was Dane's, and off limits. But this wasn't Annwyn, it was Nira and, God, Nira wanted him.

Rolf leaned forward and inhaled her scent, letting it fill him up. Using a moistened finger to ease his way, he paused when she opened up to him. *Ah, that's right. She was a regular with anal sex.* Of course, Dane said she used sex in her magic. Grabbing hold of her hips, he positioned her, sliding slowly inside her, hesitant in case he hurt her. When he was all the way in, she closed around him, muscles tightening with inhuman control. He yowled at the ceiling as the sensation of her squeezing his erection took him to new heights of arousal. He began to move, withdrawing slowly and pushing back in, always careful not to hurt her.

A growl of frustration erupted from her. 'Stop playing with me. Fuck me harder. Faster. You prick. Fuck me like a real man.'

*Hell, she was one nasty piece of work*, he thought, as she slapped her thigh and upped the pace. He grinned in satisfaction when she growled low in her throat. Finally, he detected some pleasure from her. There was something visceral in the sounds she made and the way she threw herself back against him as they fucked. While he admired the smooth line of her back, he listened to the noises she made when he thrust into her. It made him feel superior, in charge, in control, masterful. He could pleasure this woman and, right then, that was all that was on his mind. He kept himself back, rode his arousal but did not let himself come. Not until she had come again and again.

He rode her increasingly harder, surprised at how long he could maintain the pace. No wonder Dane was addicted to sex with this woman. *No*, he reminded himself, *with Annwyn, not Nira*. It made a difference and there was a spell that made them want each other.

As they fucked he was less aware of the room they were in, less aware of his breathing and the feel of her muscles squeezing his erection. Shaking his head, he tried to clear his thoughts. At sometime, he'd lost control of the situation and himself. He needed to fight back. Focusing on Annwyn, he wondered if she was gone permanently. Was Nira in possession of her own body for good? Where was Annwyn? Was she still inside that body, feeling him fucking her up the arse? He held onto that thought, tried to use it to dislodge himself from the fugue that had settled on him.

'Annwyn?' he managed to say.

Again the growl, full of desire and hunger. 'Shut up and fuck, you useless hound. Annwyn doesn't matter, only I do.'

Rolf reached down and stroked her wet folds, more to distract himself, but also to see if he could make contact with Annwyn, whether there was an element of her in there willing and able to fight against the sorceress's possession. 'Annwyn. Are you there? Fight her, dammit!'

That didn't seem to work. Nira just called out, 'Yes, more, harder. Yes.' Then she spread her knees, further allowing him access to her slick labia.

Although he was thrusting quite vigorously, he was not ready to climax. He really wanted to. It would end this encounter, though, and he would cease to be of use to Nira. Yet something was in the way, blocking his release. If anything, his erection felt harder and more painful. Was this Nira interfering? Using him as part of her magic? He tried to stop, tried to break free, but could not. He was thrusting into her and could not stop.

Nira shouted as she came, shuddering and then trembling along her arms and legs. He was free to let her go, and slid from her thinking she was done with him. He was dazed from lust, with pain gathering in his cock. How could he not come? He had heard of men going for too long and then not being able to release. Was that what had happened?

Quickly, she leaped to her feet, and faced him. 'Kneel!'

Shakily, on his knees before her, his world span. Before he could bring himself into line, she kicked him in the gut and, winded, he fell sideways onto the floor. That shouldn't have happened, he thought dazedly. It was like being drugged, he was so sluggish. *How dare she do this to him!* He wanted to wrap his fingers around her throat and squeeze.

'Get up! I am in control now. You will do as I say or die. Get on the bed.'

Rolf tried to fight her magic. Nonchalantly, he climbed on

the bed and reclined on his elbow, feeling a chuckle rise up his throat. He was 'were' and he could fight this unnatural hold on him. However, when she lifted a hand, quirked a finger, he jerked upright. He manoeuvred himself to the edge of the bed, with his legs slightly apart, his cock standing up. His view of the world altered. He wanted to fuck this gorgeous woman. Why had he been fighting it? She was beautiful and sexy and his cock just wanted to sink into her again and again. He wanted to send his seed into her, to make their life together happy.

'Now we will fuck. You will fuck for your life.'

Steadying herself with her hands on his shoulders, she straddled him, lowering herself onto his erection, hesitating slightly as she accommodated his enhanced width. 'Good boy.' She licked his face, bit his lips and teased his mouth with her tongue. All he saw was this beautiful woman looking at him with loving eyes, eyes burning with power that reached right into his soul.

He lifted her by the waist and shoved her hard along his cock. She bucked and groaned, enjoying every thrust.

'Now, little wolf, let's see you track this.' She rode him, using muscles he didn't know a woman could possess. She could sit still and still make it feel as if she was riding him. She started chanting, speaking words that flowed over him, words that lulled him further into the realm of dream. He saw the glint of metal, the shape of a knife in her hand, but he could not focus on it. He could only focus on those flashing green eyes, the burning lust in his veins and the feel of her tight cunt squeezing his cock.

His climax neared, not quite there but teasingly close. The pressure built in his abdomen, ready to explode. She was gasping now, working hard to climax. He had never been ridden before. It was against his nature. He was the alpha, he chose, he seduced, yet this was some extraordinary fuck.

'Rolf!' Dane's voice cut through the dream world he inhabited. His eyes snapped open, his head suddenly clear, his mind free. Nira had her arms raised, knife poised above him. Her gaze hardened; she was going in for the kill. Rolf blocked the knife with his arm, using the momentum to shove her sideways, while twisting himself to free his now shrinking erection. The knife flew out of her hand and landed harmlessly on the floor.

Using her elbows, she levered herself up from the floor to glare at Dane.

'You!' she spat.

Rolf saw he was no longer in her thoughts and scuttled over to the other side of the bed. The look in Dane's eyes told him some serious magic was about to erupt. Rolf had had his share for one night. Nira's magic had left him reeling as if he was hungover, except that he didn't get hangovers, not since he had had his first moon turning.

Lifting her arm, Nira went to throw a hex, but Dane must have got in first because she flew up and back to impact on the wall.

Rolf wished he had collected the knife as he'd like to skewer the bitch, but then what would happen to the other one, to Annwyn? With a deepening fascination, he watched as Nira hung suspended against the wall about a foot off the floor. The flash of her green eyes dimmed and her expression blanked as she fled. Dane let go his hold and the body crumpled as it fell to the carpet.

Dane raced over to her and caressed Annwyn's/Nira's face. 'You hurt?' he murmured. Annwyn didn't respond. Dane settled her on the floor and rounded on him.

'I told you no sharing.' Dane's posture bristled with rage as he drew in tense breath after breath.

There was an intensity in the other man's gaze that Rolf reacted to on a subconscious level. Dane was in full alpha mode, and Rolf could not fail to respond to it. He was in the wrong. Annwyn was Dane's. Rolf had not even tried to establish a claim other than to lust after her when Dane wasn't looking. Normally, he would have respected that. There was a lot to do to explain his actions.

'I know.' Rolf shifted uncomfortably, his gaze on the floor. 'It wasn't Annwyn. I know that doesn't mean much, but it was the other one.'

'So you thought it was Nira?'

'No, I didn't think it was her, it was her.'

Dane gaze widened. 'You could tell?'

'Yes, definitely. It's in the eyes.'

Dane nodded. 'So how did you come to be...'

Rolf shrugged. Dane wasn't going to kill him, but he knew there would be further discussion later. 'She initiated it. I was in control first, but then somehow—well, things changed. I was under her spell before I realised and I could no longer control myself.'

Rolf kept his gaze on Annwyn and ran his fingers through his hair. Rolf noticed that his hands were trembling. The encounter had rattled him, he guessed. First, Dane had found his friend fucking his woman and, second, then had to fight a supernatural battle to save the traitorous friend. The whole 'two people in one body' thing was pretty unnerving for them all.

'It's Annwyn now, I hope,' Dane said, his voice quiet and calm.

'Nira is not a nice lady, though she's damned kinky in the sack.'

Dane shook his head. 'Stop thinking with your prick. She was about to stab you, kill you, to be exact.'

'I can see that now, but somehow I couldn't see. I didn't even know she had a knife. Everything was dreamlike, except I couldn't come. She made me harder and larger than I've ever been before but I couldn't bring it off.' He looked down. His erection was still there, though nowhere near as painful as before.

'She had you in a spell. Perhaps you should see to it.' He indicated with his chin. 'I think there's an establishment near here that might be useful to you. I'll make you a charm against her. I have the taste of her now so I should be able to counter her influence effectively.'

Rolf grinned. 'Yeah. I'll see to it.' He reached down to pull on his boxers and paused with them in his hand. 'So what's with the knife? Why did she want to kill me?'

Dane knelt and stroked Annwyn's brow. The woman seemed to be coming around. 'Besides you being an annoying bastard that can follow her scent? I'm guessing she needs a blood sacrifice to get her body back.'

They both looked at Annwyn, watching her revive with interest. 'Do you think she's back in control? Her eyes are shut. I can't really tell right now,' Rolf said.

'Not sure. Let's put her back on the bed. Find something to tie her up with, just to make sure. Even if it is Annwyn, Nira might come back for another go.'

'And if it is still Nira, what about Annwyn?'

Dane lowered his head and stroked his chin as a glum look overshadowed his features. 'If it's Nira, then I best find the real Annwyn because who knows what situation Nira might have left her in.'

Rolf shuddered. There was something innocent about Annwyn, and he could picture her horror at being left in a sex club in a compromising position. It could quite possibly send her mad. Hell, it would send him mad to be shunted out of his own body and thrust somewhere else. It sounded much worse than a moon turning. Even with his first change, he had not felt dislocated. It was still him inside the beast.

'I think I'll take a shower,' Rolf said.

Dane moved to the doorway, blocking his friend's path to the bathroom. 'I really did mean it when I said no sharing.'

Rolf licked his lips. 'I know, but you had to be there.' He shrugged, and smiled wolfishly. 'She offered me her arse. How could I resist?'

'Next time, if there is a next time, I don't care if she offers you eternal life. She's mine and until this situation resolves itself and she can choose freely, you'll keep away from her.'

'But she did choose, well, Nira did.' Rolf shook his head, confused by the other man's words. Dane expected the situation to resolve? He expected that the woman would choose someone else rather than him? Rolf fought the urge to laugh. Spell or no spell, Annwyn wanted Dane as much as Dane wanted her. The spell, he suspected, only enhanced the attraction between them.

With a friendly punch on his arm, Dane moved out of the way. 'You know what I mean, when the Nira/Annwyn body thing is resolved or when I can reverse the spell.'

Rolf gave him a nod. 'Understood.'

With a slight acknowledgement, Dane went to pick up the woman from the floor. 'Don't forget something to tie her up with before you take that shower.'

Rolf came back in shorts and a T-shirt and carrying a shiny, orange object in his hand.

Dane looked at him. 'Duct tape?'

'You never know when you need to keep people in line.'

Together they taped Annwyn/Nira to the bed. Rolf took great pleasure in taping up her mouth and enjoyed a nice long look at her sex when they taped her ankles to either side of the bed base.

Dane noticed his interest. 'Go and get yourself laid, right now, before we come to blows. I said no sharing and that includes looking.'

'Anything you say, boss.'

Rolf left the building by the staircase. He needed to work off some energy. At the best of times he had to work a woman hard. If he wasn't careful, he could injure a non-'were'. He walked down to Coogee Beach, the cool sand giving way beneath his feet. Waves caressed the shore tempting him. A swim would help. He found a secluded spot near the south end, and left his clothes buried in the sand. A light drizzle had started and it was the best way to keep his clothes dry. After swimming a kilometre or two, he headed back to shore.

A wind had whipped up the waves making the water choppier. He visually scanned the beach, finding no one in sight. He climbed out, letting the water drip away naturally. As he bent to pick up his clothes he caught her scent. It was a 'were' female, very close and watching with interest. He could pick her out from the salt tang that laced the air.

He stood there naked, waiting for her to approach. After glancing at his rather normal-looking erection, he hoped he hadn't swum too far and that he still had enough stamina to satisfy. She wanted action. He could tell by her scent and her approach. A long-legged female strode into sight, long hair whipped up by the wind. She unzipped her short tunic dress, letting if fall to the ground as she walked toward him in a straight line.

She appraised him boldly, looking up and down before lifting her eyebrow when she centred on his erection. 'Now that wasn't what I was expecting when I headed out for a stroll tonight.'

He growled. 'Me neither,' he replied, flashing her a grin. His smile showed he wasn't going to attack her. 'Though you are a welcome sight.'

She inclined her head, showing meekness. 'Shall we?' she said in a soft, sensual voice. With her head bowed, she looked up at him, a slight smile giving her face a mischievous cast.

His grin widened and she stepped in closer. A wave of heat came off her body, and she slid herself against his wet skin. He nipped at her neck, and she growled before she caught his mouth in a passionate kiss.

'Who are you?' he asked, holding her away from him even though he wanted to shove her down in the sand and have his way with her till she screamed.

'Layla from Kaylen's clan.'

'You?'

'Rolf, alpha of the alpine pack.'

She bowed her head. 'I'm honoured to meet you, alpha.'

'Are you anyone's?' Kaylen had a ferocious reputation, and he wasn't about to get another alpha's back up by screwing his mate.

'No, I'm still finding my way.' She grinned, running her hand along his thigh. 'You want help with that?' she said as she cupped his balls. 'I think you're up for it,' she said, running her hand along his shaft and tilting her head back so he could see her smile. 'More than up for it.'

Rolf groaned as she touched him gently but confidently. 'I can't hold on for too long. I have to apologise in advance for my lack of finesse. It's going to be fast and hard.' Her eyes widened. She licked her lips slowly.

'I'm up for it.'

'Now that I know who you are, I'll come find you and make it up to you. Next time, I promise to take my time. Right now...'

He grabbed her by the buttocks and lifted her. She hooked her leg over him and held on tight as he slid into her. God, he loved tall women. Balancing on one leg, she leaned back to give him access to her breasts. She squeaked when he took a nipple in his mouth. He kept the pressure up as she whimpered with pleasure, gasping with her climax. Holding her tightly, he knelt, laying her gently back onto the sand. The urge to thrust into her overtook him. To his surprise she met him, lifting herself in time to his thrusts. 'I love the feel of you inside me,' she said, panting with the rhythm of their movement. In answer, he hunched over her, catching her mouth in a deep, searing kiss. Then she turned her head, offering her neck. He nipped and sucked, feeling her body tense. Her reaction to him was amazing. She was so sensual, so responsive. He wanted to believe it was real but his encounter with Nira had damaged him.

The sound of the waves crashing behind him and the distant traffic noises cocooned them. When he finally shuddered, filling her up with his seed, he let out a long, slow groan. He eased himself out of her, ensuring that she lay comfortably on the sand.

Quickly, he checked the surroundings, grateful that no one was about. Soon the early morning joggers would be pounding the promenade. They had been lucky to have the beach to themselves. It was a rare luxury to mate out of doors and on a beach. The only other time he had managed it was on pack territory in the hills at the back of Dane's property. He lay down and cradled Layla in his arms. Although he had his favourites, none of the pack females were of Layla's calibre. Layla tucked her head under his chin and placed her arm across his chest. She didn't speak, only lay there with him and held him close.

Then, as the first rays of the sun sent fingers of light across the horizon, she moved. Both of them dressed quickly before they were seen. 'Will I see you again?' she asked him.

'I hope so, Layla.'

She cocked her head to one side. 'Are you sure you will remember me? I sense you have someone else on your mind.'

Pulling his T-shirt over his head, he grinned at her. 'I have a lot of things on my mind. I'm not from around here. You wouldn't like my territory...'

She frowned with puzzlement. 'No beach and it's cold in winter.'

Layla nodded. 'I see, but I would have you to keep me warm.'

He grinned back at her. 'I have to go now. Thank you for your company. I'm sorry I can't offer more.'

Checking that her dress was zipped up, she scanned the beach and then nodded. With a bow of her head she retreated and was soon gone from sight. He could still taste her on the back of his tongue, the tang of her scent not easy to forget. With a sigh of regret he headed back to the hotel. Dane would be expecting him soon.

# Chapter Ten

A thumping headache woke Annwyn the next morning. The world was a blur when she first opened her eyes before hastily shutting them again, and her head hurt like it was in a vice. *What in the world happened to me?* she wondered.

With her eyes closed and still feeling groggy, she registered pain in her lower back, a throbbing as if she had fallen badly. Next, she noticed constriction around her mouth. Snapping her eyes open, she tried to scream but found herself muffled. She tried to move and found that she couldn't. She was tied to a bed. The bland ceiling of the hotel room hove into view. She was still in the hotel, in the room where she had gone to bed. Her mind flicked furiously through various explanations for her predicament, but none made any sense.

A noise drew her attention to Dane dozing in a chair by the window. Confusion threatened to undo her. *How? Why? Dane did this? But he cared for her, didn't he?* Their parting had been sweet. Yet here he was sitting in a chair while she was tied up. How could that have happened? She tried to recall the previous night's events, but nothing came to mind. Sleep, bed, that was all she could recall.

She was securely tied. How could this be? Glancing down, she saw she was naked and spreadeagled across the bed. *Oh God, this can't be happening*, she thought furiously. Thrashing her head to the side, she saw that her arms were anchored. Not in a painful way, other than to her extreme embarrassment.

Another glance at the dozing Dane, and her anger rose. He wore boxer shorts and nothing else. She felt like killing that bastard for doing this to her. Was it some kind of sick joke to tie her up? For the life of her, she could not think of any reasonable excuse for it. Yet she trusted him, and that trust went right down into her soul. Could that instinct, that innate sense, be so wrong?

The disappointment only added to her anger that was building low in her gut. She wanted to scream out, to thump and thump at him.

Dane jolted awake and crawled across the bed with careful movements. With eyebrows drawn together he peered into her eyes for some minutes. 'Annwyn?' His voice was a soft caress.

She nodded, feeling the tears of relief slide down her face. It was obvious to her that he didn't hate her. It had been a mistake after all.

Dane relaxed visibly, sighing into her ear as he tugged the tape from her mouth. It hurt, making her anger and frustration rise again.

'Oww…'

He kissed her lips softly, like a mother soothing a child's hurt. 'Sorry. I'm so sorry that hurt.'

'Did you do this?' she asked croakily, throat dry.

He nodded, concern creasing his brow. 'But it was necessary.' His gaze slid down her naked form and a small smile transformed his face from worry to something else. How dare he be amused by her predicament!

'Untie me, you piece of shit. How dare you tie me up! Are you stark raving mad?'

Dane paused, assessing her with his dark gaze. 'Apologise for that language right now.'

'I'm sorry,' Annwyn gasped. She hadn't meant to apologise as she was damned angry. Besides, she hurt all over for some reason. Why couldn't she remember what had happened? Her body felt as if she had a hangover and had been run over by a car.

Dane let a sigh escape as his smile grew larger. 'Yes, it's definitely Annwyn in there now.'

It was that spell again. His body heat and light scent washed over her. She did her best to concentrate on what he was saying. 'Now? What do you mean now?' A sick feeling grew in the back of her mind, like the left over smell of burning toast. Nira had come back again. Why did she not just take her body back and give Annwyn hers?

Dane nodded, seeing some dawning light in her eyes. 'Yes. You had a little visitor last night. One that liked shagging.'

'Did I? Shagging? Was it...you?' It wouldn't be too bad if it was Dane. She liked fucking him, even if she didn't remember.

Dane shook his head. She swallowed and gaped at him in disbelief. *Oh, heavens!* I don't want anyone else but Dane. How could I have shagged someone else? How could Nira do that? She knew the answer as she had seen into her mind. Sex was not an emotional thing for her. It was a way to draw power, to manipulate and to dominate.

'Rolf.' He watched her expression.

She gasped. Rolf could barely stand her. The man made her feel edgy. She couldn't picture herself screwing the man or he her. 'I can't have. I was in here asleep.'

Dane shifted a lock of hair that had fallen onto her face. 'Rolf tells me Nira was very insistent. He couldn't refuse what was on offer.'

Dane was very close, appearing to watch every nuance of her expression. What must he feel about that betrayal? He had not said they were exclusive. But he acted as if they were, he treated her as if she was the centre of his world. Yes, there was a binding spell muddling things. Although she was certain there was more to it than that. There was a bond between them. 'Dear God, no. It...I didn't...I wouldn't...I mean...'

The smile was back, his gaze trailing over her face. 'She nearly knifed him before I came back.'

'What? Oh, dear God! How terrible!' What was that sorceress up to? She'd tried to kill Rolf? Why?

'I arrived in the nick of time.' Relief flooded through her. Although she hadn't been in control of her body, she felt some responsibility. Rolf was Dane's friend and if anything happened to him, then Dane would suffer and she wouldn't want that.

'And what happened then?'

'She put up a fight and wasn't giving up possession of this body.' He tweaked her nipple playfully. Perhaps he was trying to belie the seriousness of the situation. Her brow furrowed in puzzlement. It unnerved her that she had no recollection. She didn't even remember the initial connection. 'You fought Nira. Is that why I hurt?'

'Yes, I'm sorry about that. It got a little bit physical. She wasn't about to let Rolf go. You hit the wall and fell. Is it bad?'

Annwyn wanted to say yes because it did feel bad. However, it was more muscle soreness than anything serious. Being tied up for the rest of the night would not have helped either. 'It's not bad. Can you untie me?'

'We had to tie you up in case Nira came back. Although I suppose now that you are back and don't look like going anywhere I can untie you, if you really insist. You do look entirely ravishing this way, though.'

Annwyn was conscious of the fact that Dane was half lying on her and that she was still tied up and naked. Despite what he had told her, she felt herself respond to his nearness. Dane was less intent on freeing her than on caressing her neck and sidling even closer.

'Dane?'

'Yes?' He nibbled her neck, sending tendrils of electricity pulsing through her body.

'Do you intend to keep me tied up like this? I mean, I feel very exposed, very vulnerable.'

'Mmm.' He kissed her mouth lightly and then came back for a deeper kiss. 'You look very sexy. I know it's the spell and all, but I want to have you right now. The thought of you tied up and begging for it is driving me wild.'

Dane's kisses sent heat straight into her belly. She began to moisten at his mention of shagging her tied up. He nuzzled on a nipple, making her arch her back to offer him more. The thought was entirely appealing to her, although she wouldn't admit it. That would make her kinky or strange. Then she laughed softly. Stranger than being in another woman's body, willingly shagging a tall, handsome stranger she hardly knew? She almost burst out laughing.

He looked up over the peak of her breast. 'Tell me to stop. Tell me to untie you and I will.'

Annwyn shared a look with him, one that ignited her

passion right at its very core. She had to be honest with him and not coy. She took a breath and cast restraint to the wind. 'No, God, just take me. I want you so much.'

Dane needed no further invitation. He was delving between her labia and sucking on her clitoris within moments. She writhed and screamed as he brought her close to climax, then eased off, probing her with his fingers before licking her once again. When she finally sagged back against the bed after climaxing, Dane freed her arms. She attacked him with caresses, gripping his shoulders while he drew her down the bed and lifted her hips. Kneeling, he thrust inside her, riding her while her feet were anchored. Annwyn gave freely of herself. Dane always seemed to bring her to new heights and in new ways. She never thought being tied up could be so exhilarating, so thrilling.

To change the pace, she wanted to be free. She thought of the tape and then her ankles were free. She hadn't noticed him tearing the tape off. Straddling him in a bold move, she lowered herself on his erection, finding taking the initiative invigorating and liberating. His cock penetrated her so deeply she shivered with the contact. He was so hard and engorged. She was impaled and couldn't move. Then Dane put his hands around her waist and lifted her while he pumped. He was so strong.

She loved the feel of him inside her and around her. Her hands rested on his firm pecs, his underlying power moving under her fingers. A light sheen of sweat glistened on his lightly-tanned skin. She massaged it in, liking how the muscles moved beneath her touch, how she moved with him. There was something wild about his movements, an edge of ferocity that she found exciting to her soul. A solid core of heat was building inside, making her breath catch, making her throw her head back as she prepared to ride her orgasm.

*Oh God, he is undoing me.* Nothing was meant to be this good. They were making so much noise she wondered if Rolf could hear. She wondered if the people in the neighbouring rooms could hear. Then Dane asked her to lean back and he took a nipple into his mouth and suckled. After that she didn't care if they heard her down on Coogee Beach. She was in ecstasy.

Nothing had been this good before. Dane completed her in ways she never thought possible.

Afterwards they fell to the bed and lay there exhausted and replete. Touching, always touching, be it a hand, a finger, a shoulder, they remained connected. How did he manage to do that, to draw her out, to draw on everything she had? When she reflected on her life with Thomas, their connection had been sweet and tender and she had no regrets about that. Yet somehow in comparison, it now seemed shallow compared to the depth of her connection with Dane. She shook her head. This couldn't be; she hardly knew Dane and was a stranger in his world.

'Come on, then,' he said, tapping her on the rear. 'You'd best have a shower so we can check out.'

With a smile, she stretched and yawned. 'Yes, sir.' She hopped off the bed and headed to the bathroom.

'Hang on a minute,' Dane said, sitting up quickly. 'How did you remove the tape from your ankles?'

'I didn't. I thought you did.'

Dane leaned down and scooped up the severed tape and examined it while his frown deepened. 'I can't recall doing that, although I was rather distracted.'

'You are distracting me from my shower.' With that she closed the door to the bathroom and got busy.

***

Dane lay back against the pillows, a smile transforming his worried frown. That had to have been the most satisfying sexual encounter yet. It worried him that he thought so because, again, he didn't know if it was that damned binding spell or actual attachment and enjoyment. He found the more he was with Annwyn, the more he thought about her, the more he liked the way she moved, her small gestures, the way she smelled. Add to that the way she reacted to him. That completely upped the attraction for him.

Shaking his head, he rolled to the side of the bed and lifted the piece of duct tape that had secured Annwyn's legs. He replayed their little interlude, picturing how her ankles had been tied. It was the reason he had brought her further down the bed, so that she would be comfortable when he rode her. He had to stop thinking like this. Lying back against the pillows, he brought the duct tape to his nose and inhaled. *Magic?* He examined it and sniffed it again. There was a trace of magic on the tape. More to the point, it was not his own. Switching his gaze to the bathroom door, he wondered. Could it be Nira? Could it be Annwyn?

He was tempted to burst in and demand an explanation, but that wouldn't work. He had to think of another way to test the idea. With that thought, the urgency leaked out of him. Annwyn seemed to be taking a long time in the bathroom and the fatigue of being up all night and being tested, combined with vigorous sex, took its toll. Dane slid into sleep. His dreams were a replay of his testing. Exhaustion filled his bones and only the sight of Annwyn tied up and willing had lifted his fatigue for a short time. Now he was caught up in sleep and memory.

A warm, damp body roused him from sleep. He awoke to find Annwyn nuzzling at his neck. She drew back when she realised he was awake. 'It's your turn to take a shower. Sorry I was so long.'

Dane kissed her briefly on the lips, then patted her behind. 'Never mind. I needed a nap. Be ready to leave. Oh, and order some breakfast. Rolf will be back soon.'

With a fleeting glance at her, he headed for the shower. If he stayed one more minute in the room with her like that, they'd be at it again in no time. Already he was rising to the occasion.

By the time he showered and dressed, Rolf had returned and a trolley with breakfast had arrived. Rolf looked to be on his second helping of sausages and baked beans already, while Annwyn nibbled on a Danish and sipped some delicious-smelling coffee.

After loading up his plate, the conversation turned to the happenings of the early morning. Annwyn blushed profusely and refused to look Rolf in the eye. Dane was pleased with her response, even though it was awkward. It was better than her making eyes at his friend.

'So, Annwyn, what was the last thing you remember after I

left.' He thought starting there might help her remember, and she had good reason not to remember seducing Rolf.

'Not much, I'm sorry. I remember dreaming again.'

'Dreaming, not drinking?' He held up two empty bottles of wine he found under the bed.

'I didn't drink them. Although I do feel hung over so maybe...but how could I do that, order wine to be delivered without remembering?'

'You also had a knife so I assume that came from the room service tray. Are you saying that Nira was in control of you while you were walking around here by yourself? You remember dreaming. What was the dream about? Now be honest.'

Annwyn's cheeks were still pink and her gaze flicked from Dane to Rolf while she licked her lips. 'I dreamed about yesterday, about Nira in the club having sex with those people. It was very real and it aroused me. Except that this time I was at your house. I mean, Nira was at your house. I remember the details, the birds chirping and the trees scratching on the windows. It was as if I was there and you were making love to me. Not Rolf.'

Dane's pulse leapt. 'You dreamed of my home?'

Her green eyes met his. 'Yes.'

Standing up, Dane paced the room. 'Damn and blast her!' he said all at once. When he turned around he met Rolf and Annwyn's questioning gazes. 'She's doubled back.'

Annwyn jerked back in her seat with surprise. 'But what about the dogs, wouldn't they keep her away?'

Dane shook his head. 'The dogs are out roaming, not locked inside the house. A couple of the troublemakers are in the dog run. They're not guarding my house.'

'Why would she go to your house?'

'Damn that bitch.'

Rolf swabbed the last of the sausage around his plate, wiping up the sauce from his beans. 'What purpose is there in going to your house without you there? Booby trap?'

'The texts. It has to be the texts. That is the only thing I have of value, yet how would she know about them? Not even the collegium knows about them.' He remembered admitting he had to them to Rafael.

Dane held out a hand to Annwyn. 'We're leaving now. Get your things together.'

Annwyn cringed as he tugged her out of her seat. 'Are you okay?' Dane asked.

'Slight headache.'

Dane sniffed. 'You've been drinking. It's only natural.'

'I have not.'

He leaned down and picked up two empty bottles of wine and waved them in front of her.

'Yes, I know about that but I…I don't remember doing it.'

'On the drive back you will have some time to think about how she got to you. I know you want your body back, but I can't have you being possessed by Nira at critical moments. You are going to have to learn some mental control.'

'I am in control,' Annwyn argued before Dane pushed her into the bedroom to assemble her things.

'Pack now.' Then he shut the door in her face.

Straightaway, he opened the door again. 'Wait, come here.' She obediently stepped forward and he placed his hands on her temples, and chanted a few words of healing. Her look of surprise was priceless.

As she turned away to pack her things he picked up his own overnight bag and headed for the door. The sooner they could check out and be on their way, the happier he'd be. He could have transferred by himself, but he couldn't leave the other two vulnerable yet again. Perhaps the dream meant nothing. The texts were well warded. He would know if she had touched them, if anyone had touched them.

# **Chapter Eleven**

For Annwyn the drive back to Canberra was awkward. She couldn't stop thinking about the incident with Rolf, and how she had apparently had sex with him. Actually, it was probably better if she didn't think that way at all. It was Nira who had had sex with Rolf. It was the sorceress's body after all. Then she thought about how Nira had been having sex in her body, and was very confused by it all. And all at a time when she had thought that a sort of normalcy was settling around her, that she could play the cards that had been dealt her, and then Nira drops by and flips them into the air.

Dane was quiet and thoughtful on the way back to Canberra. It made Annwyn fret. Was he thinking her some kind of slut? Was he going to toss her out for sleeping with his friend? Had Nira really broken into his house to steal something? All these thoughts twisted her feelings like a mass of cotton thread that couldn't be unravelled. *Oh, get a grip*, she thought to herself as they sped along the highway skirting Lake George. It was another hour or so before they would make it to Dane's place. The sunset reflected off the wind turbines on the far shore. A police car pulled someone over for speeding. Dane's foot didn't even quiver on the accelerator.

Did he do something to the cop so that he wouldn't notice him? Annwyn was dying to ask. Dane glanced her way, a slight smile on his face. She went warm inside from the way his blue eyes glittered when he looked at her. 'By the way, Annwyn, tonight I'm expecting someone for a visit. He was a close friend of my father's.'

'Oh? Did you want me to leave? I don't mind.'

Dane turned his attention to the road. 'No, no.' He reached over and squeezed her hand. 'He is coming for a reason. He wants to meet you.'

Annwyn stared straight ahead while she digested that. 'So this friend, is he a sorcerer too? Like you, I mean?'

His hand was warm as it held hers. 'Well, yes. It was him I went to see last night. It's not easy to tell you everything, but I want to assure you that he is coming to help.'

'Help with the binding spell or with Nira and getting my body back?'

'Both, I hope.'

'But isn't getting rid of that moon curse thing more important to you? Shouldn't we be concentrating on that?'

Dane moved his hand back to the wheel and she saw him squeeze it firmly. 'It's important, but there is nothing we can do for the moment. There is no immediate cure. Tomorrow night the moon is full and I will change, and there's no stopping it. After that I will have fewer than twenty-eight days to find the solution. Rafael is helping with that, too. You see, all the spells are caught up together. Although the binding curse is mine and should be easier to fix.'

Annwyn nodded and cast her gaze to the passing field. She saw a mob of kangaroos in the shade of a copse of gum trees. They looked up as they passed, apparently unconcerned. The grass was grey-looking as the region had been in drought again. She tried not to think of Dane, of him changing, and of how painful that was to him. She wanted to tell him not to worry about her and to look after himself. With a quick glance at him, she knew it wasn't worth her trying. He had a stubborn 'do not argue with me' expression on his face.

Rolf leaned forward and spoke near her ear. 'Are we stopping for something to eat?' She started at the loudness of his voice. He glanced at her and then at Dane. 'A road burger, maybe, at Eagle Hawk?'

Dane nodded. 'I'm pretty hungry myself.' He glanced at Annwyn again, a slight grin on his face. 'You?'

She lifted a quizzical eyebrow. 'Me?'

'Care for a burger? They're pretty good at this place. Not the mass-produced multinational kind. You can actually taste the cow in these. The fries are excellent, too.'

Annwyn creased her forehead. They had gone from life-changing magic spells to talking of ordinary things like eating burgers. 'Yes, of course. I'm a bit peckish. I'm surprised, though. I didn't take you for a junk food kind of guy.' She eyed him meaningfully, taking in his buff physique. There wasn't an inch of fat on him. Rolf, too, looked as if he worked out for ten hours a day.

At the roundabout they pulled in and got out of the car. Annwyn made the most of the stop to stretch her legs, then went to the restroom. By the time she returned Dane was sitting with Rolf in deep conversation.

Dane waved her over. 'I've ordered for you.'

'Oh, okay…' She pondered what delicacies he had drawn from the rather slim menu.

'Don't worry if you can't finish it. Rolf here can eat quite a bit. It won't go to waste.'

Within ten minutes several plate loads of fries had arrived and about ten hamburgers. They were huge, bursting with huge meat patties, bacon, egg, and who knows what else. Before she had eaten a handful of fries Rolf was onto his third burger. Dane had only put away one. She took a bite out of hers, barely able to get her mouth around it. Wide-eyed, she watched Dane tuck into his second. Annwyn wondered whether they were having an eating competition.

After a while she lost interest in her food. She could barely finish half her portion. It was tasty but too much for her small appetite. The distraction of watching the two men became too much for her. She sat back and watched and listened to them belching. That too appeared to be a competition. With a roll of her eyes she tried to keep the smile from her face.

***

After the light-hearted meal of hamburgers, the mood in the car grew tense as they neared Dane's property. Dane and Rolf were both alert as they scanned the fields. Annwyn kept her eyes on the red gravel driveway that curved up to the house. None of them spoke. Annwyn thought she might see Nira jump out from behind a bush and throw a spell at them, or come out waving a knife. Yet there was nothing. When Dane engaged the handbrake she opened her door at the same time as Rolf. 'Stay here,' Rolf said gruffly, before walking away and leaving the car door open.

Dane turned to her as he was getting out. With a gesture, he motioned for her to stay in the car. 'Wait here until we investigate.'

Rolf had already disappeared around the far side of the house. Dane approached the front door, pausing and leaning his head to one side. 'No one has been through this door.' He waved Annwyn over and she quickly climbed out. When she joined him he said 'We'll check the side door.'

A shrill whistle reached them. 'It's just Rolf sounding the all clear on that side. He checked the rear sliding doors and the windows.'

Dane cast a look around him, then gently kissed the top of her head. 'Wait here moment, please. Just until I know it's safe for you.'

Annwyn nodded. She hugged her arms trying not to freak out. Something wasn't right. She couldn't put a finger on it. The paddocks surrounding the house were full of grey and yellow kangaroo and tussock grasses, and dark green forest covered the distant hills. A sudden howl startled her, sending chills deep into her gut. Something was wrong. Without thinking, she ran to the side of the house where Dane had gone. The two men stood together, shoulders hunched. As she drew closer she saw that there were dark shapes on the ground.

Walking up behind them, she saw that two of Dane's dogs lay dead, their throats cut. An icy feeling grew in the pit of her stomach. She lurched to the garden and threw up the burger she'd just eaten. Dane moved to comfort her and block the bloody corpses from her sight. 'Stay there for a moment and try to comfort Rolf. Bruce and Brian were his pets. I'm going to check the door for any traps.'

Wiping the vomit from her mouth with the back of her hand, she gaped at Rolf, uncertain of what she should do. He seemed frozen, shocked, with his gaze riveted to the remains of the dogs. Edging sideways, she slowly approached him from the side, reaching out a hand to touch him gently between the shoulder blades, then rubbing gently as if soothing a cat or, dare she think it, a dog. As if sensing she was near, Rolf turned toward her, lowering his forehead to her shoulder. He did not weep, but gently brought his arms around to hold her. Annwyn found his embrace disconcerting. Something wasn't quite right. Her mouth was sour with bile, but there was something else that she could smell or taste on the tip of her tongue, something that wasn't meant to be there; something she had never sensed before. Rolf lowered his arms and stepped away from her to bend down and pick up one of the dead dogs. She averted her gaze, not quite able to look at the expression on his face and see the sorrow cut deep into his eyes. He rubbed his nose over the dead animal's head and then cradled it as he walked to the rear of the house.

The sound of Dane returning drew her gaze from Rolf's retreating form. With a quick glance at the ground, Dane noticed that one of the corpses had been removed. Rolf was then out of sight.

'Can you give me a bit of room? I'm going to tackle this door.' He studied it for a few minutes. 'This is where she entered. None of the other wards have been interfered with.' He resumed concentrating, a little hum escaping from him. She was reluctant to interrupt him, but her worry got the better of her.

Reaching out, she gently touched his forearm. 'Dane, something is wrong, something is different,' Annwyn said quickly.

Dane turned to her and touched her cheek, gently brushing his thumb against the tip of her chin.

'It'll be all right. Don't worry.' His gaze swept her face before returning to the door.

Annwyn tried to keep calm. 'It's not worry or fear. I can taste something in the air.' When he turned back to her, she shrugged. 'I can't explain it, but it's real. It's there.'

A frown appeared on Dane's brow. He nodded and turned back to the door, studying it. He moved his left hand counter-clockwise and flicked his right hand horizontally three times while uttering an incantation under his breath. Pins and needles ran up the skin of Annwyn's arms, the sensation setting her heart beating faster. She held her breath as Dane moved forward and opened the door. A noise behind her alerted her to Rolf returning for the second dog. He looked as if he'd been weeping. Dane stepped over the threshold and paused. Without looking at her he said, 'Wait. Do not enter just yet until I give the all clear. There is something I must do first.'

***

As Dane trod carefully down the hall he had to control his anger over the intrusion into his home, the sense of violation. Nira had slipped by the ward on the door, but not broken it. That is why he hadn't detected it. Clever little trick, he thought to himself. He would not be so sloppy in future. However, the house wards were flimsy compared to the others that protected important things.

Her invasion jabbed into his gut like a swift, hard punch. Nira's attacks on him were slicing closer to the bone each time. The texts hidden in his sanctum were precious to him, the only remaining link to his father. It was his duty to ensure they did not fall into the wrong hands, and Nira, or whoever was behind her, was exactly the wrong kind of hands. He could not believe she could have broken through those wards. It was this knowledge that kept him calm. The wards were a part of him and if she had broken through, he definitely would have sensed it.

What had he done to be the focus of some much hatred? Only hate could explain the depth of her attacks and the callous way she treated those in her way. The slaying of the dogs had shocked him. The dogs would not have attacked Nira and there were other ways open to a sorcerer to calm them and put them to sleep. The attack was clearly aimed at wounding him and Rolf. Nira was vindictive as well as powerful. Her character shouldn't have surprised him. The curse she had placed on him had the power to end his way of life.

Entering the hallway, he trod carefully, sweeping the floor, walls and ceiling with his senses as he searched for small spells with powerful traps. He found one at the entry to the living room and diffused it. He stood there, gazing through the tinted glass windows to the pool and continuing to run his gaze around the room. She had been inside. He could feel the vibrations of her passing, the lingering aftertaste of her power.

Kneeling down, he conjured a spell to recreate her movements. As he let the spell go, the form of Nira appeared, ghostlike, like a photo negative, all yellow and brown. He watched the recreated image of her walk down the hall, saw her tread across the room where she hovered near the door of the basement. With interest, he noted how she checked for the warding he had left. Grimly, he noted the skill in which she assessed the complex spells and measured their extent and nature without triggering them. He was grateful she had not tried to enter because the effect would have been deadly and would have ended the life of Annwyn's true body.

After he was certain there were no other traps set, he called Annwyn in. Rolf was still burying Bruce and Brian. The others, who had been in wolf form, had left to wander the pack territory for fun. Some of the werewolves liked staying in wolf form and treated it like a holiday. Dane hated the thought of it himself. He had hated his time in animal form.

Dane sighed, glad they hadn't been caught by Nira. Even though they were 'were', he wouldn't have wanted them exposed to danger. Nira had proven herself bloodthirsty, and he was glad he was not responsible for other deaths. Rolf had had trouble resisting the sorceress and perhaps the rest of the pack would find it even harder. He couldn't risk it.

Annwyn came through the door, a strange expression on her face. 'What is it?' he asked, curious about her level of concentration. She was silent, focused.

'Annwyn, what is it?'

She pointed to where Nira's trap had been. Dane instinctively pulled back. 'What do you see?'

She glanced quickly at him. 'I'm not sure. It looks like dead worms or thick threads, but not exactly. They are sort of shadows of threads.'

Dane gaped at her. What she was describing was the spell he had untangled. He could not see it, but that is what he sensed when he first encountered it. Her comment left him wondering and, even as he dismissed it, the idea it created sat heavily in the back of his mind. He remembered Annwyn being restrained and the scent of magic on the tape. The tape was associated with the hottest sex he had had in ages. Too late, his arousal returned with a vengeance. Deities above, he must learn to control himself where Annwyn was concerned.

Rolf's heavy tread sounded in the hallway. Their eyes met briefly. Rolf was grieving for his pets, and Dane's arousal faded. There were too many other things to worry about and molesting Annwyn right now wasn't a luxury he could afford. There was anger there, too, in the clench of Rolf's shoulders. Dane knew the anger wasn't directed at him, although it might have been if Rolf had caught scent of his arousal.

Rolf nodded briefly and stood behind Annwyn. When she noticed him, she jerked into action and moved out of his way.

Dane knew something wasn't right with his house, but he couldn't pinpoint it. Nira had not taken the text, but she had come for something. He walked slowly around the room, checking little spaces. Then he saw it—the gap where the photo frame had been. Nira had taken a gilt-framed picture of him as a child being held lovingly by his mother—a gift from his father. It was an item very dear to him.

He ran his fingers through the light layer of dust surrounding the space where the photo had been. 'Damn her,' he said explosively.

Annwyn started, and Rolf was suddenly on alert, ready to pounce. 'Sorry. She's taken something personal.' He shook his head. How could the situation get any worse?

Rolf inhaled deeply. 'The scent of her is still fresh. We are not far behind. How powerful is the item in her hands?'

Dane lowered his head, bracing the bridge of his nose between finger and thumb. Slowly he shook his head. 'Pretty powerful. My mother died when I was young. It was the only memento of her that survived our various moves. My father was extremely fond of it, and it was a very meaningful occasion when he gave it to me.'

Annwyn threw her head back, anger flashing in the green of her eyes. 'What further harm can she possibly want to do to you? Isn't that curse enough? Isn't this enough?' she gestured to herself, indicating the body that was not her own.

Dane's failure to solve her problem increased his frustration. 'Obviously not.'

'But what does it mean? Can she control you? Like some kind of voodoo doll? Can she harm you, access you, like she can me?'

'Yes, she could hex me, if the curse she has already laid on me isn't enough. Tracking me will be easy. I don't think she can access me like she does you. I think that comes from being connected to her native body. I'm not sure about the extent of her powers.'

'Just the extent of her depravity,' Annwyn said, her voice laced with venom.

Dane met Rolf's gaze. 'Can you track her? She can't be on foot, but it pays not to assume anything when it comes to her.'

Rolf nodded and left by the back sliding door. He looked up at the sky and around the pool area, then disappeared from view.

Dane turned to Annwyn. 'You should rest perhaps. Take a shower, a nap.'

'I'm fine.'

'Yes, of course you are. It's been a long trip after a difficult night and I was thinking that my friend, Rafael, may not come till much later. It would be best if you were fresh and not tired.'

She stood still, watching him closely with her bright gaze.

'I'm all right,' he added, seeing she was not moving, only observing him anxiously. He was touched by her concern. If only it was real and not some spell.

Nodding slowly, she came to a decision. 'Okay. Where should I sleep?'

'Take my bed.' Dane didn't want her sleeping anywhere else. He liked the thought of her between his sheets, her light scent lingering there for him to enjoy. His gaze followed her as she walked down the hall and into his room. His imagination taunted him. He wanted to go after her, to bury himself inside her. Instead, he turned away and forced his mind elsewhere. He could not continue to take advantage of her, no matter how enjoyable it was.

The beast was very close to the surface. Tomorrow night he would change. He had to accept it. There was no time now to remove the curse. The noose was tightening around his throat. Time was running out. This change would allow the curse to leave further marks on him. By the next full moon it would be irreversible. It wasn't right to drag Annwyn into that. She hadn't asked to be involved in sorcerer business, and she certainly didn't ask to be bound to a werewolf.

***

Annwyn dreamt of many things: the day's events, making love with Dane, Nira in various compromising positions, and Rolf standing naked, hot desire in his gaze. She tossed and turned as each image fought for precedence. Her feelings were running wild inside her. She was torn between desire, hate and insatiable lust.

With a start, she sat up in the bed and panted. Something wasn't right. Dane said she must learn control and not let Nira take her unawares. Yet it did not feel like Nira connecting to her. It was something else, something in the room with her.

It could be a mouse or a rat. It was the country after all and sometimes rodents invade properties. Her gaze flicked around the room, to the corners, to the ceiling. Climbing across the bed on all fours, she bent her elbows to peer under the bed and around furniture. Next to the sideboard she saw something writhing; a ball of worms, wriggling and expanding.

Wearing only a bra and undies, she wasn't going to put her foot on the floor. 'Dane?' she called out, not able to conceal the fear in her voice. 'Quickly!'

Dane's heavy step sounded as he came running down the hallway. Annwyn saw the knot of worms pulse suddenly. 'Wait. Stop!'

Dane pulled up before launching himself into the room. She pointed. 'Another set of worms. These ones are glowing.'

Dane muttered something under his breath and extended his right hand, moving it to and fro. He blinked in surprise. 'A spell,' he said. With an incantation and rapid gestures with his right hand, the ball of worms fell apart and stopped writhing. Annwyn didn't see anything from Dane, but she saw the effect he had on the spell.

'Why can I see Nira's spells all of a sudden?' Her heart beat painfully in her chest. She could see magic. That had to be it, but why?

Dane checked the room, walking around it silently. She kept her gaze on him, waiting for him to answer her question. Dane finished his circuit, then came and sat on the edge of the bed. Annwyn wanted to move her hand and touch his as it rested on the covers. 'I'm not sure what you're seeing. I'm as puzzled as you are. I can't see spells. I sense them.'

'But there was a spell, wasn't there? Exactly where I pointed?'

'Yes,' he said, reaching up to smooth her mussed hair. 'But it must be a coincidence. Like I said, I don't see spells. They are not objects to be seen, but hidden things, words and magic bound together.' He reached up and stroked her ear from tip to lobe.

She sucked in a breath and stifled a groan. A quick look at his face, and she could see his desire glowing in his eyes like embers. Her core responded to him, her pulse throbbing. If he wanted her at that moment there would be nothing she could do. She didn't want to do anything to prevent him, but couldn't quite bring herself to beg.

The longer he sat next to her, the more powerful the attraction. It was building like the steady beat of a drum. Abruptly, Dane stood up. 'Forgive me. I have things to do.' Then, without a second glance, he left the room.

Annwyn threw herself back onto the pillows and let out a pent-up breath. She was so aroused she had to do something or she wouldn't be able to function. The bathroom door loomed large in her vision. She'd have to take a shower, maybe it would help rid her of this lust.

Dane seemed reluctant to do anything about her arousal.

Surely he was aware. His lack of action puzzled her. There was a lot going on with the break-in, the death of the dogs and the threat Nira posed. She had to take back seat to those, she supposed. Yet she had seen that he wanted her. Perhaps he had gained some control whereas she hadn't.

Annwyn closed her eyes for a moment, letting the wish that she'd met Dane in better circumstances form. She shook her head. He wouldn't have noticed her. It was chance and enchantment that had thrown them together and there was no future for them.

Even though she was disappointed, she understood his reluctance. He hadn't asked for this curse. Technically, he had, but not with her. It would have been Nira fucking him instead of Annwyn. The thought made her eyes sting, and she rubbed at them. *I will not cry. I will not.* After a few minutes, she opened her eyes and stared at the ceiling. Thinking so hard had brought on a sudden headache.

Annwyn went into the bathroom and fished around in the cabinet for some headache pills. After staring at her reflection for some minutes she turned on the shower tap, anxious to wash away the unrequited desire.

# Chapter Twelve

Dane tried his best to keep his lust under control, painful as it was to ignore his intense erection. He wanted Annwyn and the desire confused him. Because of the spell he couldn't tell what was real and what was illusion, and he had no right to take advantage of her.

Mastering himself required greater control. To do this he had to use magic to tie it up in small knots. He was not proud that he had to resort to magic to control himself. It was a temporary measure and one that was not available to Annwyn. He had tasted the scent of her desire on the back of his tongue. It tasted so sweet, so damned alluring, that he knew he couldn't trust himself, and he was so close to changing. If he let himself go now, he could hurt her. The beast was savage and not under his control. It was there scratching to get out, willing him to lose control so it could escape early as it perceived the slow march of the moon.

Rolf came in, pulled a beer out of the fridge and took a long draught. He wiped his mouth with the back of his hand and swung the fridge door shut. 'Well?' Dane asked.

'Lost her at the edge of the property. She walked in from the road but had a car waiting. Impossible to track now. Where's Annwyn?'

'Shower. Rafael will be here soon. You up to cooking dinner? Just for you and Annwyn. I have to go below and do some research.'

Rolf's eyes narrowed but he didn't comment. As Dane went down the stairs he heard the fridge open and the pan hitting the hob. He tried to clear his mind of the picture of Annwyn and Rolf eating dinner tête-à-tête. Jealousy arose, potent and overpowering. He had to trust Rolf.

Down in his sanctum he picked up the spell reference book. He wanted to see if there was any record of 'seeing' magic spells rather than sensing them. Researching helped him to lose himself, to lessen the throb of desire. As he read the words in the text, he wondered what Annwyn was doing upstairs.

***

Annwyn let the orgasm wash over her, like suds flushing down the drain. It had taken her a while to come, given that she'd been highly aroused. She rehoused the detachable shower head, gasping as the movement jolted her sensitive flesh. Leaning her head against the cool tiles, she let the last of the desire drain away. It was a temporary relief. Once Dane came near her again her desire would quickly rise. All she had done was make it possible to be normal again for a short time.

She dressed quickly and dried off her hair. Dawdling for a while, she looked at her borrowed face in the mirror, trying to see the evil that was Nira. Didn't they say that people's lives were written on their faces? Nira's face was unblemished and unmarked. Perhaps the saying didn't apply to a sorceress. The smell of cooking meat reached her, making her stomach growl. When she thought back to the burgers they'd eaten at lunch she couldn't understand how she could possibly be hungry again. *That's right*, she thought as she nodded to herself, *I threw up*.

With soft steps, she trod down the hall. Dane was nowhere to be seen so she tried the kitchen. She was brought up short by the sight of Rolf cooking. He cocked a smile at her, turned off the gas and slid two steaks onto plates, which already had fresh salad on them.

'Sit,' he said, jutting his bearded chin in the direction of the large dining table.

'Aren't we waiting for Dane?' she asked, staring down at the steak, which oozed blood into her plate.

'No, he said he's not eating and doesn't want to be disturbed.'

Rolf's gaze never left her face. 'I see,' she said, looking down at the table to hide her pain. He was staying away from her. It was such a chore to be around her, she supposed. Having to make love to someone because of some curse and not because you wanted to.

Rolf stood up halfway through eating his steak and placed a

glass of red wine next to her. 'Sorry, I forgot to serve the wine.'

She whispered her thanks and took a sip. It was a good wine from a local boutique winery. She took a longer pull and placed the glass on the table. 'Do you find me attractive?' she asked suddenly, surprising herself as well as Rolf. What did she mean anyway? This body or her real one?

'You're attractive enough,' he said without much conviction.

'Enough for what?' she asked, narrowing her gaze and frowning at him. She was annoyed at herself for asking such a dumb question in the first place and now she didn't like his tone.

He dropped his knife and it clanged against the plate. Gazing at her with irises that glowed yellow, he said, 'Don't go there. Just don't go there. Isn't it enough that he's crazy for you every minute? Now you want to drag me into it.'

Puzzled, she shook her head at him. He glared at her for a minute or so, until his irises lost their unnatural light and returned to his steak. Annwyn reached for her glass and took a few more sips. Dane's retreat from her made her feel insecure, unwanted, unloved. Possessing Nira's body confused things further. She had no idea if Dane would find the real Annwyn physically attractive. Her mind must have wandered because Rolf calling her name drew her back to the moment. Leaning back slightly, she gazed up at Rolf. 'Finished?' he asked.

'Thank you, yes. It was very good.'

Without a word, he took her plate to the sink and started washing up. Annwyn looked around the room and wondered what she should do next. Without warning, the door of the sanctum opened. Dane came out and held it ajar. Her heart leapt at the sight of him. Then an old man appeared, whether from the stairwell or thin air Annwyn couldn't say. Her gaze shifted between the two. This must be his friend. The old man was a head shorter than Dane and much thinner. He had long waist-length grey hair and a mid-length salt and pepper beard. He was wearing floor-length red robes and a strange knife in his belt.

'Rafael, let me present you to Annwyn.'

Annwyn erupted out of her seat and then slowed herself

down. She did not want to make a fool of herself by tripping over in her haste.

The old man stepped forward and bowed his head 'So you are Annwyn.'

'Why yes. You must be Rafael. Dane told me you were coming over for a visit.' The old man's eyes glittered as he appraised her. Annwyn sensed he was looking inside her.

'Do you know me, Annwyn? Have you seen me before?'

Annwyn's gaze shifted to Dane and then back to the old man. 'No. I don't think I've ever seen you.'

The old man turned to Dane. 'Does that alleviate your mistrust of me, my friend?'

Dane paled. 'I meant no disrespect. However, I thank you for putting my mind at rest.'

'Of course, if I was behind this plot it would be Nira who would know me and not this human.'

Dane tilted his head to one side considering the old man. 'You speak true.'

He moved to Annwyn's side and touched her arm gently. She glanced at him, doing her best to suppress the groan of desire his touch elicited. 'Yes?' she asked him.

'Rafael would like to examine you. He will not harm you. I'll be here the whole time.' He smiled at her and nodded reassuringly.

She found herself nodding too. 'What does this examination entail?'

Rafael's voice was deep and gravelly. 'I will place you in a trance.'

'Hypnosis?'

'Not quite but the definition will suit.'

'Very well. Go ahead.'

'Dane, if you could bring a chair for Annwyn. She will need to be comfortable.'

Rolf instead brought a chair and then sank back into the dark shadows of the room, pretending he wasn't there.

***

Dane swelled with pride about how calmly Annwyn accepted

117

Rafael's presence and acquiesced to his examination. She had such pluck. He couldn't help but admire her and this was quite apart from the attraction, he thought. He shook his head slightly. He had to stop thinking of this thing they had as any kind of real relationship. Why, even this night Rafael might unravel the curse and set them both free. What would happen then? She'd be free of him. Free to be with whomever she wanted.

Rafael did not take long to put her under his spell. 'So Annwyn, tell me about your life.'

Annwyn did as she was bid and told him about her job and her house. 'And what were your dreams, Annwyn? What filled your nights?''

'Thomas. I dreamed of Thomas every night.' Her voice was a whisper, full of longing and disappointed hopes. Dane's heart clenched. It wasn't fair that her life was filled with grief.

Rafael lent in close. 'Every night?' he asked, his face full of concentration.

'Yes,' Annwyn replied. 'He was my life.'

'You say you are a widow. How long ago did Thomas die?'

'Three years and two months.'

Rafael beckoned Dane closer and whispered in his ear. 'There is something not quite right here. There is some tampering.' Dane nodded, understanding dawning. There was a clue here as to how Nira had managed the body swap. His hope rose. It had been the right choice to seek Rafael's help and to join the collegium.

Again Rafael leaned in close to Annwyn and spoke softly to her. 'How strong are these dreams? Did they change recently?'

'The dreams are strong. Always he makes love to me in the dreams. Lately, in the past month or so, they grew stronger.'

Rafael's eyebrow arched. 'Stronger in what way?'

'They grew more real.'

'And the most real one you experienced?'

'That was when I ended up here. In this body, with Dane. He was making love to me. I saw her eyes. She tricked me by pretending to be Thomas.'

Rafael stood back and rubbed his chin. 'Interesting. It is

possible that she was exceedingly attached to her husband. It is more likely, though, that there is something unnatural in her dreams. After three years you would expect the occasional dream. But to dream of him every night for three years, well, that defies reason. There is something there. I can sense it. Your binding is there and also a strong connection to someone else. Nira, I suspect, and yet I can't quite put my finger on what the other thing is.'

'If I loved someone deeply, I think I would dream of them all the time.'

Rafael turned to him. 'Tell me, do you dream of your father every night?'

Dane rocked back on his heels. 'No, I don't. I did at first, though, but they grew less as the months passed.'

'Exactly. It is normal for one to grieve, but the grief lessens over time. Memories fade. Life goes on. For some reason for Annwyn, life did not go on. I'll try something else.'

Dane watched Rafael use a different spell. There was no change in Annwyn. Her eyes were closed, her breathing slow and relaxed. 'So, Annwyn, have you ever met Nira before?'

'I don't recall. No, I don't remember.'

Rafael's eyebrows drew together and he released a subtle spell, breaking down a barrier. Annwyn's face clenched as if it hurt. 'And now…what do you remember?'

A conjured vision sprung up in front of Annwyn. Dane leant back and Rafael's power encircled it. In the image, Annwyn was sitting on a couch, sipping a glass of water. It was the real Annwyn, the one in the photo, the one he had not met.

'Where are you, Annwyn?'

'I'm at a party with Thomas. It's at Ned's house. A friend. One of the weirdo ones who thinks he's a warlock. I'm in the sitting room alone, taking a break from the rest of them. They're outside, dancing around a bonfire naked and stuff. Thomas likes to join in, and we have good sex after so I don't mind really.'

In the image, the door opens and in walks a lithe, dark-haired man with a face covered in freckles. In one hand he has a ceramic cup. Behind him come Nira, and he is holding her hand.

'Hey, Annie, why are you sitting there all alone and what the hell are you drinking?'

Annwyn smiles at him, her gaze travelling to the woman, eyebrows rising in query. Thomas looks to Nira. 'This is Nadira and she wants to meet you. Here, drink this. It's a negus, a hot spiced wine. It's delicious.' He passes the cup to her. Annwyn smiles her thanks, then takes a sip.

Nodding, Nadira says, 'Go on. It's very nice.'

Annwyn goes to put it down on the coffee table.

'No, no,' Thomas says. 'You must drink it all. It's the last of it, and you can't waste it.'

Annwyn frowns, but picks up the cup. She takes a large swallow. Thomas sits down next to her, leaving Nira standing there, looming. He runs his hand across Annwyn's neck.

'Come on, love. Drink the rest. The alcohol is cooked away. It won't hurt you.' He kisses her neck lightly, then licks and nips at her throat. Annwyn lifts her shoulders, her gaze flicking up to Nadira, obviously not comfortable to be so intimate in front of a stranger.

Annwyn takes the last drink, her eyes turning glassy. Thomas takes the cup from her flaccid hands and puts it on the table.

Thomas and Nadira stand in front of her while Annwyn gazes at them, a bewildered expression on her face.

Dane took a step behind Annwyn and this brought the faces of the two others into view. Rafael had created a three-dimensional image of this memory from the past. The edges were smudged. He could see the door but not the far wall.

Thomas's eyes lose focus, but there is a hunger in his gaze. Nadira's green eyes glow faintly with power.

Nadira turns to Thomas, reaches up and cups his chin before catching his mouth for a searing kiss that leaves him gasping. Nira moves to one side of Annwyn and Thomas moves to the other.

Thomas lifts Annwyn's chin, nips it with his teeth, then probes her mouth with his tongue. Nira whispers in her ear. Annwyn becomes pliant, opening her mouth to her husband's kisses, groaning with desire as he unbuttons her blouse and slides his hands into her bra. White, firm breasts strain against his hand.

Nira reaches behind and undoes the clasp, tugging the garment free. Thomas's head descends and takes a dark, erect nipple into his mouth. Nira chants in her ear and Annwyn flings her head back. Nira leans forward and takes the other breast into her mouth. Annwyn cries out; neither of her assailants are gentle.

Dane can see from her face that she is close, hovering on the cusp of pleasure and pain. Dane closed his eyes, dreading what the memory will show and knowing that now that Rafael has found it and exposed it, Annwyn will remember it too.

Thomas unbuttons Annwyn's jeans and slides his fingers into her panties. Nira scuttles to the floor and pulls them over Annwyn's hips, leaving them gathered at her ankles. Then, together, they probe Annwyn, taking turns to stroke her sex, occasionally tongue kissing and then giggling while they molest her.

Annwyn responds.

Dane could see her arousal, see how she opened herself to them giving them greater access. He wanted to ask her about this scene, but couldn't interrupt the moment. There was a clue here.

'Good,' Thomas says, a leering expression on his face. 'You were right, Nadira. Having power over her makes my erection more powerful.'

The sorceress closes the space between them, their lips meeting in a searing kiss. Breaking apart, she speaks softly in his ear. Before she has finished the words of the spell, Thomas's face loses its expression.

'Stand up!' Nira commands him. He does as he is bid, leaving Annwyn partially clothed, her gaze riveted to her husband.

'Take off your jeans!' Thomas stands up and unzips his jeans. He isn't wearing underwear and his erection springs free. He is engorged, and Dane suspects unnaturally so, given what Rolf explained about his own encounter with Nira.

Nadira whispers some more words, casting a spell tight around the unsuspecting Thomas. She kneels in front of him and takes him into her mouth. Nira licks and sucks, teasing his tip with a long, moist tongue. Thomas closes his eyes as if feeling every invigorating slide of wet flesh against his arousal. He groans loudly in a voice full with ecstasy.

From his breathing it is clear he is close to climax. She quickens her pace, drawing him in and out. He cries out as Nira drinks him, taking his load. Thomas stands there with knees shaking as the sorceress goes to Annwyn, burying her face between Annwyn's legs.

Dane turned to Rafael, eyebrows raised in query. The old man seemed unfazed by what they were witnessing. He answered Dane's unvoiced question. 'She is using his seed to form a bond, to seal her spell,' he said quietly.

Dane swallowed as he watched Nira tongue Annwyn, pushing her legs apart so she could reach the very core of her. Dane's arousal came sharp and hard, and with it came guilt. This scene, this memory, was of Annwyn being betrayed by her husband and his sorcerous girlfriend. Annwyn had grieved for a man who didn't deserve her, didn't deserve her loyalty or love. He thought of the years she had wasted pining for this man and shook his head.

A spasm rocks Annwyn as the powerful orgasm tears through her. Nira stands over her, speaking her spell. Annwyn jerks once as Nira gestures sharply, testing her control.

The image went dark as Annwyn lost consciousness.

The scene then opened again, with Annwyn sitting fully dressed on the sofa.

Thomas sits beside her, chatting to another man as they drank beers. She stretches catlike as she wakes up. 'I'm sorry, Ned,' Annwyn says to Thomas's friend, stifling a yawn. 'I must have dropped off.'

Rafael ended the vision. When Dane turned to look again at Annwyn she had tears streaking her cheeks and her eyes were red and puffy. Again Dane's heart clenched. She had relived a scene from her past that had been blocked from her, hidden by Nira's sorcery. How fresh must be the feelings of hurt and betrayal?

He knelt beside her, not sure whether he should touch her. As soon as he got close, she threw herself at him, clinging tight around his neck. He let her cry it out while whispering soothing words. Rafael looked on.

'Oh. Dane. It was Thomas. Thomas who gave me to her. I can't believe it was all a sham. I thought he loved me, but how could he when he did that?' She burst into tears again. He could see that her mind was thinking through the lonely days and nights, thinking of her husband, unnaturally amplified by a spell.

'It's over now. You have your whole life ahead of you. It must hurt now but it will get better.'

She clung to him and he buried his face in her hair, marvelling at how he could empathize with her pain and sorrow. He stroked her back and soon her sobs ebbed.

'Annwyn?' Rafael said after a few minutes once her sobbing had died down. She didn't look at the old man, just clung to Dane like her life depended on it.

'Yes,' Annwyn responded in a small voice, her face turned away.

'What you have just witnessed is how Nira prepared you for a vessel of exchange. She could have prepared others, although it would take time and power to do so. The husband that you mourn was not worthy of your love or your grief. He betrayed you, I think, knowingly. I'm not sure what he gained from it. Perhaps she gave him a small power, some small gift that he used until it drained him dry. Nothing comes without a price.'

Dane clung to her, hugging her, knowing what it had cost her. Three years of her life spent mourning her husband and the loss of her life, and now the loss of her body. Annwyn pushed away from him and turned to face Rafael again.

'There's your link, the pathway,' Rafael said, confirming Dane's own thoughts.

'So Nira laid the groundwork. But that was so long ago.' Dane was amazed at how long Nira had been at large.

Rafael nodded. 'Yes. This has been long in the making. Whether it was made to escape from you, or a general escape plan, I cannot say. I will take her with me now. I wish to test her.'

'Take? Test me? For what?' Annwyn clung to him, and Dane did not want to let her go.

'Magic. Power.'

Annwyn stiffened in his arms.

'But she is human,' he replied, his view of the world distorting uncomfortably.

Annwyn released her hold, setting herself back to gape at Dane and then shake her head.

Rafael considered them for a moment, his gaze flicking between them. 'She was human. Now she is changing, becoming something else, I suspect. Let me confirm my suspicions.'

Dane nodded. Annwyn gripped his hand and he patted it. 'Rafael will not harm you.' Annwyn's chest was heaving, though, and he saw the raw panic there.

Rafael cast a spell, a rapid gesture, and Annwyn's eyes rolled back in her head. Dane eased her back into the chair, pausing to stroke her forehead. 'I have noticed things,' he said to Rafael, staying close to Annwyn and fighting his protective feelings. He could see that Rafael could help them. He had to trust. He was still reeling himself from Rafael's dramatic statement. He recollected the duct tape and how she could sense spells, see them, actually. Initially, he had thought it a coincidence.

Rafael was gazing at him, stroking his chin. Dane shrugged. 'Until you spoke about it, I did not suspect. I did not think it through. Do you need my help?'

'No, only to witness her testing.'

'But she is unconscious.'

'Her mind finds it hard to accept what she has inside her. This is best. The testing will help her realize and perhaps come to terms with it.'

'Perhaps?'

Rafael lifted an eyebrow. 'This is no pubescent sorceress coming into her power, but a grown human woman. The transition will be difficult for her. She will need to be trained, if only not to be a danger to herself and others.'

Dane nodded, not quite comfortable at the prospect of

separating from her. He was bonded to her and she to him. To be apart for an extended period would cause them both discomfort. Images of their lovemaking came to mind. Perhaps she would do better without him lusting after her, rutting with her whenever they could fight the urge no more.

'Annwyn, it is Rafael. Let me into your mind, let me see who you really are.' There was a moan from Annwyn as Rafael slid his presence into her. Dane hoped the old sorcerer wouldn't be too interested in memories of their lovemaking as he watched the process silently. The testing consisted of several questions, some which brought displays of power. These Dane formally witnessed. Annwyn was becoming a mid-weight sorceress.

As Rafael ended the test, Annwyn opened her eyes. She appeared calm. 'I have magic?'

'Yes, my dear, and some special talents.'

Dane's head jerked up. 'Talents?' He feared she had inherited Nira's tendencies, that the power was somehow leaking back to the body that owned it.

'I think she may see spells, not just sense them.'

Rafael rocked back on his heels. 'A rare talent indeed.'

Annwyn reached out to squeeze Dane's hand, and he assisted her out of the chair.

'So that knot of nearly invisible threads I saw was a spell?' Both men nodded.

'You said you can't see spells?' she asked Dane directly, her green eyes a challenge.

'No, I can feel them, sense them, but not see the construct of them. Only a few of us can see spells.'

Annwyn nodded. 'Am I like her? Do I need sex to power my spells?'

'No, my dear,' Rafael replied, sharing a look with Dane. 'Your poles are perfectly balanced.'

Annwyn frowned. 'But...where does this power come from? If this is her body, then isn't it her magic coming back to it? Isn't it her possession of me that caused it?'

Rafael shrugged. 'I cannot say for certain. I can only say that you do not have her perversions. Perhaps this is the way she would have been had she chosen a different path. I suspect it is something latent in you. Time may reveal a bit more about its origins. Now, my dear, I would like you to accompany me. There are many things you need to learn and not much time to learn it.'

'Is Dane coming too?'

'I'm afraid that won't do. It would be a distraction for both of you, and Dane's curse is upon him.'

Dane agreed silently. The moon's power was flowing along his bones. Soon he would not be able to resist it. Soon the beast would take over, and he did not want Annwyn to see him like that. She did not need to feel pity, nor to fear him.

'Can we have a few moments together?' Annwyn asked, her manner self-assured with Rafael. In less than an hour, the old sorcerer had managed to build trust in her. Dane was impressed by the old man's skill, and his care and concern. He had been right to trust his father's dearest friend. Most of all, he was very proud of Annwyn.

***

Annwyn glanced between the two powerful men, conscious of her new status. She caught a glimpse of Rolf hovering in the unlit dining room, looking on. She had neither sought nor desired power, but she had it. Rafael was right that she needed to know how to use it. Her heart was heavy at leaving Dane even for one night. She feared for him and regretted the separation. If only there was time for one last lovemaking session. There was so much to say and feel.

Dane moved to the door to his basement, his 'sanctum', as he called it. 'My friend,' he said to the old man. 'I would be honoured if you were to view the texts I have below. I have removed the wards. I will need a few minutes only.'

Rafael nodded, his eyes alight with intrigue. 'I would be honoured.'

He disappeared quickly down the stairs.

Annwyn sucked in a deep breath as Dane enveloped her in a huge hug. She clung to him, letting the heat of him wash over her. *Oh lord*, she thought, *he feels so good*. How was she going to bear the separation? She looked up at him and his mouth descended, hungrily kissing her. Her hands ran over his back as he squeezed her buttocks, lifting her as he pressed her against him. It pleased her to know that he was aroused and ready. If only they had the time and the privacy to sate themselves. She arched back so she could see his face, see the vivid blue of his eyes. Her hand cupped his strong chin, stroking upwards toward his ear. 'I will miss you so much. I already ache at the thought of being apart from you.'

He didn't answer, just pulled her close and ravaged her mouth with a kiss that left her gasping and in no doubt of his desire for her. 'I will come for you when the change is over.'

'How long?' she asked, her voice husky with emotion.

'A day, maybe two. Don't worry, Rolf will look after me.'

'I wish I could look after you.'

Dane's eyes narrowed. 'Rolf is a werewolf. He is quite capable of looking after me when we are with the pack.'

Annwyn reeled, rocking back on her heels. 'Rolf is a werewolf? I thought…' She shut her mouth. Why advertise her stupidity? *Oh my God*, she thought, *I fucked a werewolf, well, Nira did, but still…*All the little hints fell into place, and she remembered their amusement at her comments. She punched Dane lightly on the arm. 'You should have said.'

'Well, now you know.'

He shrugged in a gorgeous way that made her throw herself at him and hug him tight around his neck. 'I'll miss you, and I'll worry about you.'

Dane's eyes darkened to indigo and his mouth tightened. With a nod, he acknowledged her comment. However, Annwyn sensed that there was something more he wanted to say. Footsteps sounded as Rafael came up the stairs.

Annwyn stepped away from Dane, wanting to capture an image of him to take away with her. She noticed threads around him, slightly unravelling. She unconsciously picked at them, willing them away. A long thread unwound from around his waist. She gave it another tug, and another, revealing layers like bandages.

'Time to leave now, Annwyn,' Rafael said, beckoning to

her.

'But…'

'Don't keep Rafael waiting, Annwyn. He's an important man.'

Annwyn stopped unpicking the threads. Stepping up to Dane, she stood on tiptoe to give him a peck on the lips. She hovered there, taking in the scent of him, feeling the pull, the attraction to him in her gut. This was going to be hard, the separation, the wrench. How was she to bear it?

'Goodbye, Dane.'

'I'll see you again soon,' he replied, his voice thick with emotion. She gave a nod to Rolf and joined the old man.

# Chapter Thirteen

'Come,' Rafael repeated. She reluctantly backed away. The separation was already a physical ache.

The old man grabbed her hand. His skin was dry and lined, but not repulsive. 'You may experience some dizziness, my dear,' he whispered. Her gaze met Dane's and then the world went blank. It was pitch dark for a few moments, then colours exploded into her vision with whirling spiral patterns that made her feel odd. The disorientation sent her head spinning. Suddenly, there was a hard surface beneath her feet. Dizziness made her lose focus, and it wasn't until she found herself horizontal in a strange young man's arms did she realise that she had keeled over.

The young man gaped at her, his eyes wide. 'Thank you, Max, for catching Annwyn,' said Rafael's disembodied voice.

'Annwyn?' He blinked a few times, mouth gaping. He was young with short dark hair and startling hazel eyes that appeared to have violet pigments. He was very pale with a smooth complexion. Dressed in a light-coloured suit, he hoisted her back up to her feet in one fluid movement, retaining a hold on her as she swayed.

'Yes, my name is Annwyn,' she said as she removed herself from the young man's embrace. He politely stepped away from her and his expression closed over. Looking at him, he seemed surprised by her arrival.

Max bowed swiftly, a short nod of his head. 'I'm Max, Rafael's assistant.'

Offering her hand to shake, she dropped it quickly when all he did was glance at it. To cover her nervousness, she turned around to take in her surroundings. 'Goodness, is this a castle?'

Stone archways towered over cathedral doors and the interior walls were clad in dark wooden wainscoting. Overhead, a timber ceiling rested on heavy, wide beams. Annwyn turned full circle, taking in the room, the heavy but comfortable-looking furniture and the large fire, throwing golden light onto a cowskin rug.

Rafael looked embarrassed. His face reddened and he shrugged. 'It's not that big a castle, but it has been in my family for a few generations. Max, can you show Annwyn to one of the guest rooms? The tartan room I think will be best.'

Max bowed sharply from the waist. 'Certainly, sir. Should I order some food for you both? Cook is due to go to the market soon, but she had made lunch.'

Rafael waved his hand. 'Not for me, but see to it that Annwyn is fed well. She is on a different time. No doubt it's nearly breakfast time where she was.'

Annwyn thought it wasn't long since dinner, but then she had lost track of time, being hypnotised and tested. If they were in Scotland then it was ten or so hours behind.

'As you wish,' Max replied before indicating which direction she should go.

Impulsively, she hugged Rafael. 'Thank you.' He started, then relaxed as she pulled away. 'Thank you for everything.'

He squinted at her. 'You're welcome, my dear. Have a sleep now, and I'll call for you around noon tomorrow. We will start on our sessions then.' Annwyn tried to calculate how long that would be. Nearly a day, she thought. She did feel rather tired so perhaps she could sleep that long.

The old man watched her as she walked up the wide staircase in Max's wake.

'Are you a sorcerer too?' Annwyn asked Max as she trailed her hand along the banister. The wood was very smooth and it glowed warmly.

He turned his head and peered at her over his shoulder. 'No, my role is to serve.'

'Oh.' Annwyn could think of nothing to say to that. They traversed the second floor and stopped about five doors down. All the doors looked identical. Looking back up the hallway, she saw row upon row of red Persian carpets. Dim portraits adorned the walls. Figures from the past, she supposed.

A cough drew her attention. Max stood by the door. He had opened it so she could precede him. 'This is the tartan room. I hope you will be comfortable.'

She stepped over the threshold. It was a large room with an antique desk in the corner, heavy tartan drapes at the window and a rather large bed. It would be large enough for Dane to fit in comfortably. She shook her head. There was no point in thinking along those lines. She wasn't about to share this bed with anyone or anything but those rather large continental pillows.

As her gaze travelled the room Max hove into view. 'So, Max, can you tell me what I should do if I need anything…or anyone?'

Max gave a small smile. 'There is a buzzer beside the bed.' He moved to the left-hand side and pointed to panel in the wall. 'It will alert me or Jane, the housekeeper. You can talk into the grille there as it is also an intercom.'

Max moved toward the door. Moving forward to intercept him, she smiled and held out her hand again. Max looked at it, his head tilting to the side. After a slight hesitation, he shook her hand, then dropped it. Annwyn decided it was a weak handshake without much character.

'I'll bring up some food presently,' he said as he exited the room.

Annwyn went to the doorway and hovered there, watching Max walk back down the hallway. Turning back, she re-entered the room. While not surprised by the four poster bed, she felt the tartan was a bit overpowering. Something you would expect in a kitsch bed and breakfast on the tourist road in Scotland.

The counterpane was a block of deep blue with a ruffle of red patterned tartan, which matched the curtains. Stepping forward, she noticed that the bed had its own drapery of tartan material, too. She ran her hand down one of them, wondering what it would be like to sleep in a curtained bed. Stewart tartan, she thought, all bright red and merry. Royal Stewart, that was it. She must remember in case Rafael was particular about his clan or something.

Her mind wandered as she looked around the room. Rafael didn't sound Scottish but, then again, what did she know about Scotland? Not much, except that one or other of her great grandparents came from a small place near Fort William.

Slipping off her shoes, she placed them under the chair, suddenly realising that she had forgotten her things. Her gaze swept the room as she chewed her bottom lip. Should she disturb the staff now or sleep naked? Just then her eye caught sight of her overnight bag. With a grin, she went over to it and took out her toiletries and her night clothes. There was something to this magic after all. Dane must have sent it.

A knock at the door signalled Max entering with a tray. On it was a fresh baguette with thick slices of ham off the bone and lashings of fresh salad and egg mayonnaise.

After thanking Max as he departed, she ate slowly. Brushing the crumbs from her hands, she continued to explore the room. To her surprise, she found a small bathroom, behind what she thought was a cupboard. A shower was just what she needed. The hot water was a luxury after the terrible evening she had had. Now that she was alone, she let the feelings of betrayal wash over her.

Thomas had been part of a plot to make her mourn him for longer than what was right, and with such an acute intensity that she had trouble moving on from. Lucky for her, she did not have a suicidal bone in her body. She had been brought low by grief and now she was confused. They had had a good marriage. It wasn't her imagination. But something must have changed before the end, before he became ill. Before Nira entered their lives. She had felt guilt about caring for Dane while mourning Thomas, but now she was right to let that grief go. She had loved Thomas, but now he was gone. Rather than fill herself with anger, she chose to recall the good times they'd had together. Perhaps her Thomas had been a victim as well. She found it hard to believe he would inflict such harm on her. Nira had no right taking away the happiness of the past, as well as jeopardizing her future as well. But now that she had sorted it all out in her head she felt she was free to love again, free to allow herself to enjoy

Dane without the guilt of hurting Thomas, or betraying those feelings she once had.

For a long time her heart had been empty, but now it was full to bursting. Dane had filled it up with passion and power. Now she had power too, her own power. Or was it Nira's power? She would find out soon. The next few days would reveal more. As the hot water cascaded down her back she sifted her thoughts concerning all that had happened. Rafael had hinted that the power he detected in her was normal, not skewed as Nira's was to the sexual poles. It was a comforting thought.

As much as she loved being with Dane and revelled in how he made love to her there was no way she wanted to get into the kink that Nira preferred. Dane's tendencies tended toward the normal, she thought. Her feelings for Dane suffused her with warmth. Yet those warm sensations were tinged with fear. What if he couldn't ever love her? Then what if he could, but she had ruined it by what had happened with Rolf? What if he couldn't overlook Nira's possession of her and the sex with his best friend?

As she dried herself off the indignation rubbed, like the brisk movements of the towel. It hadn't been her fault. Yet he had been angry with Rolf afterwards. Rolf was a powerful-looking man, all muscle and inner strength. For a moment, she wished she could remember their sexual encounter. With a stab of guilt she thrust that thought aside. *You don't lust after your lover's best friend. Trouble. That was all that could come of it.*

Annwyn slipped her nightgown over her head. Dane had said Rolf was a werewolf. No wonder the wolves were friends with Dane and that horrible curse of his. Did that mean Rolf had magic of his own? Was it magic that turned men into wolves? She shook her head as she tidied up her belongings. She hadn't realised werewolves were real. Rolf was rather frightening in his way, silent and brooding. She recollected how tenderly he had picked up his dead pet. *Yes,* she thought, *he was capable of deep feeling.*

Frowning at her thoughts, Annwyn turned down the sheets, her mind awash with questions and fears. As she slipped between the covers she came back to her central fear. What if Dane only lusted after this body and had no interest in the real her? 'Oh, Dane,' she whispered to herself. 'How did life get so complicated?'

Annwyn struggled to sleep in the strange room. The curtains were closed, serving well to block out the daylight and, even though the castle was quiet, sleep eluded her. The time difference, that must be it. She thought it best to turn her mind to something pleasant. What did she find the most pleasing thing? Dane making love to her. So she let memories of her time with Dane flow into her, the memory of his mouth on her sex, driving her wild until she shrieked with pleasure and shook from her orgasm.

Annwyn touched herself, letting her finger trace the pattern of Dane's tongue. She used those memories with the stroking to bring herself close. God, she wanted release. Yet she didn't want to go too far in case she touched Nira's consciousness. Annwyn shut down her thoughts and concentrated on her rapid stroking, feeling herself closer and closer to climax. Her buttocks clenched, enhancing her arousal. It came in wave upon wave. As her body shook she threw her head back against the pillow and whispered, 'Oh, Dane. What have you done to me?'

Indeed, she thought, I've never been this hot in my life. She lay there letting the tingling effervescence of her ecstasy slide away, leaving her with a mild glow and a mind ready for sleep. There's no use in worrying about it, she told herself as she rolled over and went to sleep. In the dark recesses of the tartan room Annwyn found her sleep untroubled as if there was a barrier there keeping her concerns at bay.

***

A knock at the door woke her. At first she had no idea what time it was until she checked her phone which had reset to local time. It was 12.30 pm. 'Yes,' she called out in answer to the persistent knocking. She squinted at the date. She had slept for nearly twenty hours. Amazing!

The door swung open. A woman in uniform stood there. 'Gud mornin', mam. I've brought yer breakfast tray.' Annwyn lifted an eyebrow as the woman's accent was very thick. The woman turned to the side and picked up a tray. Walking in, without a smile or a nod or any kind of acknowledgement, she placed the tray on the desk with a brisk movement. She was in her forties, Annwyn guessed, rather plump and plain.

'Thank you. You must be Jane.'

'No, mam. I'm Morag. Mrs Jane's the housekeeper. I help her out when there be guests.'

'Well, thank you, Morag.'

Morag walked out and shut the door quickly behind her. Annwyn stared at it for a moment, blinking. She was really in a castle in Scotland. It quite suddenly and completely came home to her. With a groan, she climbed out of bed and staggered over to the breakfast tray. She was glad Morag hadn't called it a 'wee' breakfast because it looked like the kitchen staff didn't know what she ate so had catered for all contingencies. There was oatmeal porridge, orange juice, tea, coffee, bacon, grilled tomatoes, sautéed spinach, a kipper, poached eggs, scrambled eggs, four different kinds of toasted bread, and three different kinds of milk. She picked up one of the tiny jugs. This one was soy as it looked thick and greyish so were the others low fat and regular? She shrugged and settled down to eat.

After spooning some scrambled eggs and bacon onto her plate, she decided to drink the tea first, then have coffee afterwards. She gave the oatmeal a miss, even though she liked it. She wanted to eat a reasonable amount of the food without giving offense or feeling guilty about the waste. Now if Dane had been here, there would have been no problem.

'Not again,' she groaned and took a bite out of her toast. 'Get a grip, woman. You've been apart for one day. You'll live.'

Within the hour, she was going down the stairs, hoping to encounter either Max or Rafael so they could begin. She was keen to know what was happening to her and to learn something useful, if at all possible. She wandered around the main hall that skirted the living room, trying to decide which direction to take. She heard a voice from a room further down so followed it along the corridor.

As she drew closer she picked out Max's voice. It was a one-sided conversation so perhaps he was on the phone. 'I don't care about that,' he said. 'I'm just telling you what is going on here.' There was a pause. 'No, I agree it's not the best situation.' He was quiet again. She heard him pace as the floorboards creaked. 'You come up with a plan. I'll keep thinking.'

'Annwyn?' Rafael's voice came from behind. She swung around, her face flushed. She had been caught eavesdropping.

'Rafael. I was looking for you.'

Rafael gestured for her to join him, and she hastened back up the hallway. She looked over her shoulder and saw that Max had stuck his head out of the room and was looking at her. *How embarrassing*, she thought, *being caught listening in*. Well, she argued with herself, I didn't do it deliberately.

'I hope you slept well, my dear. Do you mind coming down stairs into my sanctum? It's the best place to do these things, you know.'

'These things?'

He turned slightly, a light in his eyes. 'Yes, sorcery.' He shrugged. 'Magic, you call it, although that is not quite encompassing enough a term for me.' He grinned at her, then waved his hands at a piece of wainscoting. It sprung open, revealing a secret door. Annwyn felt a rush of excitement and then she paused to examine the doorway. It glimmered faintly and then faded from view. Was this magic she was witnessing? She was of a mind to ask Rafael but he had already started down the rather narrow staircase. She hadn't seen Dane's sanctum so she was agog to see what Rafael's looked like. The thought that she could be a sorceress thrilled her. What if the power was all her own? If so, how did that come to be? She was about to learn it all.

The risers squeaked beneath her feet as she followed Rafael. It got so dark she lost sight of him and had a moment of panic as the walls seemed to close in, the oppressive gloom tightening. A scream fought its way out of her throat.

A hand grabbed her clenched fist and tugged. She found herself clasping onto Rafael's robes, panting heavily.

'Sorry about that, dear. I forgot about the final ward. It doesn't like strangers.'

Her eyes were wide with shock. 'That was magic? I thought…I thought I was having a panic attack.'

Rafael tilted his head. 'Really? It should have made you run the other way. Interesting. I'll have to work on strengthening that one.'

He bowed slightly, his robes rippling around him. 'Welcome to my sanctum. No doubt you realise that this isn't for visitors normally.'

She rubbed at her upper arms, feeling a damp chill rising off the floor. The room was very plain. No windows, but there was light coming from somewhere. She scanned the room. There, she thought, a number of lamps attached to the walls and a couple more beneath far benches. There was something about the lamps, too, a kind of glow, like the secret door. She could see the magic in them.

Shelves held books and papers, or perhaps parchment for it looked thick and curled at the ends. There was not much else of interest in sight. Annwyn assumed that this was probably only part of his sanctum, but she took no insult from that. He hardly knew her. Dane had said he was a powerful man. She should be glad he was willing to help her.

'What do you see?' he asked her quietly. She realised he had been silently studying her reaction to his room. He raised an eyebrow when she described the lights.

'Stand there, will you? Watch and tell me what you see.'

Rafael did nothing. There were no gestures or incantations, but Annwyn took a hasty step back. A small ball of golden light about the size of a tennis ball appeared. It expanded rapidly, making her flinch. As the sparkles retracted a demon-like figure appeared, chilling her to her very bones. Her scream made Rafael smile.

'Interesting,' he said and turned away.

Annwyn bit down on a retort. It wasn't funny and he'd better have more to say than interesting by the time they were done.

'Now, see this device?' He held up a little machine with wheels and small turbines on the top and a box beneath. It was the size of a regular shoe box. Annwyn nodded. 'I want to see if you can move the turbines but hold the wheels steady.' She reached out a hand. 'With your power, Annwyn.'

Annwyn frowned as she examined the machine. She did not see how to move the turbine without moving the wheel. On the surface, they seem to be attached.

Chewing her lip, she knew she was failing the test badly. It occurred to her that there might be a trick to the machine and that what was on the surface may not be what was beneath. She focused on the box. Her senses delved into the dark space. She could feel the machinery rather than see it. Trust Rafael to try to trick her. There she saw a thread of magic and tugged it loose.

Drawing her mind from the box, she flicked the turbine with her power and it spun fast. The connecting wheel remained stationary.

'Extraordinary,' Rafael said. This time there was a glint in his eye, and a smile teased the edges of his mouth. She thought he was pleased.

He set another test for her, and another. When they finally climbed up the narrow dark staircase again she felt as if she had been flattened by a bulldozer. They must have been going at it for hours.

Max waited for them as they re-entered the hallway. 'Master, Miss Annwyn. I have bad news.'

'What is it?' Annwyn burst out, thinking it was news about Dane.

Rafael half turned to her, his expression serious. 'Be calm, dear. It takes a lot to damage Dane Archwright.' He returned his attention to his assistant. 'You're going to tell me dinner is ruined and cook isn't prepared to serve it.'

'Dinner?' Annwyn said dumbly. Her stomach rumbled. Had she been below that long? 'God, what time is it?'

Max bobbed his head. 'It is near ten pm. You have been below for more than eight hours.'

Annwyn drew her head back in surprise and blinked. 'Eight hours?'

Rafael waved his hand dismissively. 'Tell cook to serve the dinner as is. I'm sure it is fine.'

Max bowed from the waist and then headed down the hall.

Rafael grabbed her elbow. 'I'm sorry, my dear. I kept you so long that our roast beef is sure to be well done, and our roast potatoes less then crispy. Otherwise, I'm sure the meal is fine. My cook is temperamental and likes to see me waiting patiently to be amazed by her culinary feats. She does not like to be the one kept waiting.'

'I see. Do I have time to freshen up?'

'Yes, my dear. Hurry along and I'll keep the rabid hordes of servants at bay.'

Annwyn ran up the stairs, surprised at the time that had elapsed. Rafael had a small bathroom and they'd had some herbal tea during their short breaks, but eight hours? Really?

The dinner, when she sat down to it, was superb. Rafael provided a delectable red wine. 'Australian, and a gift from Dane. Australians make big wines. I see you have an appetite so the food is not that bad then. Cook will be pleased.'

Rafael cut into his roast beef. It was well done but amazingly tender and the vegetables were just to Annwyn's liking. She shoved another piece of meat into her mouth.

'I must warn you, my dear,' Rafael said as he placed his knife and fork gently on his plate and placed his elbows on the table to regard her seriously.

Annwyn swallowed her half-chewed mouthful. 'Yes?'

'You must leave room. Cook makes the most excellent desserts.'

Max had joined them for dinner but had stayed mostly silent. His head shot up from where he was regarding his plate. 'Sticky toffee pudding and double cream.'

Annwyn turned toward him. 'Would that be something like what we call sticky date pudding?'

Max shrugged and left the table to tell the kitchen that they were ready for the next course. Annwyn made inroads into her wine. How she wished Dane was there. Drinking his wine made her feel warm inside, as if he was there in some small way.

'Penny for them?'

Annwyn's gaze flicked to Rafael. His smile seemed sympathetic. 'It's nothing. Silly, really. I miss him.'

Rafael nodded. 'I see no trace of the binding spell on you. It has faded already.'

Annwyn was taken aback. 'But that means…'

Rafael was grinning now. He saw her perturbed look and picked up the bottle for a refill, tumbling the rich red liquid into the deep bowl of his glass. 'You are in love with him.'

Annwyn sat back in her chair, feeling deflated. It had been easier when she had the spell to blame. She could let her feelings go wherever they willed and only had to worry about controlling them and worrying about whether he could love her in return.

Now it was not some mystical spell ruling her destiny, but her own heart. It seemed outrageous. What if Dane was also free? Where did that leave her—in love with an unwilling man? She groaned and leaned on the table, her head supported by her hand.

'It's not that tragic, my dear.'

Before she could respond, they were interrupted by Max bringing in a tray with three steaming bowls on it. He placed the dessert in front of her. It looked and smelt just like sticky date pudding. Lovely hot caramel toffee sauce glistened on the spongy cake with a huge dollop of thick cream. Food, at least, would console her and there was no use in fretting now. She would find out how things stood with Dane soon enough.

So, with a sigh, she stuck her spoon into the bowl and began to savour the delectable flavour of sticky toffee pudding. By the time Rafael served her a second glass of port she was feeling done in and positively tipsy.

'I think we'll put off our chat until tomorrow. However, I have left a book in your room that I want you to read. It should help you with some exercises.' Rafael reached over to pat her head affectionately. 'I'll see you in the morning.'

As Annwyn wasn't leaving the room just yet and Rafael didn't seem to be either, she assumed she had been dismissed for the evening. Leaving Rafael to his warm fire and his assistant,

Annwyn managed to climb the stairs and fall into bed. She undressed as each piece of clothing became uncomfortable, deciding to delay her shower until morning. Her shoes were somewhere by the door. She'd find them later. In a haze of wine-filled drunkenness, she drifted off to sleep.

***

Dane leaned against the wall, staring out the window, a cool beer in his hand. The sound of Rolf's empty bottle hitting the counter brought his attention back to his friend.

'We should drive out to the ridge now. The rest of the pack will be gathering. I'd like to keep to pack custom and all change together at the full moon.'

Dane was on edge. His skin itched and the beast prowled along his defences, ready to trample them down. He ran his fingers through his hair, the sensation like daggers pressing into his scalp. He shook his head at Rolf. 'I'm not sure I'll be able to control the spell until then. I feel the moon's pull on me now.' He let out a little growl. Dane's head jerked back in surprise as he had not meant that literally.

It was close but he wasn't about to transform at that moment. Dane realised his friend had little patience with his whinging about his curse. If anything, Rolf was well adjusted to his condition. He considered the benefits rather than the downside. Most of the pack did, too. It was Dane's resistance that made them want to help him. Perhaps they didn't want a reluctant wolf in their pack.

Dane couldn't help his reaction. He dreaded the change—dreaded what he would do while a wolf and the changes the curse would etch into him this time. Would Annwyn find him desirable after the change? What if she couldn't stand to be with him, to look at him? Dane widened his eyes, then shook his head. He needed to get those feelings of permanence with Annwyn out of his brain.

As soon as they got her body back and shucked that binding spell, it was over. Period. There was no 'us'. Still, his mind went back to the question. What if in a couple of days, when Annwyn came back, she was revolted by him? *Well*, he said to himself, *you'll just have to keep away from her. There, problem solved.*

Rolf slapped him on the shoulder. 'Come on, lock up the house and do your hocus pocus or whatever it is you do to keep the bad guys out. The pack is waiting and you're safer there with us than here on your own. Like you said, there is nothing you can do now before the full moon. The curse is still there. We enjoy your company.'

Dane met his gaze, unable to hide his dismay.

Rolf shook his head. 'Really, Dane, being a werewolf is not that bad. It has its rewards, believe me. Give it time and you will adjust.'

Dane shook his head. He'd had fun with Rolf, but there was something important at stake here: his identity and the collegium. Rafael had suspected that it was an attack on the collegium itself that was the root of his problem. He couldn't walk away from that, not now, particularly when he had given his oath to protect the collegium.

'No offence to you and your kind, but I was not meant for your way of life. I have to fight it even if, in the end, I can do nothing. Each time I change I lose part of myself. I become less than I was.'

Rolf's gaze trailed over him and then he drew his shoulders back. 'It's the woman, isn't it? You're worried she won't want you.' Rolf shook his head slowly.

Dane steadied himself for his friend's disdain, but said nothing. His silence only confirmed to his friend what he'd been thinking about moments before.

'She loves you and she won't care what you are—man, wolf, or sorcerer. She is committed to you, heart and soul.'

'It's the spell. Not her. She can't control her attraction to me or even her obedience.'

Rolf shook his head. 'It might have been that way at first but it's something more now. I can smell it. I can sense it. God, I can almost feel it.' Rolf turned away and headed to the sliding door, pausing before opening it. 'Come on. I'll get the car warmed up while you close up.'

Dane nodded and went to set his wards. While he chanted

and set each spell he tried to calm his mind for the fever of change that was to come. He closed his eyes, begging the deities to give him the strength to be ridden by his inner beast and come out the other side intact.

143

# Chapter Fourteen

Annwyn thought it was a noise that woke her sometime later. For whatever reason, she was wide awake and had an incredible headache. She thought to take a shower but was reluctant to wake anyone with the sound of water gushing through pipes so she flicked on the light. In her overnight bag she found some headache tablets and swallowed them dry. She climbed back into bed, sitting up and rubbing her forehead.

The headache began to shift but she didn't feel like sleeping. Next to her on the bedside table was the book Rafael had given her. She picked it up. It had a plain cover and seemed to be handcrafted.

After frowning at it for a few minutes, she remembered that Rafael suggested she read it. As sleep and morning seemed a long way off she began to study the book. A few bumps and thumps in the house caught her attention, but the book was fascinating. She stopped now and again to try the exercises and was pleased with the results. This book was teaching her how to use her gift.

Before they came out of the sanctum, Rafael had explained to her that she had a rare gift. She could see magic spells. She could even see the residue of them. With practice she could learn to undo them.

Her capacity for magic was reasonable and appeared to be growing. Rafael could not explain it, nor did he think it was Nira's power. He thought that when Nira possessed her, that she left a residue behind and that it had ignited a dormant power within her.

It appeared that many humans had some dormant magic within them but, without a trigger, it never amounted to anything. 'It is not deliberate, my dear. Nira has done this unwittingly. You must learn quickly to hide what you can do from her. I fear she will destroy you if she discovers it.'

'Why would she do that?'

He shrugged. 'Defence, my dear. If she is clever, she could do worse. She might access your power, drain you and add it to hers.'

A cold sensation sliced through her centre. That evil woman had done enough already. Look at what she had done to Dane. Access to more power would make her invincible. Annwyn did not want to be at her mercy. She remembered the cold horror of discovering that Nira had taken her over. Dane had seen that, had caught Nira in this body having sex with Rolf. Although Dane had not blamed her she understood his frustration that she couldn't control herself, couldn't block out the other woman.

Some of the instruction Rafael had provided that day was going to help with that. She tapped the top of the book he gave her against her chin. She'd finish this book before she went back to sleep. She had a lot to learn and not much time.

It took a good four hours to go right through the book. She practised some of the exercises. Lifting the book in the air using magic worked eventually, as did switching the light on and off. These were simple manipulative magic exercises that were sometimes useful and sometimes less so.

She would wait until morning and then revise what she had learned before moving onto more complex actions, such as creation magic and spell-casting. Although these were only simple introductory lessons they had to be done with care. If she mastered these before her next session with Rafael, she would be happy.

Rafael also wanted her to study the shape of the spells, and learn the pattern types. These he couldn't instruct her in too deeply because so few in the collegium could see them as she did. He suggested she start her own notebook to catalogue what she saw. That way she could decipher patterns over time. What really excited her about her ability was that, because she had such a rare gift, there was now a place for her at the collegium. She couldn't help but think of a future with Dane, despite the impossibilities of her situation.

Now that her mind had wandered to Dane, she wondered what he was doing and whether he was safe. She didn't conjure memories of their time together as she didn't wish to unwittingly summon Nira. Luckily, Rafael had put up a ward to alert him if there was a change in Annwyn, a sort of alarm bell to let him know if Nira had taken her over. It wasn't much comfort, but at least she wasn't in danger of doing something evil.

***

Nira placed the photo of Dane and his mother back into her carry bag and wiggled on the park bench, trying to find a spot that didn't irritate her sore behind. Fog hovered low over Lake Burley Griffin, its mirrored surface glistening. A few cyclists sped by and black swans squawked as they searched for leftover bread.

The object she had stolen was good for forming a connection. She could skim his mind without him noticing. She smiled to herself. Her curse was building. How he hated it: how it hurt him. Smiling grimly, she savoured those emotions. They fed her emptiness. The connection revealed the depth of the moon thrall curse, the corrupting nature of the spell. The curse had been one of her own devising, even her master had been surprised at how well it had sunk into him, how it shaped him. He had everything: position, power, a great blood line, while she had nothing except what she created herself. Her master had cultivated her, but her methods for enhancing her power were her own. He offered her a place in the collegium only if she served him, though she had not earned it yet. The time was not ripe.

Her mind returned to the visit to his house. His house wards were easy to subvert. Greater care and craft were required if he wanted to keep her out. He'd lived in Australia too long and hung around too many humans and that made him lax. His wards were flimsy, except the ones guarding the sanctum. They, at least, had increased her level of admiration for him.

Her master had not expected her to retrieve the items he wanted. The quality of the ward, though, confirmed that what Dane kept hidden was important, valuable. A sudden thought of Annwyn in his mind nearly made her scream in frustration. How dare he lust after her, desire her! It was Nira's body, not that

146

lame woman's pale-limbed pile of flesh. He should try fucking that! Anger burned deep in her gut at the thought that either of them could feel something good from all this, that his stupid, waning binding spell gave them pleasure. She would deal with them both. Nira sank into cold rage.

***

When Dane and Rolf pulled up, dirt billowing behind them, they saw that there were about twenty cars parked up on the ridge. It looked like there were a few more to arrive before all members were accounted for. Rolf was greeted with howls as he exited the car. He was popular, a good alpha leader of his pack. When the other members of the pack saw Dane they nodded politely, their gazes wary.

Dane shook his head. They were worried he'd challenge Rolf for leadership. Dane stifled a grin. It was the last thing on his mind. A future where that might happen was something he tried desperately not to think about. Another four cars pulled up, tyres grating on the loose gravel. In these were four females and Dane could almost sense the ripple of excitement that went through the male members of the pack. Straightaway, helpers appeared to carry groceries the women had brought with them into the small hut. There would be a barbecue before the moon ascended above the Tinderry ranges.

The pack gathering for moonrise put Dane on edge. He could feel the moon coming, feel its pull and walk along his bones. The excitement and anticipation of the other werewolves only made it worse. It was as if it had invisible claws scraping off the vestiges of his control.

Dane paced, nodding to those of the pack he knew—a mechanic based in Queanbeyan, a secretary of a department of state, a local politician and two federal politicians, a leading mining magnate, and a rather burly young man who was an up-and-coming sculptor. Dane wondered at how well concealed the paranormals and the supernaturals were within the general populace.

The barbecue was fired up by Joe Mazelli, a celebrity chef, and he fired off chitchat with Delia Morgan, the most senior female pack member. He thought she was a government auditor. She looked too dainty and sweet to be either a werewolf or a zealous figure-chaser. The smell of the raw steaks hit him and it was enough to push him over the edge. His control frayed.

Ripping at his shirt, he let out a tumultuous howl as heat and the great paws of the beast began its rampage beneath his skin. The tattered remains of Dane's T-shirt dropped to the ground. Small whimpers escaped as his skin burned like a hundred lit cigarettes were being pressed into him. The beast's claws began to shred through Dane's unwilling flesh. Dane's consciousness fled as the curse transformed him into the beast.

***

Rolf kept a surreptitious eye on Dane. His friend was even more on edge than usual this close to the full moon. The sight of the raw meat being lined up on the grill served to tease his hunger forth, tempting his beast closer. The steaks were driving him crazy and he only needed the meat warmed slightly to satisfy his craving. He liked them blue.

With an ear-splitting howl, Dane's beast erupted. The poor man had no time to remove his clothes properly and the moon was a good hour off rising. Rolf stripped off his own shirt, baring his chest to the brisk night.

'There goes the barbecue,' he said to the pack, a cheeky grin on his face. They'd take the meat before they headed for the run. He howled in a way only a werewolf can, signalling the pack to begin the change. Dane's transformation would only set the rest of them on edge so it was better to go now. The mechanics of dealing with a werewolf when the rest of them were in human form were difficult. Dane was technically a new werewolf, although the curse made things trickier. It was easier to communicate if they were all wolves at the same time. It reduced the amount of misunderstanding.

Rolf peeled his jeans off his hips and let them drop to the ground. He kicked them, along with his shirt, through the open door of the small hut they used for storage. His boots he placed just inside the door. The other pack members followed suit, shucking clothes and storing gear. The pack women shed their clothes too to stand naked amongst the men. Dane howled again.

Dane prowled around the clearing, growling as each member of the pack changed, and let out a surprised bark when two changed together. Rolf stayed close to Dane, nudging him with his muzzle. Dane whined and then began to settle.

Rolf held the pack in the clearing until the moon rose above the ridge, majestic and bright. At the sight, the pack howled in unison and Dane right along with them. With a nip to his hindquarter, Rolf got Dane running with the pack.

Soon they were deep in the dark bush, leaping over gnarled roots, inhaling the scent of rabbits, foxes and possums. Further in, they disturbed a mob of kangaroos grazing in patches of wild grass. They bounded off to escape as the pack slammed along worn paths between the wattle, eucalypts and pines. Bats shrieked and flew up into the night. Rolf revelled in the freedom of the bush and the power in his sinews.

Dane ran alongside him. Rolf acknowledged that Dane was a notable wolf, large, powerful and with good instincts. The only issue was what Dane's ability was to exert himself when in wolf form. Rolf had been a wolf for so long it was second nature to him. He worried that Dane's sense of self was weakening with each transformation, which was the opposite of what would happen if he was a natural born wolf. The damn curse was not natural and this worried Rolf. Really worried him.

A hare darted from the undergrowth. Dane went for it and Rolf followed close behind, bounding over a fallen log and dodging a rotting stump. The smells of the bush came alive around him and the scent of the hare pulled him along. The rest of the pack started to hunt too. Rolf could hear and smell them wending their way along tiny trails in pursuit of animals.

By the time he caught up with Dane there was nothing left of the hare except a head and a bloodstained pelt. Rolf wolf-grinned and set Dane running into the night again. A wombat was foraging close by. They must be near the creek. Rolf did his best to head off his friend. Dane would not like to kill native animals. He was pretty calm about the feral pests, but natives he agonised over. Rolf intended to spend his post-change hangover indulging himself in drink, women and fast cars, not guilt. There was a grunt up ahead. Rolf sped off to head off Dane's assault. He let out a howl to let the pack know where he was. As he raced after his friend he found himself cursing. Sorcerers!

# Chapter Fifteen

The next morning, Annwyn was up in time to forestall a servant bringing her a tray. She found Max in the dining room reading the paper while he absent-mindedly pushed scrambled eggs around his plate. He swallowed a mouthful and made to stand up when she came in.

'Oh, please, stay seated. I thought I would join the household for breakfast today.'

Max sat back down. 'Thank you. You are most welcome to join us. Rafael is not awake yet. He works late most evenings and sleeps late.'

She helped herself to an English muffin and some scrambled eggs from the chafing dish. She tossed some crispy bacon onto her plate.

'He works very hard.' She sat down opposite Max before going back to the sideboard to pour herself some potent-smelling coffee. While she was pouring Max added, 'He sometimes pops out for meetings, but mostly he leaves me messages and instructions. Just in case you find he's not here one day. Don't worry about it.'

Taking her seat, she took a sip, relishing the aroma and the mellow taste. It was very good coffee. 'I'm sure I can manage without Rafael for a little while. Although I'm keen to return to Australia as soon as I can.'

Max shook his paper out and began folding it. He looked up, meeting her gaze. 'I'm sure you are, and when Rafael is finished with you I'm sure you will be free to go.'

There was definitely a sinister undertone in Max's words. While she gaped at him stupidly, he got up from the table and left the room.

Picking up a piece of her muffin, she pondered that exchange. Of course, the young man must resent her presence. It was as simple as that. With a shrug, she tucked into her eggs.

Morag bustled in. 'Mornin',' she said as she plonked down a bowl of cinnamon and clove-spiced stewed fruit.

'That smells delicious. I'll have to try some.' She rose up in her seat to look at the contents.

'As you wish,' Morag replied without a smile, wiping her hands on her apron she bustled out. Annwyn contemplated the shut door. *Friendly bunch,* she thought. No point in taking offence. She savoured her coffee and reached out to drag over Max's abandoned paper to read. When ready for a second cup, she helped herself to a portion of the stewed fruit.

As she finished off her second helping Rafael ambled in, gaze slightly unfocused.

He poured himself a coffee then started when he turned to the table and saw her sitting there.

'Oh, good morning, my dear. Forgive me, I didn't see you. Have you been down long?'

'Not long at all. I've had a nice leisurely breakfast and an excellent night's sleep. Thank you for your hospitality.'

He harrumphed. 'It's nothing. You're a very exciting discovery.'

Annwyn saw her opportunity. 'That's very sweet of you to say so but I'd really like to get back to check on Dane.'

Rafael's eyebrows shot up and then came slowly down. 'Ah yes, best leave him at least another day. This curse thing and the effects of the full moon may linger for a few days. He was quite adamant that you stay with me during that time. Besides, he can always come here and fetch you himself.'

Annwyn's gut clenched. What if Dane didn't come to fetch her? What if he didn't want her in his life? The binding spell was effectively dissolved. She knew that, but Dane didn't. But even then, the uncertainty, the fear of rejection, almost crushed her. She tried to smile for Rafael who still regarded her under his brows as he sipped his coffee. Seeing her complacency, he helped himself to breakfast. She noticed that he took only the stewed fruit.

Rafael excused himself. 'Meet me at the door to the

sanctum in half an hour, will you? I've some things to discuss with my assistant.'

Annwyn returned to her room to prepare for another day of lessons. She collected her lesson book after making herself presentable and tidying the room. She didn't want to upset Morag by leaving an unmade bed.

Dressed in comfortable jeans, a long-sleeved top and runners, she was ready for anything Rafael had to throw at her today. Her excitement threatened to spill over. She had power and was learning how to use it. Surely, it would bring her closer to Dane.

Once down in the sanctum Rafael got straight to work in training her in how to use her power. First, he created a number of small spells, then asked her to note down in her notebook the particular patterns, and they discussed how the spells looked and the function of each curve, twist and knot.

Soon Annwyn was able to differentiate between hexes, love spells and bindings. She practised making the spells to the same patterns. She managed to create a spell that would turn a black cat white, and also how to disguise a hex within the spell so that if the cat rubbed up against someone, it would leave a black mark on their skin or clothing. Quite a harmless little hex, but the pattern was there—a complex weave running anticlockwise. She could tell that Rafael was rather excited by her progress. With the advantage of being able to see the pattern of the spells, she could replicate them exactly. Rafael told her that her ability was an innovation because usually sorcerers learnt by feel rather than sight. They even tried it with her eyes closed, and she could still sense the patterns.

Rafael scratched his beard. 'You will have to learn that the traditional way as well,' Rafael said after a thoughtful pause. 'To develop the greatest potential of your gift you will have to do it the hard way. So now I'm going to blindfold you, and I want you to try and recreate the spells.'

Annwyn was a little bit disoriented without the ability to see. However, she found that by using hand gestures, the incantations she had learned, and the image that was left of the spell, she could still turn the black cat white.

Rafael had conjured a black cat for them to experiment on. When she asked about it he laughed. 'Actually, it's my cat. I've just swept him up from outside and brought him here. Don't fret about it, though. Vester has been my assistant most of his life. He'll get a nice treat from the cook when we're done.'

Annwyn stroked the cat. Its warm fur was soft against her hand and the robust feline purred loudly, not distressed in the least at having been changed from black to white and back again. Annwyn's jeans were covered in black stains from where the cat had rubbed up against her, leaving its small hex. With a flick of his wrist, Rafael wiped the trace of the hex from her clothing.

'Now, my dear, we will try something a little bit more complex. I want you to send a message to Dane using your power. First, I'm going to demonstrate it to you and send you a message. Then I want you to copy me. But, in your case, you will have to picture Dane and also consider his location. You will need a little bit more power to give the message a push than I will need to send one to you because you're right here next to me.'

'Is there anything in particular you want me to ask him?'

'No, Annwyn, the message will be entirely your own and between yourselves. I only ask that when Dane replies to you that he includes me so I know that you have been successful. But, remember, he may not yet be himself so his response may not arrive until tomorrow at the earliest. However, later on this evening, I want you to send me a message before you go to sleep. Do not worry about waking me for I'm likely to be awake until the early hours.'

Annwyn beamed a smile at him. 'I will. I won't forget, and I'm very grateful for your instruction. I'm so excited by this new world opening up to me.' Annwyn closed her eyes so that she could think of a message to send. This message she wanted to be very special as it was her first, and communicating this way was entirely intimate.

Rafael coughed into his hand. 'My dear, you need to watch me first so that you can copy me.'

For Annwyn there was not much to copy. Rafael did most of it in his head and had to explain it to her. She began to worry that she could not quite accomplish the task. Then Rafael actually sent the instructions in a silent message. 'A-ha, now I see what you mean.'

All she had to do now was to compose a message and package it up in the way Rafael showed her.

*Dane, this is Annwyn. I'm learning to use this power. Rafael is taking very good care of me and teaching me. I miss you very much, and I hope you're well. Please respond to this message when you can so we know it has arrived. Rafael sends his regards. Love Annwyn.*

The 'Love Annwyn' came so smoothly and naturally that she didn't hesitate over including it. She had to get over the fear that he could not love her in return, had to accept that she had feelings for him and deal with them, come what may. Wistfully, she smiled and turned her attention back to her lesson.

Annwyn's stomach rumbled noisily. 'Annwyn, my dear, we should take a break for lunch, I think. He checked his watch. 'Perhaps an early dinner, given the hour.'

Annwyn rubbed her stomach, feeling a little bit embarrassed. 'I'm sorry, I thought I'd eaten a very substantial breakfast today.'

'Never mind, dear, I'm feeling quite peckish myself. When you think about it, what we are doing is quite complex and a break will do some good and allow some of that heavy instruction to sink in. However, I expect a vast improvement tomorrow.'

'Does that mean that we won't be continuing today?'

'No, my dear, it does not mean that at all. We will resume after our break. I'm just saying, generally, that I expect a lot from you tomorrow. And I'll have another book of instructions for you to study tonight.'

As they climbed up the stairs she asked. 'Do all new sorcerers have to learn so quickly?'

'No, my dear, unfortunately current circumstances require a

crash course, as you would call it. You have come quickly into this power, and you have come into it in circumstances of danger. Your knowledge will be patchy, but I must give you enough instruction so that you will be able to protect yourself and not harm others. It will take you years to fully master all there is for you to learn.'

Annwyn pushed open the secret door and climbed through the narrow space into the hallway. She turned slowly, ready to help Rafael when he emerged after her. In the light of the hall she could see that he was very tired and looked poorly. The sight of him like this brought her a feeling of compassion. She was full of gratitude but also concerned for his welfare.

'Rafael, are you sure you need to spend time with me again this evening? Surely you need time to spend on other things, or to relax a little bit.'

'My dear, there are a lot of things that weigh me down. If I was not teaching you, I would be on some other collegium business. Do not fret over me. I am well enough.'

With that, he pressed her gently in the small of her back, urging her to precede him into the dining room. Rafael left to search for the staff in order to rustle up a meal. This allowed Annwyn time to ponder her situation and to consolidate the lessons she had learned that morning.

She realised that they had left Vester, the cat, in the sanctum. As Rafael's wards permitted her entry, she reached out with her power, following it down the dark stairway into the sanctum and groped for the presence of the cat. There she found it, asleep on top of one of the work benches. She wondered if it was right to transport the cat outside at that moment. She hadn't really pictured the outside because she hadn't been out there and doubted her ability to do so. She decided that as the cat was asleep and not in any way distressed that she would leave it. However, she thought it was probably a good idea to go outside and check the surroundings so she could transport it at a later time as part of her practice. It was entirely possible that she could transport the cat to Dane's house. It would, unfortunately, cause havoc with Australia's quarantine laws and might prove distressing to the cat, considering the presence of dogs and werewolves.

Not long after, Max walked in and pulled up short when he saw her sitting there. 'Oh, I didn't realise you'd be upstairs already.'

'We're taking a short break. Having something to eat. Will you join us?'

Max hesitated. 'Thank you, I might just do that. Could you tell me where Rafael is at this moment?'

'He said he was going to look for some lunch. So I suppose he went in the direction of the kitchen, to see the cook, perhaps?'

Max nodded with a slight smile. 'Yes, quite right. I'll pop down to the cellar then and select a wine.'

Annwyn smiled and nodded her head. 'I'm sure that would be lovely, thank you.'

Max backtracked out the door and disappeared. Annwyn was left alone again, twiddling her thumbs. Shortly, she was interrupted in her contemplation by the arrival of Morag who had come in to set places for lunch. She did not take well to hearing that Max would be joining them. She stomped out of the room to fetch more plates.

Rafael came in about five minutes later with a handful of glasses and a bottle of wine. 'I met Max downstairs. He'll be joining us shortly. But, my dear, I fear you should not have any wine this afternoon. You need to have all your faculties sharp and unclouded by alcohol. I hope that's not a problem. You may have as much wine as you like this evening.'

Annwyn smiled and assured him that she didn't mind going without wine. The cook served them an excellent roast lamb with dainty little potatoes and fresh green beans. While Max and Rafael chatted over a glass or two of wine, Annwyn excused herself and went to explore the outside of the castle. She wanted to make sure that if she did transport that poor cat, she would do it properly. As she passed the kitchen door she overheard the cook and Morag complaining about the demands of their master and his guest. She noted that they were particularly vitriolic about Max and his high-handed manners. Wasn't he a servant like them, they said. Annwyn shrugged, thinking to herself. Like that, is it?

A rocky path led from the back door into a lovely vegetable garden. The grounds were not overly large, but she knew she was in the country. Rubbing her upper arms against the chill breeze, Annwyn took a walk around, interested to see the castle in all its dilapidated glory. While it appeared well looked after from the inside, the ravages of time were quite evident on its exterior. Some of the outer stones were cracked and crumbled and some were missing altogether.

One of the turrets had completely collapsed although the stone had been cleared away. At the front there was a long drive that disappeared into some woods. She expected it was where the access road was located. In the distance, under a marbled grey sky, she could see rounded barren hills slightly pink with gorse and heather. The wind picked up, sending fingers of ice into her skin so she hurried back inside through the backdoor. Once inside, she jumped up and down on the spot to bring warmth back into her arms and feet.

She arrived in time to hear Rafael call for her. Running fingers through her hair, she hastened to the hidden door where he was waiting for her. 'There you are, my dear. How did you find the outside? The highlands chilly enough for you?'

'It was lovely, thank you. And rather chilly. It's autumn here, isn't it?'

'Yes, though the weather here's a bit unpredictable. It has certainly been warmer than normal for this time of year.'

Rafael flourished his hand, inviting her to open the hidden door. This she did without mishap, smiling to herself with not-so-secret satisfaction. She couldn't wait to see Dane and tell him everything she had learned and how wonderful it was.

Again down in the sanctum, they continued their lessons. Rafael let her transport the cat outside into the vegetable garden. Next, he asked her to bring in a few of the turnips that were growing there. Annwyn closed her eyes and tried to picture the vegetable garden. 'You should have seen them. They grow like weeds, the damned things.'

On her quick foray outdoors she hadn't noticed any particular type of vegetable. However, she remembered what the garden looked like and, mentally, she sorted through the weeds and found the green tops of turnips. She wasn't quite sure how to extract the turnips and bring them in, although, she did her best. Rafael's hoot of laughter made her jump back in surprise. She'd deposited a lump of earth with a few turnips in it on the floor. 'Oh dear. I'm sorry I've made a mess.' Her hands covered her mouth.

'Never mind, my dear. It's quite all right. You can send the dirt back to the garden and the turnips to the kitchen. Go on then.'

With a wave of her hand, Annwyn sent the vegetables to where they belonged and deposited the dirt back into the garden. It was actually quite hard separating the dirt from the turnips. Rafael had his arms crossed and an amused expression on his face. He nodded. 'It was very well done. I'm surprised at how far you have gone in such a short time.'

Annwyn could not hide her delight at his praise. She had been working hard but now it was feeling natural to her. He was right that being able to see spells gave her a distinct advantage.

The remainder of the evening was spent working on one spell alone. Annwyn had to study the theory of it and recite it back to Rafael before she was even allowed to see him cast it or attempt it herself. This particular spell involved conjuring an image, a plausible and tangible image of a person and having them move and speak as if they were alive.

When she asked Rafael why he was being so cautious he replied that the spell could be dangerous. It was possible to invoke something dark into the conjuring, which would essentially let something loose into the world that shouldn't be there. Annwyn frowned and bit her lip. 'I'm not sure I want to try to spell now.'

'Yes, well, magic or sorcery is not to be taken lightly, my dear. Every time we interfere in the natural course of the world we take risks. When we make mistakes, the ramifications can be quite far-reaching.

'Consider Dane, for example. The ramifications of his curse are quite devastating. He faces the loss of his position in the collegium, and he even faces the loss of his humanity, if you will. Because he is affected by a curse to become a werewolf at each moon's turning, it is not a natural event. He is not an actual werewolf with a werewolf's awareness or control. That comes from being a natural werewolf and from learning within the pack. Werewolves are a very ordered community, with their own brand of politics and cultural codes. They follow pack rules, even broader rules than among the paranormals.

"If Dane's curse is not stopped, he may lose his life for the pack will not be able to live with a werewolf who has no control over himself while in wolf form. If the worst comes about and his curse cannot be removed, then perhaps he will develop the skills he needs to survive among the pack. I fear for him if he does not develop that capacity, though.'

As she listened to what was in store for Dane, Annwyn grew more and more appalled. Her stomach dropped and she had to fight to remain standing. It was like a punch in the gut. The ramifications were huge. It was a death sentence. She shook her head. 'That's horrible. He deserves so much better.'

'On that we agree.'

***

It was very late when Annwyn went to bed. She was so tired she crawled under the covers half undressed. She did not even have the energy to take a shower or take off her clothes. Sleep took hold of her before she had even rolled onto her side. It was a long, deep sleep and when she woke in the morning it was if she had been dead to the world. Crawling out of bed, she didn't check the time before she struggled into the shower, hoping that a good scouring with strong hot water would revive her somewhat.

Runnels of water massaged her back and after a few minutes her head began to clear. She had failed with the final spell. Rafael had been good about it but his disappointment was clear. It was probably the fear, the fear of doing wrong that had held her back, made her less positive in her actions and thoughts.

Oh, well, she thought, there is always today.

She took time getting dressed. Today, she wore a new pair of jeans and a warmer top. Even with the central heating in the castle she could feel in her bones that the day was chillier than the one before. Coming from Canberra meant that she knew a cold day when she felt one.

When she went down to the breakfast room it was empty. There was no food laid out. She wandered through to the kitchen and all was silent. Scratching her head, she opened the back door and peered out into the kitchen garden, wondering whether the staff were out there for some reason. It was raining and the sky was a dark, nasty grey. The wind was up. She retreated inside and shut the door with a snap. The staff were definitely not out there, not willingly in any case.

Running up the hall she called up the staircase. 'Max! Are you there, Max?'

There was no answer. Climbing the stairs, she went to her room to check the time. It was 11.30 in the morning. It seemed odd that there were no staff present. If she'd missed breakfast, surely they would be preparing lunch.

Deep in thought, she ran a hand along the banister as she walked slowly back down the stairs. There was still no of sign of any staff. She walked further, hoping to find the room where Max had been talking that first day. There was no sign of him. Her stomach grumbled. She really needed to eat and have a cup of coffee. As she'd always looked after herself she had no qualms about going to the kitchen and making herself a sandwich, at least.

It occurred to her to wait a while before she went looking for Rafael as he usually slept late. There was no point in alarming him because his staff had absconded. Perhaps they'd gone to church or something. She laughed to herself at the thought that she really had no idea what day it was.

Food was reasonably easy to find in the well-organized kitchen. She found slices of ham off the bone and a lovely fresh baguette that looked like it had been delivered that morning. The coffee machine took a little bit more work but she managed to get something that resembled coffee to dribble out into her cup. By the time she finished eating there was still no sign of anyone in the house.

Later, she sat in the lounge room staring at the ashes of the dead fire, wondering what to do. It was now after lunchtime, the time that Rafael usually began lessons. He had still not appeared. She eased back into the comfortable leather chair and stared at the ceiling, wondering what to do. He had said to send him a message last night. With a skip of her heart, she remembered that she hadn't. She'd been so tired and had gone straight to sleep. *Rafael, can you hear me?* She sent the message and waited. When he didn't respond within half an hour, she assumed he must still be asleep or that her message did not work.

She was tempted to send a mental message to Dane, but she was unsure the first one had worked as there had been no answer. And what if he was still a werewolf when she sent it? Was it like email? Did the messages queue until he accessed them? The thought made her giggle, despite her trepidation. In the end, she decided she would contact him but not at that moment. She would give Rafael another couple of hours before she called in reinforcements.

While she stared at the ceiling she heard an abrupt thump overhead that made her nearly jump out of her seat. Sitting forward, she was soon standing up, balancing on the balls of the feet and ready to run. She waited to see if the sound came again. Long moments passed before she heard another sound, the sound a faint footstep. Someone was on the second floor.

Annwyn slipped out of the room and scanned the stairs. She couldn't see any movement from the base of the stairs so she carefully climbed up the risers, one at a time, clinging to the banisters and hoping that her weight did not cause them to creak. About halfway up the stairs, she heard the noise again and paused. It was coming from down the corridor, from her room.

When she reached the top of the stairs she let out a pent-up breath. She tried to move quietly, keeping to the carpets to muffle the sound of her footsteps. As she approached her room she saw flickering shadows, the sign of someone moving around inside. Her heart beat hard, her pulse thumping in her neck and pounding in her temples. What was going on?

Garnering her courage, she pushed the door so it flung open quickly. There in the room was her. Her body. It was Nira.

'You!' they both said in unison.

Before she could react she felt a presence behind her and was shoved hard between the shoulder blades. The floor loomed large as she was propelled forward. Caught off guard, she couldn't anticipate the fall and fell awkwardly onto her wrist.

'There she is!' Max said from behind her. A foot prodded her in the butt. 'I still can't believe you aren't you.'

Annwyn crawled into a sitting position on the floor, nursing her wrist. Adrenalin made her heart beat faster but her mind was alert. Something must have happened to Rafael otherwise he would have been here. Was Max some kind of traitor in cahoots with Nira?

'Put her in that chair and tie her down.' Nira said with a swift swing of her head, sending her short bangs flying. Annwyn was spellbound. It was her, but not her. The gestures were all wrong and the sneer on her face seemed alien.

The air of menace intensified as Annwyn ineffectively fought off Max. Before she even thought about it she sent off a mental message to Dane, a quick scream of terror, in the vain hope that he could answer. There had been no response to her trial message. Maybe she was feeling overconfident, but she was sure she could use her power to send messages just as Rafael had showed her. Yet Dane hadn't answered so far.

'What do you intend to do with her?' Max asked with a sneer.

Nira looked up from what she was doing. She was unwrapping a dagger with a double-edged blade, an 'athame', Dane had called it. 'I'm getting my body back. Then we'll deal with your master.'

Max swallowed and paled somewhat. 'Deal with?'

Nira snickered. 'Yes, deal with. You're too soft. We have to be tough to get what we want. We can't have soft hearts because someone is nice to us. The collegium has locked us out for too long. It is time to make a stand, to take our place and throw those in power out.'

'I thought the curse of Dane Archwright was all we needed to show our strength. That once the collegium saw what we could do, it would make concessions. Let us join.'

Nira was shaking her head. 'That was only the beginning. That got their attention. It made them realise they're not the only ones with power. The collegium restricts us because its members think we're not good enough, that we don't have the right bloodlines, but now they'll know they're wrong.'

'Yes,' he said, responding to the ardour in her voice. 'How will you get your body back?'

'I need blood.'

Max's face lost its expression as realization hit. 'A blood sacrifice?'

'Yes.'

Max looked at Annwyn and back at Nira. Too late did he realise that he was to be the sacrifice. He turned and took two steps before she threw the dagger, catching him to the right of the spine. He went down. She pulled out the knife. Blood gushed as she chanted.

Annwyn struggled. She had no doubt what Nira would do next, once she had her body back. With a grunt, the sorceress pushed Max's inert form onto his back. He was still alive, mouthing words. Annwyn thought it might be a prayer. Nira checked Max to make sure he couldn't get away. She returned to the bed for a chalice. Annwyn began to fall apart.

'Look, you don't have to do this. I'm sure Rafael can help us get our respective bodies back. You really don't...'

Nira ignored her, slashing Max's neck and catching the gushing blood in the chalice. Annwyn threw up over the arm of the chair, then fell back. She felt sick and faint. As she fought for consciousness, she heard Nira's voice chanting loudly, the words tangible as the hovered in the air around her head.

A blackness descended on her, like many crow wings beating in her mind. She tried to fight, but then hot blood trickled down her face and neck. She screamed once in terror as her consciousness drained away.

# Chapter Sixteen

Dane woke up on the floor of the hut. His head ached and he was parched with thirst. He cracked open an eyelid and shut it again quickly. The sharp slant of sunlight peering through the door made him recoil. He tried to moisten the dryness in his mouth with saliva, only to feel his thick, dry tongue. Again he attempted to peer through his eyelids, this time shading them with his hand.

Rolf slept peacefully, sprawled on his side, head resting on his hands. Naked as the day he was born, Rolf was having one hell of a dream if his hard on was anything to go by. Glancing down at his own nakedness, he saw that he had accumulated some scrapes, a few minor cuts, and he smelt of blood.

Dane's gaze then took in the hut as he leaned forward to flick the door shut. He noticed that someone had folded what was left of his clothes; they were ripped beyond repair. His shoes were misshapen. Dane considered them. He'd turned before undressing. Shaking his head, he tossed them to the floor. Lucky he was on his own property and he had plenty more close at hand. Rolf stirred.

Dane glanced over his shoulder and lifted his T-shirt. It fell apart in his hands so he tossed it to the floor. He'd have to drive back to the house naked. Rolf was on all fours, retrieving his own clothes.

'The pack is gone,' Rolf said as he stuffed his feet into his boots.

'How long?'

'About three days. You took a while to shake off the change this time.'

'Three days?' Dane gaped at him. Three days of his life gone. He had no memory of what had happened to him, only the ghost of the beast like fire in his blood. He jerked back at a sudden realisation. 'Annwyn must be frantic.'

'Be calm. She is in safe hands with Rafael, isn't she?'

'I hope so. Nevertheless, she will worry. She's vulnerable. While I'm sure of Rafael's friendship, I am not so confident about the others in the collegium.'

Dane ran his fingers through his hair, fighting to calm himself. The beast's presence made him more anxious than normal. He hated that lack of control, the inability to hide what he was feeling.

Rolf nodded. 'We'll have you back home in no time.' The other man's gaze lingered.

Dane's hands went to his face. 'How bad is it?' he asked with a hoarse voice. 'What little gift did the curse leave behind this time?'

Rolf lowered his gaze and shrugged. He took out his pen knife and began cleaning his nails, examining his fingers from different angles. 'You look the same to me,' he answered without looking up.

Dane swayed unsteadily. The room spun and he reached out to the wall to steady himself. Damned curse was taking its pound of flesh from him, weakening him when he needed to be strong. He touched his face, fearing it was now a snout and let out a sigh when it was just rough from lack of a shave. He skimmed his hairline. He thought it was different but he wouldn't know for certain until he saw his reflection in a mirror.

He moved an arm and paused. He squeezed his bicep. His muscles were larger. He examined his legs and his other arm. His physique was more powerful. Did this mean he had more strength too? Did it mean he was more beast than man?

Rolf smiled and nodded slowly. 'I told you there was a good side to being a wolf. You're built, man. More built that you ever were before.'

Dane growled low in his throat. It was a growl full of vengeful promise. The answer in Rolf's eyes spoke volumes. His werewolf friend would help him track down who did this to him. 'Let's go home then and get cleaned up. I have to check up on Annwyn.'

'Sure. You owe me a couple of steaks, by the way.'

Dane looked puzzled. He didn't remember any steaks. As they settled in the car Rolf explained. Dane could tell his friend was concerned about his lack of control, but didn't try to draw him out. Dane was already worried enough for both of them.

Later, Rolf cooked while Dane cleaned himself up and tried to put his mind in order. He felt different. He detected a change after every time he suffered the curse, but this time it was more pronounced. Shaking his head, he tried to think of something else. Annwyn came to mind. The change had left him with unsated sexual urges. His cock stiffened, quickly and painfully, imagining the scent of her skin, the taste of her mouth and the soft velvet of her sex.

He pulled on his jeans, adjusted himself, thinking it might be a good time to visit Annwyn. Perhaps she could come back with him. Shaking his head, he berated himself for his impractical desires. There was no point in him staring at his reflection either looking for signs of the beast, which is what he caught himself doing.

The smell of cooking meat reached him, making his stomach punch with hunger. When he walked out to the dining area, Rolf was sliding a huge T-bone steak onto his plate. Dane pounced on it, not even waiting for Rolf to sit down. Rolf didn't seem to mind. He put the pan in the kitchen and in no time had polished off his own meat.

Dane finished the last of his and, using his tongue to dislodge bits of meat from his teeth, sat back in his chair. 'That was…'

He stalled. Something strange happened. 'Annwyn?'

Rolf sat forward. 'What?'

'Gods! Annwyn!' He shook his head. She could send messages with power? 'She's in trouble.'

'What about your friend?'

'He must be in trouble too, if he's not there protecting her.'

'Where are they?'

'Scotland.'

'Scotland?'

Dane held out his hand. 'Come with me. I need you, Rolf.' His friend's eyes were wide with fear. Dane knew that Rolf had not travelled the sorcerer's way. The man understood the concept but not the actuality and was deeply suspicious. It was the wolf in him. He was happier when his feet were firmly planted on the ground.

'What is it?'

'Come on! It's urgent. We must travel this way,' Dane replied, a quaver in his voice.

Rolf stood there unmoving, only his nostrils flaring, a sign that he was contemplating Dane's request. 'Please,' Dane said as he held out his hand.

Rolf gave a nod and took his hand for the transfer.

***

They arrived in Rafael's castle in the living room. The fine leather chairs were unoccupied. All was quiet and there was no one around. Rolf moved in the direction of the kitchen to check it out. Dane sent a mental call to Rafael—something he should have done as soon as he heard that quick burst from Annwyn. In his haste to reach her, he hadn't thought to contact his old friend in whose care she was.

Rafael wasn't answering. Being in the same building, the response should have been quick, almost instant. This did not bode well. His gaze tracked around the room, following the line of the banister to the second floor.

His skin prickled on the back of his neck. Something was definitely wrong. He could hear Rolf searching out back, even opening the back door. Dane shook his head.

A scream from upstairs alerted him to Annwyn's presence and her danger. He ran up the stairs, taking them two at a time. He heard Rolf responding close behind, his feet thumping on the floorboards as he ran down the corridor and then muffled by the carpet as he headed for the stairs.

'It's her. Her scent is strong.' The gift from the beast enhanced Dane's sense of smell.

On the landing, Dane hesitated as all the doors looked the same. He prayed for Annwyn to make another noise but feared that scream might be the last sound she would make. Nira had no care for her. She would kill Annwyn if there was no danger to herself in the act. He trod carefully, not wanting to alert Nira to their presence.

Rolf came up behind him silently, his nostrils flaring. From his nod, Dane knew that Rolf had Annwyn's scent too. Moving in front of Dane, he led the way to one of the identical doors.

Dane listened. A muffled sound emanated from within. He lifted a querying eyebrow to Rolf, who nodded in response. Nira was in there. Something else was on the air, a familiar, tantalising scent. *Fresh blood.* The beast within him responded to it instinctively.

With a nod to each other, he and Rolf stepped back ready to throw themselves at the door. Dane didn't want to alert Nira to their presence by using magic. He wanted to take her by surprise.

Their combined weight smashed the door down with an explosive whoosh! Annwyn screamed, unable to fight off Nira who was in the process of tipping warm blood from a chalice over her face, trying to pour it into her mouth by holding her jaw open.

Half kneeling on Annwyn, chanting as she did so, the sorceress turned at their entry. She let out an explosive expression of frustration. 'No!' She threw the chalice at them.

Dane deflected it with his forearm, sending it to the wall in a spray of dark blood. A quick glance at Annwyn, and relief flooded through him. The blood wasn't hers.

Nira climbed off Annwyn, readying a spell to launch at Dane, but he got there first, sending a hammer of power into her chest, rocking her backwards. She managed to deflect most of it, but it hurt. Her gaze strayed from Dane to his side. Dane slanted his gaze sideways and saw that Rolf stood immobile.

'Fight her, dammit. She's got a hold of you.'

Rolf shivered and shook his head. After Nira had tried to kill him during sex, Dane had given Rolf some assistance in fighting off spells. The devilish woman had a subtle way of getting into one's brain. Rolf reached up to clutch the charm around his neck. No wonder Annwyn's husband had betrayed her as that woman had a way about her that was hard to resist. Rolf nodded, signalling that he was in control, his grin evil. However, all his sinister intent was focused on Nira.

'Mutt!' Nira cursed, when she realised that Rolf had broken her hold. 'Mindless brute!'

With a backward flip of a hand, she lifted Rolf with her power and flung him to the far corner of the room where he landed face-first on the floor. Dane could only spare a quick glance, enough to see Rolf lift himself up by his hands and shake his head. He was whole. It was enough.

Nira focused her gaze on Dane, derision dominating her features. 'I see the beast has left its shadow in you, cursed one. It is wonderful to see the collegium's finest, its elite, fall to the lowest depths. Too long have you ruled over the rest of us. Too long have you set yourself apart. Now you see that we can be as powerful as you.'

Her scathing remarks set Dane's blood afire. 'You attacked me to make a point? That's bullshit. You're not smart enough. Someone else is behind this. Tell me who.'

'You'll never know. You'll become a mindless savage beast and you will never know who put me up to it.' She gave a little laugh. 'I don't care how you rot before you die.'

Dane let his gaze fall on Annwyn. She was in a kind of stupor still, with blood running out of the corner of her slack mouth. He couldn't tell if any harm had come to her. She appeared whole, but what of her mind? All he knew was that he had prevented Nira from taking her body back. Max's corpse was placed beside the chair, his throat cut—the source of the blood. He sighed with relief. At least it wasn't his precious Annwyn's.

He knew that being distracted with Annwyn would allow Nira to think she had an advantage. He hoped she would fall for it because he was ready. Nira built up another spell but, before she could release it, Dane thumped one home. She flew up and back, right past Rolf, who was now standing poised on the balls of his feet. His head tracked her passage. Instead of impacting against the wall, Nira disappeared.

'No.' Dane slapped his hands together. She was a sneaky, wily sorceress. How had she done that? He had to do more work so that he could predict her use of magic. At least this time she hadn't achieved her goal. She couldn't complete the ritual with Dane there, and with Rolf at his side. Dane inhaled a breath and let his tension out. Nira wouldn't be back any time soon.

Dane hurried over to Annwyn, his hand brushing the curve of her face. Rolf stood behind him. 'Look for Rafael. He's probably in his room on the floor below.'

'I have his scent. I'll find him.' His gaze flicked over Annwyn's unconscious form, a knowing look in his eye.

Dane ignored him and continued to try to rouse Annwyn while Rolf slipped out the door. Dane went to the bathroom to wet a towel so he could clean the blood off Annwyn. He didn't think she would take it well if she woke up covered in blood, particularly the blood of someone she knew. With his ministrations, she began to moan and mumble although she was not answering to her name or giving any sign that she knew where she was or what was happening.

His gaze went to Max's body on the floor. Rafael's aide must have been a traitor. He tried to remember what he knew of the man and realised he knew little. All he knew was that the man had no magic and had been with Rafael for just over a year, maybe two. The man was from a respectable family, but perhaps this was not true after all. Dane wasn't sure but wondered whether Max had been involved with Nira. How else could Rafael be put out of action? How else could Nira have got in? He had to have been betrayed by someone close to him and who closer than his trusted aide? Since the moment he met him, the man had set Dane's teeth on edge.

And where were the staff? Hopefully, Max had given them the day off rather than harming them. Rafael had often complained that getting staff to work in this part of Scotland was difficult. Having all his staff go missing at once would send the locals gossiping and make recruitment a nightmare. He knew Rafael would feel the betrayal deeply.

Dane couldn't work out what Max's motive might be,

except that the man had no magic and, therefore, did not have a place in the collegium. He could work at the collegium, but he could not take pride of place among the sorcerers or achieve greatness within its ranks. How many secrets did he know? How many of the collegium secrets had this man been privy to? To many, he thought. Too many.

Dane took one of Annwyn's hands. He caressed it in his and kissed her fingers tenderly. He lifted her palm to his face and rubbed his cheek against it. 'Please, please, Annwyn, be well. Be unharmed. I don't know what I'd do if anything happened to you. You're the most important person in my life. And I think it isn't the spell that makes me feel this way. It's you. I only wish that you could feel the same for me.'

The sound of footsteps hurrying down the corridor alerted him to a new arrival. He turned ready for another assault but was relieved to find Rafael standing there, a stunned expression on his face and dark circles around his eyes.

'Deities! How could this happen?' Then he saw Max's body. His hand went to his mouth. 'Max?'

Rafael came forward and knelt by the dead man's side. Gently, he smoothed Max's hair back from his forehead. His eyes travelled along his torso and up to his gaping neck. A sob escaped him. 'Max, I have failed you. I should have listened. I should have listened to your warning.'

From his position by the corpse, Rafael looked to Dane. 'So Max betrayed me. He used a potion to knock to put me out of action. He was working with Nira?'

'Yes, I think so. Annwyn, when she recovers, will be able to tell us more. I arrived in the nick of time. I didn't realise Annwyn had the power or the knowledge to send me a message. Thank the deities that you taught her and that she was strong enough to call me. She must have been desperate.' Dane was on the verge of coming to see her anyway, but her warning allowed him to come prepared and with Rolf for support.

Rafael climbed to his feet, his knees creaking. 'Thankfully, Max didn't know about her power. It was something I kept from him. I gave him another reason, one close to the truth, to explain why she was here. Annwyn and I spent time in my sanctum away from the others. I didn't know the specific nature of the threat, but I knew that she was threatened. I knew she was in danger, but I didn't think Nira could reach her here. I was careful and thank all the powers that I was careful. If Nira had known, she would have taken steps to prevent Annwyn calling for help. She may have thought of other ways to use her in her power struggle against you and the collegium.'

'You taught her well then, although I can hardly believe she grasped the intricate ways of sorcery so quickly to accomplish this. It's been, what, two or three days at most? It took me two years, from memory.'

'Ah… yes, but you were young then. Annwyn has a special gift—a rare gift and a sharp mind. I trust you with this knowledge, knowing she cares deeply for you and you for her,' he said. 'Annwyn is a seer. Not only can see the fabric of spells she can replicate them and even unravel them. Because of this gift of hers, I was able to teach her quickly. By showing her the shape of the spell, she was able to duplicate it. Her power, I think, is growing. It has been enhanced by the spell that had been placed on her and by mixing with sorcerers.'

Dane shook his head in a mixture of disbelief and profound relief. His Annwyn was one of them. 'All sorcerers? Or just her connection to Nira?'

'Hard to determine exactly, but I think the connection to Nira is a particular cause. The latent power in her seems to respond to Nira like an antibody. It fights Nira like a human body fights a virus. The more Nira links with her, the stronger Annwyn instinctively tries to be. Once aroused her power will now grow and expand until it reaches its natural limits.'

Dane let the news sink in. It gladdened him to hear that something good was coming from this tragedy. Annwyn would be a special sorceress, one with a kind and loving heart. She would not deliberately do harm to anyone, except to protect. Unlike Nira.

'I'm afraid Nira got away,' he said to Rafael. 'Thank the deities she didn't complete the ritual.' He looked down at

Annwyn's unconscious form.

'I'm not sure what damage she has done, but I hope that we were in time.'

Rafael gestured at Annwyn with his right hand. 'With your permission may I examine her?'

'Please do.'

Dane noticed how tenderly Rafael touched Annwyn, gently brushing his fingers along her arm and then peering into her eyes. Rafael said a few words under his breath that Dane didn't quite catch. With his hands on either side of her forehead, he called to her. 'Annwyn?'

Annwyn's eyelids flicked open. She sucked in her breath as if she hadn't breathed for a long time.

'There, there, my dear. Take it easy. All is well.' Rafael soothed her, patting her on the head.

Fluttering her eyelids, Annwyn calmed. Her gaze took in Rafael and then shifted behind him to Dane. 'Dane…you heard me?' her voice soft and barely above a whisper.

Dane could only nod as his throat tightened with emotion.

'No permanent harm from what I can see. I will leave you two alone for a moment but then we must talk further. I will find out what has happened to my staff. Nothing dire, I pray.' With that Rafael gathered his robes around him and left the room.

Dane took the opportunity to move closer to Annwyn, not able to stop from touching her. Her fingers trailed along his hand, brushing the fine blond hairs. Neither of them said anything for a few minutes, and just gazed at each other.

'Thank you for coming so quickly,' she said at last, a tremulous smile on her lips. He so wanted to kiss them. Instead, he rubbed a finger along her chin.

'Thank you for calling me. You're amazing, do you know that? You saved yourself.'

'I was terrified, truly. And taken by surprise. It was all I could do to call you before she descended on me. Is she …'

She turned to check the room. Dane caressed the curve of her head. 'Escaped. I'm sorry, she is a bit clever. Got away before I could stop her.'

'Can you stop her though?'

A shrug came automatically. 'I don't know. I do know that I should be able to defeat her.'

Her hands moved up his arms. He almost sighed at her touch. Now, looking at her, he had a big lump in his throat. He had almost lost her.

Her expression softened as she gazed at him. Reaching out to touch him, her fear slid away.

Dane wanted to hold her to him, but was suddenly hesitant. On one level, he had no right and on the other all the rights. She was his, if only she could be.

Dane thought about Max's body and how difficult it probably was for Annwyn to be sitting there recuperating with a corpse next to her. 'Shut your eyes for a bit. I'm going to move you.'

Her eyes widened. 'Shut my eyes? What is it you don't want me to see?' Immediately, she looked around and then leaned over the side of the chair. He saw her expression, the reliving of the horror of what she witnessed and the blood draining from her face. She fell back in a faint.

When he slid his arms under her she didn't protest. He held her to him and carried her from the room. It would not be appropriate to whisk her away to his place straightaway. Rafael needed support, and it wasn't good manners to remove a guest without due notice.

A room a bit further down the hall seemed perfectly adequate. It was a room that he had stayed in on a long-ago visit. It had a king-sized bed. He laid her down, gently placing her head on the pillows. In the bathroom he found fresh towels. He wet one with warm water and some sweet-smelling soap. He wanted to make sure he cleaned her up before she rested. He pictured tucking her naked body into that bed.

He shook his head as he ran the water. He really had to get a hold of himself. They'd been apart just over three days and it felt like a lifetime. How was he going to cope with losing her? He studied his reflection in the mirror as he wrung out the towel. The change had left its mark and he hated it. What if she now found him repulsive? What if he couldn't remove the curse by the next full moon? That change would be the end of him. He would lose it all.

175

# Chapter Seventeen

Strong hands removed Annwyn's clothing, piece by piece. Instinctively, she knew it was Dane and relaxed into his tender care. She was drowsy for some reason, couldn't quite shake off the effect of Nira's presence in her mind. She knew it was him, by his scent, by the way his breath brushed against her skin. Gently, he wiped her face, removing the traces of sour vomit that lingered there. He washed her arms, her hands, her breasts and dried them as he went to ensure that she did not take cold.

Part of her mind rebelled at being so weak and exposed and letting Dane see her this way. She worried that he would not respect her afterward. That she had lost some of her dignity. When he was done, he gently lifted her to the centre of the bed and placed the covers over her. She heard him removing his clothes, then the weight of his body shifted the mattress beneath her. His hot skin moved against her body. He nestled her close to him and slowly brushed the hair from her face. He didn't speak as his strong fingers combed her hair and massaged the tension from her scalp. Sleep pulled at her.

There was a need in her, though. She wanted more of him, wanted him to hold her. Desperately, she wanted to speak her desire. She opened her eyes and found his face close, his blue eyes vibrant as they gazed back at her. 'I want you,' she said in barely a whisper. 'Stay with me.'

A slight nod of his head, and she realised he had heard her and that she had spoken aloud. A cloud of mystification enveloped her once again and her consciousness began to float away, but not before his embrace tightened, his large, warm body enveloping her, his lips nuzzling at her neck. As her mind slid away to sleep, she revelled in his closeness. It was not a sexual encounter. There was comfort and love in that embrace. She felt so safe and so free to love.

Dreams and images assaulted her as she tried to free herself from the tendrils of fugue that Nira had left behind. Reality, though, waited, and vivid memories slashed into her mind. She shivered at the knowledge of how it felt to be in Nira's power. The ritual had begun before Dane arrived to save her. She remembered the black talons reaching into her mind, trying to claw her out of her body. This would be no welcoming exchange, no sweet return to her own body. With Nira's anger and desperate need Annwyn could tell that the sorceress wanted her out and didn't care where she sent Annwyn's consciousness. She would have gladly ripped Annwyn from her body without a care, chiselling away bits at a time and tossing them anywhere.

Images of blood assaulted her and the smell of it and the taste of if on her tongue. She must have moaned loudly for Dane whispered her name.

'Annwyn, wake up. You're having a bad dream.'

She opened her eyes. By the light streaming through the curtains and the feel of Dane's bristles on her bare shoulder, she knew it was morning already. She had slept the night through, wrapped in Dane's tender embrace. Tears welled in her eyes as she felt suddenly profoundly touched at his care. Crying was like the final humiliation. She turned to hide her face in his shoulder.

Wordlessly, he comforted her, caressing the back of her head until she quietened. She leaned back, catching the questioning look in his eyes. Smiling tremulously, she brushed her fingers along his jaw. She swallowed a few times before speaking. 'Thank you. Thank you for coming. Thank you for your care.'

'Hush, hush.' He kissed her fingers. 'I'm glad I got here in time. Glad that you're safe, though I can tell from your dreams that you're not unscarred. I would that Nira had left no permanent mark on you.'"

'Shhh…It's not your responsibility. You know for a fact that she's had a link to me for many years. It is circumstances. Neither of us is at fault.'

He gazed at her with eyes full with compassion. 'True. But it's up to me.' Her eyes widened. 'Us. To put things right.'

Annwyn nodded, a brief smile finding its way to her lips. 'Yes.'

He hugged her once, then gently disentangled himself from her and sat up. Glancing back, he caught her questioning look.

'I best go find some breakfast. I smell bacon cooking. Either Rolf is in the kitchen or the staff are back.'

Annwyn felt surprisingly good now that she had let her pent-up emotions out, and that Dane was there. Her stomach felt empty, though. 'I'll get up too.'

He nodded and the rolled to the edge of the bed. Annwyn got a very healthy view of his smooth-skinned buttocks as he left the bed and reached for his jeans. Her smile grew wider, as she watched him don is T-shirt, admiring the way his back muscles flexed. Yes, she fancied him and wanted him despite all that had happened.

'Stay here. I'll bring up a tray.'

She lay back against the pillows. 'Thanks, that would be great.' There was no great hurry, she thought, and luxuriated in feeling safe.

He paused before leaving the room, making intricate gestures. She saw a thin film of translucent yellow climb the walls, smother the windows and web the door as he left. A warding. So that is what one looks like. Its pattern was a fine web and then it sank into the fabric of the room and disappeared. Dane wasn't taking any chances, was he? The fabric of the warding intrigued her so she climbed out of bed to study the wall. Surely, if she could see spells, she should be able to detect it. However, after witnessing the initial placement, she could no longer see it. It was another thing she made a mental note to ask Rafael about. It made her feel uncomfortable that she couldn't see magic that she knew was there.

Dane's heavy footsteps sent her hurrying back to bed. She didn't want to explain what she was doing. Her magical development was to be a surprise.

By the time he opened the door with magic and carried in the tray, she was sitting up in bed, feeling perky and ravenous.

The smell of crispy bacon and poached eggs almost made

her swoon. Dane placed the tray across her lap and locked the tray legs. He poured her a coffee. 'I'll be right back. Start without me.'

Not long after he came in with a tray of his own. They ate in companionable silence, sharing tender looks and shy smiles. Why was that, she wondered, when there seemed so much to say and not enough words to say them.

Later, as she passed her tray to Dane, who took both trays to the door for Morag to collect, she sat back against the pillows savouring her coffee as she studied him. She was grateful to have Dane with her again. The ache to have him close during their separation had at times been unbearable. Yet the experience with Nira, with what she had witnessed, made their reunion even more bittersweet. She could see in his expression how much he feared for her, but also she could see the guilt he carried with him. 'It's not your fault, you know.' Her voice was soft, full of warmth.

Dane placed his coffee on the bedside table. 'I know, but I can't help feeling this way, feeling responsible for what happens to you. It's this damned binding spell. I can't help but feel your pain.'

Annwyn scanned him from head to foot and took a deep breath. They had to discuss it, even if it meant he left her because of it. 'I can't see the binding spell on you any longer. There were some threads before I left, before the full moon. But they are gone now. From what I've learned from Rafael, I had inadvertently unpicked the last the spell. It was weakening anyway.'

Dane's eyes widened and his brows grew into a frown. He shook his head. 'No, that can't be possible but I wish it were so..'

With a shrug she replied, 'Perhaps you could check with Rafael later?' She didn't want to argue about it. His belief in the spell was as firm as hers had been. It would be difficult for him to digest this, just as it had been for her.

'I will.' He smiled tenderly. 'Now, I think it's back to bed for you.'

Annwyn shook her head. 'No way. I have some studying to do.' She threw off the covers and then had a sudden thought. 'Oh? I assume Rafael was unharmed?' Her gaze fixed on Dane. The way his eyes drifted over her nakedness made her blood rise.

She reclined on the bed as Dane's body covered hers. The kiss was searing, snatching her breath, boiling her blood. Thoughts of study fled as he ran his hands up her sides to cup her breasts. He took each nipple into his mouth and suckled them in turn. Her breath caught and her back arched. A gasp escaped her.

Rolling off her, he held her close, forehead to forehead as he spoke to her. 'I'm sorry about that. Lack of impulse control.'

Annwyn shook her head, not quite able to form words. He was such a shocking tease. Surely he could tell she was ready, wanted him. She decided to lift her eyebrows and continue the conversation. 'Rafael?'

'Yes, he is fine. It appears Max drugged the wine. He put Rafael out of action but did no permanent harm. He called the staff and gave them the day off. To Rafael's relief, they turned up as usual this morning.

'So Rafael is expecting me soon?'

Dane shook his head, a mischievous, sexy smile lighting up his face, and putting fire into his gaze. 'I said you'd be down later this afternoon. I said we had some urgent business to discuss.'

'We do?' Her gaze was focused on his lips. His head descended as his mouth captured hers. Annwyn felt an emotional heave as a connection between then snapped tight. He moved her, moved her to her soul. Their tongues battled it out and the kiss deepened. Annwyn clung to him, as desperately as he clung to her. After they broke off the kiss they gazed at each other in wonderment.

Their breathing regulated, and Dane's forehead creased, an unspoken question. With a slight nod Dane lifted himself away from her and crawled backwards to stand at the end of the bed. While she watched, he ripped off his T-shirt and stripped off his jeans in record time. A sense of utter joy blossomed within her chest. She had to stop herself from thinking forward to the future, a future they didn't have. As he cradled her she tried to focus on him, on the moment, and on the amazing feeling of connection. Brushing her fingers through his hair, she urged his head down for another kiss. She wanted to lose herself in him.

What was she going to do when one long searing kiss brought her to the edge? Dane was in no hurry, he lingered there, licking her lips, nipping at her chin, smiling at her with happiness in his eyes as he cradled her head in his hands.

Annwyn wanted to shove him over onto his back and have her way with him, but he was having none of it. She was anchored there under his broad frame. His presence surrounded her, infused and penetrated her. He nuzzled at her neck, kissed along the column of her throat until he found the sensitive spot that sent shafts of desire straight to her core. Her breath caught, and he drew response after titillating response. As she lay there gasping he shifted further down to take his time in pleasuring her nipples.

'Oh, God,' she cried out as he drew her nipple deep into his mouth. Erotic thoughts invaded her head, igniting her passion further. She tried to grab a handful of his hair but couldn't get a grip as it was too short.

His eyes darkened with desire as he reached up to catch her mouth in another searing kiss. Restlessly, she moved under him, trying to get her hands on him, to pleasure him, to make him take her now.

'Patience,' he whispered as she held her hands to the mattress and he recommenced kissing her down the neck and breasts. As he moved lower his hands slid along the line of her arms until he was cupping her breasts while his clever tongue slid between her already moist labia.

A shuddering cry escaped her as he nudged her clitoris back and forth and then sucked on it so gently she thought she would scream. A sudden and powerful climax rocked her, leaving her shuddering and weeping. Still Dane turned his attention elsewhere, pushing a finger inside her wet sex and then adding another.

Annwyn was beyond control. She knew she was making

noise, lots of noise, but she was so caught up in Dane's sensual hold she didn't care. It was only this moment and the exquisite feel of him pleasuring her that mattered. His fingers were expert in seeking out erogenous zones. She writhed and groaned and begged. She wanted him inside her, fucking her with that marvellous cock of his. His hot mouth descended again. Her surprised cry fell on deaf ears. Dane was determined to bring her to climax again, by the way he teasingly and gently put his hot mouth on her.

He left off massaging her breasts and nudged her legs open wider. With his hands under her buttocks, he lifted her as if she was a melon and ate her. Her legs were twitching and her voice was hoarse from excitement. When the second climax hit she was barely sensible.

They'd had sex before and it had been good. There was something different in this coupling. He'd touched something in her. Maybe it was the separation or the near-death experience. She didn't know, but she detected something from him—an honesty, a fearless honesty. Perhaps he didn't believe that the spell was gone. She didn't care. This was powerful.

'How do you want me?' he whispered hotly in her ears. Was he done torturing her already? What position did she want? She wanted him deep within her, she wanted him hard and in control. 'From behind.'

Before she knew it he had flipped her onto all fours. She angled herself up to give him easy access. Because of his height he stepped from the bed, dragging her toward him. She locked her elbows as he pushed inside her, deep and no-nonsense. Her shuddering gasp filled her ears, just as he filled her. He put his hand on her back to steady her and she held still while he thrust into her, his powerful body slamming into hers. Another climax hit as he took her higher. She kept her thoughts centred on him, the feel of him inside. She refused to let anything else get between them at that moment. The connection held. He grabbed a fistful of her hair. Annwyn cried out. It didn't hurt; it increased the tension, the pleasure, as he drove himself deep inside her. She cried out again.

'Please,' she begged. 'Come! Please come.'

Another wave of pleasure rocked over her. Dane's hands locked on her hips, pulling her back against him in a perfect rhythm. 'You're mine,' he said in a deep voice. 'You're mine,' he repeated as he thrust into her for emphasis.

'I'm yours. Oh God, I'm yours,' she answered as a surrender so sweet settled over her. Dane withdrew, and suddenly she felt bereft.

'You're mine.' With that he thrust into her again, the pace extraordinary until he shuddered as his climax swamped him. Annwyn wept and couldn't stop. It was such a profound encounter.

Dane didn't ask her silly questions like whether he'd hurt her. He held her until the sobs subsided.

A soft knock at the door woke her some hours later. Dane still slept, his body completely covering her nakedness. Rolf put his head in through the doorway. There was no change in his expression when he saw them both on the bed, sheets in a tangle on the floor, Dane's leg over her, his arms wrapped firmly around her.

He didn't come any further into the room. 'Rafael is looking for you. I'll tell him you will be down soon.' She saw his nostrils flare. He slid out the door after inhaling. Must be a werewolf thing, she thought.

'Dane?' she whispered.

He didn't stir. Being this close she took the opportunity to study him unobserved. There was something different about him. It wasn't the lovemaking so much. That was all Dane and something from within her. There was no disguising of feelings of attraction. It was open and honest lovemaking. Yet she could see his hairline had changed, new hair was growing around his hairline. His eyebrows were more pronounced as if the bone underneath had thickened. Her fingers traced the contours of his ears and, yes, there was a difference there, too. It was the moon turning curse, leaving its mark.

Damn, Nira. She had momentarily forgotten that Dane's life hung in the balance. They had fewer than twenty-four days to force Nira to remove the curse.

A sudden urge to talk to Rolf overcame her. She needed to know about what happened to Dane during the curse. She needed to know more about werewolves, about living with one. As Dane's sleep was deep, she carefully extracted herself, putting a pillow in his arms in her place.

With a smile she glanced back at him on the bed from the doorway. She'd managed to shower and dress without disturbing him.

Rolf was sprawled on one of the leather lounges reading a graphic novel when she came downstairs. He lifted his head. He'd shaved off his goatee. 'Rafael has popped out on some business. Literally popped, I mean. He said he'd be back soon.'

'That's okay. I want to talk with you.'

Rolf sat up and rolled a shoulder before settling back in his seat. 'Sure. Fire away.'

Annwyn had dressed in a demure skirt and a high-necked blouse. She wasn't exactly sure why; perhaps it was because she had been caught having sex with Rolf without her knowledge. She sat opposite him. 'Can you tell me about Dane? I want to understand what happens to him when he becomes a werewolf. I want to know what will happen if we can't shift the curse.'

Rolf stared at her, his gaze sliding from the top of the head to the skirt covering her knees down to her stockinged feet. 'You love him,' he said quietly but firmly.

She nodded, not quite able to speak. 'It's as if we were meant for each other, despite curses and spells…'

A smile flitted briefly over Rolf's face. 'I know what you mean. Dane, he is a lucky man. You're good for him. Give him a little time and he'll see the truth of his own feelings. He thinks it's the spell but we both know the spell is gone. It didn't survive Nira changing bodies that long.'

Annwyn nodded, quite taken aback by Rolf's keen perception. 'So… can you tell me?'

Rolf's expression changed. It grew sombre and a little sad. 'The change for him is not normal. Physically, he looks like a werewolf but, mentally, it's not the same. When werewolves change they retain a lot of their human personality. They can think and act like they would if they were human. The main difference is that the beast within them has control and sometimes can take them over when they are frightened, threatened or protective of anyone in the pack. The times I've seen Dane change, his ability to maintain that sense of himself is diminishing. In the last change it was all I could do to keep tabs on him. There was no way to truly communicate with him. If he was to change permanently, which we think will happen in the next moon turning, he wouldn't be able to stay with the pack. It would be dangerous for him. I don't know whether he'll be even able to change back into his human form.'

Annwyn fought back tears. 'Are you saying that he may become a wolf permanently? That he will be unable to exist as a human?'

Rolf nodded, his expression turning even sadder. 'I'm saying it's a very strong possibility, given the current trend. We don't know for sure. But you have to be prepared for that eventuality.'

'No, no, no.' She stood up and paced along the carpet, fists balled. 'We can't let that happen.' Then swinging around to face Rolf she clenched her fists and blurted out. 'I can't let this happen, and I won't let this happen. I won't.'

Rolf stood up and grabbed her by the shoulders to stop her frantic pacing. They faced each other. 'What can you do? You are powerless where Nira is concerned. I have seen this with my own eyes. I have fallen victim to her through you.'

Annwyn turned away but he pulled her back. She met his ferocious gaze, all animosity and feral hunger. 'Rafael is teaching me. I will stop her. By my life, I will stop her. She can't do this to him. By God, I'm not going to let it happen.'

The sound of Dane walking around upstairs alerted them that he was awake. 'Can I get you a coffee?' Rolf asked.

'Yes,' she nodded. 'I could really do with one and probably a burger or something. I'm starving.'

Rolf's fleeting smile disappeared when he heard her door open upstairs. Dane was on his way.

'I guess he'll be hungry too, and probably for the same reason that you are. I'll order the kitchen to prepare lots of burgers.' He left the room with an obvious smirk on his face.

Just after he headed for the kitchen Dane thumped downstairs. Annwyn stood to meet him and went toward him for a hug. He embraced her when he reached the bottom of the stairs, but she could tell he was upset, slightly moody. 'What's wrong? Is everything okay?'

'You weren't there. I woke up and you weren't there and it didn't seem right.'

Annwyn stood on her tippy toes, reaching up to brush her fingers through his hair. 'I tried to wake you but you were dead to the world so I thought I'd come down here to see where Rafael was. Rolf said he popped off for a little while. Are you hungry? Rolf's gone to rustle up some burgers.' Her stomach rumbled noisily. 'You see, I'm hungry all of a sudden. You?'

Dane's gaze searched her face, and then his tense expression relaxed. 'You're very beautiful this morning.' He drew her close and bent his head to whisper in her ear. 'You were very beautiful last night.'

A shiver of delight shot from her sex to her heart. His words alone could excite her beyond measure. She couldn't lose him and she'd give anything to save him. 'It was amazing. You can make love to me any time you want. I'm giving you a license.'

She turned to walk away. He swatted her lightly on the butt. 'You can't give me what I've already taken.' Annwyn smiled at the arrogance in his voice, glad that his confidence had returned. Now that she'd had a chat to Rolf she understood the magnitude of the curse that hung over him and the threat to a long-term future together.

Rolf returned, bringing a tray with a steaming cafetera of coffee and three cups. Annwyn almost swooned when the aroma reached her nostrils. Dane dashed to the tray before Rolf had even set it down and poured himself a cup, downing it quickly. Then, with a more measured pace, he poured Rolf a cup and handed it to him and then made Annwyn one, making it exactly how she liked it.

She took it gratefully, taking her time to inhale the smell of freshly roasted beans. Rafael was rising in her esteem with his good taste in wine and coffee.

Rolf and Dane settled themselves down, ribbing each other about sleeping habits, snoring and smelly socks. Annwyn savoured the scene, sipping her coffee and enjoying being alive in the moment. She knew it couldn't last. And it didn't.

Rafael walked in. He seemed distracted at first, not noticing them until he pulled up short. 'Oh, you're all here.'

Dane stood up. 'We've just had some coffee. Would you like some?'

Rafael waved his hand dismissively. 'No, no. I thought that you'd be gone by now and that Annwyn would be waiting for me in the sanctum ready to continue her training.'

Rolf sniggered in the background. Dane stood his ground and crossed his arms. 'We have matters to discuss first. I prefer if we do that privately.'

Annwyn stood up to and inserted herself between the two men. She crossed her arms and gave them both a long look. 'If it is me you're discussing then I'll be in the room too, thank you very much.'

They both gaped at her and then at each other. She could feel their hackles rising.

'Now wait a minute—

She cut Dane off. 'You don't think you're going to go away and discuss this in private, do you? No way. If you're talking about me, I'm going to be there. No point of negotiation available.'

'Annwyn,' Dane said.

Rafael spluttered. 'Now, my dear. Let's be reasonable about this.'

Annwyn challenged Dane, narrowing her eyes and turned her full attention to Rafael. 'I owe you a lot, Rafael, and am grateful for all you have done. But you have to include me in this discussion. I don't understand what the problem is. Don't you trust me?'

Rafael's cheeks began to blush as if he had drunk too much

wine. His eyes widened. 'Of course, I trust you my dear. It's just that...'

'What he means is that he wants to discuss my presence here.'

Annwyn shifted her gaze from Rafael to Dane. 'Your presence?'

Rafael sighed and rolled his eyes. 'Very well. It seems that we are discussing it in any case. You, my dear, need to concentrate on your training. You had a little reunion with Dane last night, most naturally, of course, after what happened. However, I feel it is time that he left so that you can continue your training.'

'Oh?' Annwyn was a bit nonplussed.

Dane squared his shoulders and crossed his arms, again looking down crossly at his old friend.

'I'm not leaving her. You can't ask that of me. Not after...'

Rafael stood straighter, his chin rising. 'The danger has passed. Nira has struck out and was defeated. She had help from the inside, and we understand how. It was as I feared. Those who have been repulsed by us are banding together to destroy us. It's you who has to fight now. Your time is running out. Go home. Study that text I told you about. Look at it with new eyes and then you might find the answer. The best I can do is make Annwyn ready, prepared to take on Nira, if she has to. I'm sorry to say this but to start her life among us, even if you aren't here.'

'No, please don't even say that.' Emotion clogged Annwyn's throat. How could the old man say it, put into words her most horrible fears? She had to fight back the tears. What a dilemma. What if they only had this time together? She didn't want to spend it apart.

'Can we talk privately, Rafael?' This from Dane. He ignored Annwyn's injured look.

The old man nodded. 'Come with me.' The old man's shoulders slumped as he walked out of the room. He was defeated already. Whatever Dane wanted, it looked like he already had it.

Rolf came close and put his arm around her. 'Don't worry.

Dane will handle it. You will get some more time together. He needs it, you know. He really needs to be close to you.'

'Was the last change so rough?'

Rolf nodded, his look desolate. 'He feels he is losing more of himself every time. He was afraid you would be repulsed by him. I knew it wouldn't be the case, but until he believes it himself he is adrift emotionally. He needs a bit more of your time to regain his equilibrium.'

Annwyn reached up and patted Rolf's hand on her shoulder. 'Thank you for telling me. Thank you for sharing that with me. It's really important and makes such a difference.'

With that Rolf returned to the couch and picked up his graphic novel. Rafael and Dane weren't away for long. When they emerged from Rafael's office it appeared they had reached a compromise.

Dane came forward, kissed the centre of her forehead and went to sit on the couch opposite Rolf. She switched her gaze from him and levelled it at Rafael, her eyebrows rising slowly.

Rafael ignored her silent gesture. 'You should be down in the sanctum, waiting for me. Move along,' he said, his tone playful as he made shooing motions and ushered her to the secret door.

Once inside, he was all business as they recommenced her training. After they had recapped their previous session Annwyn remembered her question. 'About wards, they are visible and then they disappear into the fabric of what they are warding. Why is that?'

'A very good observation, my dear. It's true the weave of a warding spell merges with the specific object it is guarding. That is, if there is a specific edifice, so to speak. One can place a ward around oneself or establish a ward in the location around where a person is standing, for example. However, the person can move out of the ward and will no longer be protected. Also wards need to be renewed, otherwise they dissipate and become weak and ineffectual, even breaking up completely as if they were never there.'

Annwyn nodded, understanding now why Dane had this habitual approach of setting wards whenever they left the house.

'So Dane will have to go home soon to renew his wards? Is that what you have agreed?'

Rafael rubbed his chin and looked at her sideways. 'I can see why he is attracted to you. You don't miss much, I think. Yes, you have a few more days with young Dane. But I need you to stay here a little bit longer to hone your skills and there is someone, several someones actually, I want you to meet in the collegium. You will need to join the collegium formally. Your testing has been recorded in the archives. However, there are formalities to be observed. I won't have you being a recalcitrant like Dane.'

Annwyn slid off her stool and paced. Her excitement was hard to contain. She turned suddenly. 'You're saying that you want me to join this collegium so soon, that I am going to be a sorceress already? But that's so hard to believe. I didn't think...I didn't connect. Well, not really...'

Rafael made himself a little taller and crossed his hands over his belly. His robes fell squarely from shoulders, almost regal. 'You are no ordinary sorceress, my dear. You have a special gift, a rare one. You will have a place in the collegium, there is no doubt about that. Dane knows this and welcomes it. Now, let us continue without further distraction.'

They worked for a number of hours. By the end of it Annwyn could cast her own wards, although she had trouble detecting them once they sunk into the fabric of the wall. 'I hope you are much better at detecting wards in future. Or that you are at least able to detect one in the open air, where they have nowhere to hide.'

Rafael decided to give her practical experience. 'Come, my dear, we will need to go upstairs and outside. You will wait in the kitchen while I cast a ward, a very small one in the back garden. When I call out, you will have to detect it.'

Morag gave her a rather funny look when she took refuge in the kitchen. Annwyn tried small talk but that proved ineffectual so she poured herself another coffee, which was still warm on the stove. She found a little bit of cream in the fridge and, after ascertaining that no one needed it, tipped it in her coffee, added sugar and sipped it slowly while she waited for Rafael.

It took quite a while to find the ward. Not only had Rafael put it in a strange place, he had made it very small. Visually, it was disguised by the bark of an old oak tree and it wasn't until she approached from behind that she noticed it. The ward revealed itself as a slight distortion in the air. It did not have colour or shape. The only tell-tale sign was a slight wavering effect similar to heat rising off a tar-sealed road in summer. Rafael then taught her a spell which assisted in finding wards.

'Tomorrow, I will start teaching you how to disassemble wards and to do it without alerting the creator, which I think you are up for. However, you must keep that knowledge to yourself. No sharing, even with Dane. Do you understand?'

'But why?'

'No questions. A sorcerer has his own special knowledge and only teaches it to his apprentice. That knowledge is a bond between them.'

'Oh, I see. I understand.' Hopefully, Dane would not ask her. She hoped she hadn't already told him something she shouldn't have.

'Now, I think it's time to join the others for dinner. As it is a special occasion I think I'll ask us all to dress up.'

Annwyn gave Rafael the appropriate thanks for his time and for his care in teaching her. She realised that what he was doing for her was a special honour. She also realised that he was doing it for her, and not only because he was a friend of Dane's. Somehow, she had earned the old man's respect. Perhaps it was the nature of her gift.

When they emerged from the Sanctum, Dane's eyes latched on to her immediately. Rafael told them of his plans for a dressy dinner. Rolf growled and Dane nodded. Annwyn excused herself and went upstairs. Max's remains were gone and the room had been cleaned. She used her gift and saw it had been done by magic. Traces of a spell still lingered in the carpet. She took a shower and dressed with care.

The pale mint-coloured gown she wore was simple and

elegant, the cut clinging to the curve of her hips and the hem sweeping the floor. The colour accentuated the green of her eyes. Her straight blonde hair was tied in a French knot. She realised she was at home in this body and no longer thought of herself as an interloper. The old Annwyn felt distant. If she never her got old body and her old life back, she realised she wouldn't mind.

Dane was dressed in a dark, well-cut suit that enhanced his large frame. The jacket fitted close, as if he had gained weight. He had become more buff, she realised. Returning Dane's regard she smiled at him, trying to keep herself from responding to his presence. She was not sure it was working because her cheeks radiated heat and certain parts of her anatomy had other ideas.

Rafael wanted to talk after dinner, but the attraction between Annwyn and Dane was undeniable. Quite insensible to the absence of conversation around them, she was startled when Rafael said a rather loud good night. Her gaze swept the table. Rolf was smirking again, and Dane was deeply flushed.

'Oh? Good night, Rafael. See you tomorrow.'

Annwyn made to stand up and Dane was there instantly, guiding her chair out of her way and then offering his arm as he led her from the room. They were so absorbed in each other that they forgot to wish Rolf good night.

***

Dane made love to Annwyn with a kind of desperation. Even though she thought she was ready for another lovemaking session, she didn't realise she would get one long continuous one, interspersed with short naps. It was as if he knew something was going to happen, something was going to interrupt them. It was the best kind of exhaustion she had ever experienced.

Annwyn nestled close to Dane, resting her head on his chest while he slept. Every part of her ached, but it was a good, satisfying ache that made her feel replete rather than drained. If she were to express it coarsely, she would say she had been well and truly fucked. Dane jerked suddenly as if having a bad dream. Annwyn rolled away to avoid being hit by an errant arm and watched as his eyes snapped open.

'What is it? What's happened?'

Dane's gaze was alert as it met hers. Sitting up suddenly, he was nearly half out of the bed before he answered her. 'Someone's breached my wards. I have to go back. I can leave Rolf here.'

Annwyn gathered the sheet around her and followed Dane as he headed to the bathroom.

'Rolf would be more comfortable with you, I think.' She did her best to hide her disappointment. Yet she knew the time for separation was near and grumbled to herself about her lack of emotional control. She wouldn't cry. That would be ridiculous.

Dane nodded and quickly performed his ablutions and donned his clothes. After a brief hug, and a longer and rousing kiss, he left the room. She heard his footfall on the stairs as he went to get Rolf. She stood there looking at her reflection, tempted to berate herself, before gathering up the sheet and returning to the bed.

The scent of Dane was all around her, in the air, on her skin, in the bed and the room. She hugged the sheet to her chest, letting her senses fill. She didn't know when she would see him again. There was an aching, empty hole in her heart.

She had a few more hours before her training with Rafael began and so she chose to climb back into bed and catch up on some sleep before the day began in earnest. After that, a long soak in a bath would be in order. She hoped Rafael didn't mind if she commandeered the large bathroom down the hall. A shower in her ensuite wouldn't quite cut it.

# Chapter Eighteen

Nira found it hard to draw in breath so she held her side and took shallow breaths, wincing at the pain. She'd barely escaped that last encounter. How had things turned out like that? How did he know that the little cow needed help? Dane Archwright's last thrust had wounded her deeply. Drawing up her skimpy top, she angled her head to look at the wound. A weeping burn about ten inches long spread from her back around to the side of her ribs to under her breast. *Fuck, it hurt.* Dane was proving more and more difficult to predict. He was definitely packing some heavy fire power, more than her master had prepared her for. *Mid-range sorcerer my ass!*

As well as the wound, Nira's energy levels were shot. There was nothing to do but lie low for a while and try to recover. The one-room hovel she had taken refuge in offered little comfort. She could hear the toilet cistern running on and on, its constant dribble setting her nerves on edge. Yet she had no strength to do anything about it, no will to even eat.

***

As she walked slowly down the steps to the first floor Annwyn felt clean and revived after her long bath. Tears had flowed and mingled with the steam as she'd eased the soreness from her muscles. There was no shame in letting her emotions out, she decided.

So much uncertainty in one's life was bound to cause upheaval, and feelings of love and desire only added to the mix. She tried to tell herself that it would all work out, that love would conquer all, but she knew she was kidding herself. If she wanted a life with Dane, she was going to have to fight for it, fight for him. The thought alone made her stomach curdle and her heart race.

She had been an early childhood teacher, with nothing more exciting in her life than paper cuts and scraped knees. Now she was fully embroiled in another world, learning magic and spells and loving a sorcerer who was cursed. She ate breakfast alone, but that suited her. She was in no mood for chitchat and as she had to study for the rest of the day, it gave her time to mentally prepare herself.

Rafael undertook his training with fervour. Where at first his instruction had been gentle and patient, he now grew more exacting. He expected perfection from her, which on the day Dane departed was difficult and frustrating for Annwyn. At first, she thought her lack of success was due to fatigue. A full night of vigorous sex and little sleep did little for her concentration, neither did the separation from Dane. She couldn't help thinking of him and worrying.

However, as the days wore on, she realised that Rafael was requiring a higher and higher standard from her. As she made each small achievement he patted her on the shoulder and asked for more. Just when she thought she was ready to burst, to let out her frustration and tell the old sorcerer what she thought of him and his teaching, he complimented her, catching her off guard.

'Well, my dear, you have exceeded my expectations. I know I have driven you, and I truly have been your tormentor these last couple of weeks, but there has been a dividend. You have grown so much in power and in skill, beyond what I thought possible. I am so pleased. I didn't know what you could achieve; I was acting on instinct.'

'Instinct?' Annwyn couldn't repress her smile. She was delighted with his praise and in the success of her hard work.

'I felt in my bones that there was more to you and that this gift you had had greater depth than I first thought. I know it was hard to separate yourself from Dane. I have seen your sorrow. But I feel that it was worth it as his absence allowed you to concentrate and your anger propelled you forward because I was so hard on you.'

Annwyn gathered the old man in a hug. He patted her gently on the shoulder. 'Don't cry on my robes, dear. They are terribly difficult to clean.'

She pulled back. She hadn't been crying but his words

instigated of a major flood. Relief, excitement, pride—all jumbled together. After she dried her tears she asked, 'Can I send Dane a message now?'

'Of course,' he said with a smile. 'Now I think you are ready, as ready as I can make you. Tomorrow we go to the collegium and you will meet the rest of the triumvirate.'

Her breath caught. She did not realise that she was that ready. Shaking her head, she cleared her mind and calmed her breathing. She didn't want to communicate her distress or emotional state to Dane. He had enough to deal with, and she didn't know if she could carry on a conversation without letting something of her feelings out. She only knew that messages worked—short ones.

Annwyn pictured Dane and his home and then she distinguished him; a strong bright mind. They had not been allowed to contact each other, on Rafael's orders. The mind-to-mind messages could be very intense and would have served to distract Annwyn from her studies. Now, though, as she sensed Dane and readied herself to send him a message, the emotion nearly overwhelmed her. Her success with magical power was something she had never imagined before she met him. To get where she was she had gone without the comfort of his touch or even the sound of his voice. Pushing the emotion down, like filling a cushion, she prepared a set of words.

*Dane, Rafael says my training has been very successful. I'm going to meet the triumvirate tomorrow. I'm not sure but I think that means I can see you again soon.*

The reply when it came was infused with love and pride and longing. Annwyn almost wept at the intensity of Dane's sentiment.

*I'm so proud of you. I will be with you soon.*

Because the emotion was so overwhelming she overlooked the fact that the message didn't really tell her anything, except how he felt about her.

After this, she was definitely going to push for a visit with Dane. This time she wanted to visit him at his home, to see how he was living and how he was coping. It didn't escape her notice that time was growing short before the next full moon.

Later, she sat on the large leather sofa, turning over her thoughts as she stared idly into space. Rafael called to her. With a jerk, she blinked a few times and saw him standing before her, a set of robes drapes across his arms.

'For you,' he said. 'For the presentation tomorrow. First impressions and all that …'

The robes were glamorous and otherworldly. Something akin to robes worn by the nobility when being presented to the monarch. Hers were a rich deep green, trimmed with silver braid. She also had a hat: a cross between a beret and a beanie, she thought with a laugh as she put it on her head.

'Shall I try them on?' she asked Rafael.

'Yes, of course. You will want to look your best. You have already been tested and registered with the collegium, but I think you will be requested to demonstrate your special gift. Don't worry. I believe it will be a simple process after the reading of a spell. You will then need to swear your oath.'

She took the robes and kissed him tenderly on his weathered cheek. 'Thank you, Rafael. For helping me. Helping Dane.'

Rafael nodded. 'I have not been as good a help to Dane as I should have.'

'Has he found nothing in the texts yet?'

Rafael lowered his chin, his gaze dropping. 'No, nothing.'

Annwyn frowned at the lack of progress. 'After tomorrow I must return to Dane.'

Rafael's nod was slow and careful. She caught his eye. 'Yes, my dear, I agree. You are perhaps more useful there than here. We can take up further training later…when things have settled.'

'He will not be a wolf forever,' Annwyn said forcefully. 'I won't let him be alone like that, lost to everything. You must speak to the other members of the triumvirate, maybe they can help.'

'You are right. It is time to seek their assistance.'

'They are ignorant of his curse?'

'Yes, at Dane's insistence I stupidly agreed.'

'He doesn't trust them, does he?'

'No, my dear, he does not. Now off you go. I won't be here for dinner this evening. I'm sorry to leave you alone but I have to prepare for tomorrow.'

'But first you will see me in my robes.'

His grin was wide. 'I wouldn't miss it. Off you go.'

Annwyn had to be satisfied with that. Despite her lingering despair over Dane's suffering, she was energised. She was going to meet the rest of the triumvirate, she was trained and ready for anything, and she was going to be with Dane.

Upstairs in her room she tried on the robes. Her reflection in the mirror surprised her. It was like looking at her own body now, she'd been in Nira's body for so long it had become her — Annwyn. There was no more feeling of disjointedness, or of feeling violated and ripped away. She had grown into this body in the same way that she had grown into her power. It really made her see that there was an Annwyn that was separate from her physical body. She shook her head at the wonder of it.

Which part did Dane desire? The real her or this body? He certainly liked the body and was turned on by it. Would he be equally attracted to Annwyn's own body if she returned to it?

It was all too hard to think about. She had to expect that if it was this body he wanted, then she'd have to live with his decision. There were too many other factors at play affecting their futures. She didn't have the luxury of dwelling on just one aspect.

Rafael was waiting for her at the bottom of the stairs as she glided down. He smiled at her, like her own father had when he walked her down the aisle to give her away to Thomas. He'd been gone a long time now. Her parents were killed in a car accident on the Hume Highway—a truck driver changed lanes without checking his rear view mirror and wiped them off the face of the earth. It seemed as senseless now as it did then. They would be proud of her, though, she thought. Really proud of her hard work.

Rafael kissed her on the forehead. 'You will be wonderful tomorrow. You look so full of sorcery it makes my heart skip a beat. I'm sorry to leave you alone tonight. I asked cook to make something special for you.'

She thanked him and he left her there standing alone. She climbed the stairs and changed back out of her robes. To the dining room she wore track pants and a big sloppy jumper with thick woollen socks. Morag brought her dinner on a tray: a big juicy steak, with thick-cut fries and a great mound of spinach. Next to her plate was a dusty old bottle of red wine. Not to be one to refuse such hospitality, she poured a glass and savoured its rich tones. For the first time, she found Rafael's music system and played a rousing Beethoven symphony and a number of other classical pieces from Rachmaninov, Chopin and Dvorak. When she was done she had consumed two full glasses of wine.

With a mellow feeling she climbed the stairs and went to bed. Tomorrow seemed a long way off. Closing her eyes she went out like a light, only to be roused by the sun creeping through the imperfectly shut curtains. When she checked the time she realised that she had overslept and had to move quickly to be ready for the meeting at the collegium. As it was she barely had time to fix her hair and check the fall of the robes in the mirror before Rafael called her from downstairs, urging her to hurry.

As she rushed down the corridor she reflected that Dane hadn't mentioned much about Brun and Vollos, other than that they were old and cranky. Rafael was so sweet—how he could work with the others if they were so cantankerous?

Rafael was waiting for her and clasped her hands, smiling gently. 'You ready?'

Annwyn nodded. This was her moment of truth.

Rafael transferred them smoothly. This time she knew what to expect and the nausea was only slight. As the room took shape around her she realised that they were in an ordinary-looking office space. She glanced at Rafael, sending him a querying look. 'It's the collegium's headquarters in Denver. To everyone it looks like an office building.'

Annwyn shrugged. 'It certainly looks like one.' She was expecting something a little grander, something a little more elaborate to go with the robes.

'Come along, dear. They are waiting.'

With a swirl of robes, Rafael headed to the door with Annwyn close behind. They walked along a dingy corridor across very boring carpet and entered another room, three doors down. Rafael walked in ahead of her. The door opened as they approached. Annwyn hesitated at the threshold seeing that it was a large boardroom with heavy wooden furniture, drapes covering the walls and an amazing view across the city. It was in striking odds with the plastic and aluminium theme of the building.

At the end of the table two elderly men climbed to their feet. Their robes were the same colour as Rafael's. One man was tall with striking features. The other had papery skin so thin she could see the pattern of blue veins beneath. Under his hat she could see straggly white hair that clearly hadn't been cut for a long time. This must be Vollos and the slightly younger one Brun. There was something odd about Vollos, something that made her tense and wary as she approached.

'May I present my protégée, Annwyn Flaydin, who I propose for the position of honoured seer.'

There was a hard crack of laughter from Vollos and harsh intake of breath from Brun. 'You overestimate this mortal's worth, Rafael,' Vollos said, his whole body quivering in outrage. 'She has not yet been tested or accepted.'

Rafael took their reaction rather calmly. 'She has been tested and her result recorded in the register. However, she is willing to demonstrate the manner of her gifts. First, she will make her oath to the collegium. After that, there are other matters that require considered discussion.'

Vollos sat back down as if he was folding up his bones in a pile. He waved his hand dismissively. 'I don't have time to sit here all day and listen to oaths. Take her away and come for me when you've sorted it all out.' He coughed, a sharp phlegmy bark.

Annwyn looked away, not quite sure of what she was seeing when she looked at him. Rafael guided her out of the room and Brun followed close behind.

'I will have one of the stewards come and witness her oath.'

He didn't quite smile and Annwyn thought he was wary.

'I'm afraid some extra testing will be required,' Brun added. 'tto demonstrate her worth for the position of seer.'

***

*Come! Come now!* The voice of the master reached into Nira's mind, spearing into her stupor. I need you here.

Nira cracked open an eyelid. The world around her was blurry and the stink of her own filth met her. *I can't. I don't have the strength*, she replied, using what was left of her power to respond.

The master's mind reached out and slapped her. Flung back onto the floor, her head spun. How had he done that?

*Don't make excuses. You must get here within the hour. Your body is here. Come and claim it.*

The master withdrew his presence. Nira laughed, feeling her hysteria rise. He wanted her to go to the collegium. He says that Annwyn is there. *What the fuck was that bitch doing there?* Rafael must really be taken with her to present her to his colleagues. Perhaps the cow had seduced him. A picture of her rutting with the old man brought a grin to her face. *The old fool.*

The master left her a small package of power. It unravelled and spread through her limbs, and her energy levels rose. Peering at the chair in the corner, she saw he had sent a robe. Climbing to her feet, she stumbled to the small bathroom to quickly make herself presentable.

***

For Annwyn what followed was a gruelling and exhausting experience. She thought Rafael had been hard on her but she was wrong. He had given her only a taste of what the additional testing might be. However, she was joyful at the result. She had been officially accepted into the collegium and her power was recognised as the rare power of the seer— ne who can see the fabric of spells.

After Brun and Rafael congratulated her she was invited once again to present herself to the triumvirate. This time they went to a different room, one that better-matched her imagined meeting place. It was no boardroom this time, but a large space rather like a meeting hall. The ceilings were high with gold filigreed cornices and red plush drapes. The floor was tiled in white marble and already sorcerers were gathering wearing their ceremonial robes in a variety of shades.

Rafael left her at the door with hastily whispered instructions on how she was to walk up through the sorcerers gathered and present herself to the triumvirate. 'I have to take my place with the others. Fear not, you will do well.' With a quick pat on the back, he raced off. Annwyn waited and wished with all her heart that Dane was there. While she looked on people appeared in the room, filling up the empty spaces. She focused and calmed her breathing, ready for when she was called.

Rafael called the room to order. 'A meeting of the triumvirate will begin. The first order of business is the presentation of our new seer, Annwyn Flaydin.'

Annwyn began her slow walk down the aisle which appeared as the gathered crowd parted to let her pass. Males and females robed for the occasion formed regular lines. Black robes, red, brown and varying shades of pink. None wore green robes like hers.

Ripples of whispering rippled out as she walked past. She did her best not to be distracted by the commotion she was causing. She kept her gaze ahead and focused on Rafael. His expression was sombre, but not unwelcoming.

The other two members of the triumvirate stood either side of Rafael. Brun flashed a grin at her that made his pale blue eyes twinkle. He seemed genuinely pleased to have a new seer. Brun had witnessed the testing and had lavished high praise on her at the end of it.

Vollos's grey visage wavered in front of her eyes. There were threads of something black, oily tendrils, stretching out behind him and weaving through the crowd. Annwyn thought it strange and began to track these dark threads. Someone in the crowd had a connection to Vollos. The closer she came, the more she detected dark ripples of evil emanating from the threads. Drawing back her gaze she met Vollos's face and stopped. Dark malice washed over her, rocking her back on her heels.

'Annwyn?' It was Rafael, taking a step toward her. 'What is it? What's wrong?'

Under attack, Annwyn could barely speak. Vicious and so cutting were the claws of magic that ripped into her mind. The magic tasted foul and the putrid stench of it was overpowering. Taken aback, it took a moment for her to pull in her strength, to centre herself and build a defence. With a mighty shove, she pushed the malice and gut-rotting stench out of her body.

Vollos began to screech, a sound that set all to action. He gestured wildly at her, thankfully not hurling a hex. 'Kill her! She's an imposter.'

Shouts rang out around her. The gathered crowd broke its orderly ranks and began to mill about, some trying to leave by the door, others conjuring themselves away. A few tried to grab her, but she used her power to thrust them away.

The knives of hate directed at her mind needed to be dealt with before they did her permanent harm. The old man was in her line of sight. She drew a spell that would repel him and shove him far away. The power manifested itself as she let it go as a streak of violet flame. The old man, Vollos, flew back, hitting the wall about eight feet above the floor. The stunned look on his face remained as he hung there. Abruptly, his crumpled body dropped with a thud to the floor.

While she watched, some of the black tendrils had retreated back to Vollos. The other section of the tendril slithered into the crowd of milling sorcerers. She tracked the withdrawing tendril and saw it shrink away from her and into the robes of an escaping sorcerer. Annwyn ran forward, trying to follow to the path of the black tendril. Rafael followed behind, calling to her and asking her what she was doing.

'Are you mad? Do you know what you have done?'

'Yes,' she called back. 'Hurry, he's getting away.' To save her breath she sent him a quick message and image of what she had seen.

Rafael didn't respond but stopped yelling at her, hopefully no longer thinking she was some kind of traitor.

As the crowd dissipated, she caught a glimpse of someone. Someone in collegium robes and who quickly conjured themselves away once all the tendrils had slid beneath their robes.

Annwyn pulled up short. Just one quick glance was all she got before the sorcerer transported away. Rafael came up beside her, panting.

'Did you see who it was? Do you know who it is?' she asked breathlessly.

Rafael shook his head, not quite able to speak from exertion. Annwyn clenched her fists, annoyed that she had not spotted the dark tendril earlier and that the sorcerer who had been manipulating Vollos had managed to escape.

Rafael reached out to her and Annwyn turned to his embrace. Looking up into his face, she asked, 'What was it? It seemed to be some sort of controlling spell. It was very dark and dangerous. I think it was controlling Vollos or at least connected to him.'

Rafael comforted her. 'There, there, my dear. It was unexpected. None of us knew. We can't see the way you do. I knew you would be a boon to us. But it's all so distressing.'

'Vollos?' Still within the circle of his arms, she looked up and asked, 'Is he…I didn't…'

Rafael shook his head. 'He lives. Just.'

Rafael escorted her to a small room. Within was Brun who leaned over Vollos who lay on a cot. The old man's breathing was hoarse and thin. As he tried to lift a quavering hand his strength gave way and it flopped onto the blanket that had been hastily pulled over him. 'Forgive me. I couldn't stop once it had begun.'

Annwyn wasn't sure what he was talking about although she kept quiet, certain that the others did.

Rafael came forward. 'Vollos, did you kill Tord?'

The old man's eyelids flickered. With a voice that was a wheeze, he replied, 'Yes, he suspected me. I had to silence him.'

'Who are you working with?' Rafael asked, kneeling beside the bed. 'Tell me.'

Vollos turned his face toward Rafael. 'It was…I…was…' Vollos convulsed. It was as if all the years of his long life had arrived at once. He looked so old and frail. He did not speak again.

'He is still alive but not for long. This event has weakened his hold on life,' Brun said after a quick examination.

Rafael waited at his bedside while Brun tried some healing.

'Nothing. He has no will to live now. The bindings on his life are undone,' Brun said as he moved away from the body.

They stood for a while, watching the old sorcerer's faint breath pass in and out of his frail body. There was nothing that could be done. Rafael let go Vollos's hand and stood to his feet.

Brun raised his hand. 'Wait a moment. You said there were other matters to discuss.'

Rafael nodded. 'Events have made a leisurely discussion difficult. Dane Archwright was right. There was a conspiracy and his father was murdered. However, it did not end there. Dane himself has been attacked. Cursed in the most terrible way. I must go to him. I must take Annwyn back.' Annwyn detected a light touch, like the hum of electricity. She realised Rafael was sending a communication to the remaining member of the triumvirate.

Brun lowered his head and shook it. When he lifted his face again Annwyn could see the shock there. 'I had no idea. He hid it so well. If Vollos couldn't withstand this evil, how can any of us?'

'Let me take Annwyn back now. I hope you can manage the situation here. I'll be back soon as I can, and we will find how big this conspiracy is.' He clasped Brun on the shoulder. 'We must show strength and hold the collegium together. Our enemies may strike while we are weak.'

Brun gave a quick nod.

Rafael ushered her out of the room, but Annwyn resisted. She remembered Dane's father's name.

'Are you saying that the old man killed Dane's father?'

'Vollos confessed to it. It burdens my heart to have to tell Dane that he was right in his suspicions that there was rot within the collegium. That the threat to him may originate here.

'I wish I had better looked at that sorcerer you chased. I thought all the leads went to the vampires and the other malcontents who envy us, those who are disgruntled by not being admitted to the collegium. Yet the thread seems closer to home. Perhaps he killed on the orders of somebody else? Vollos was a master, long-lived and powerful. If he could be subverted, then any one of us could be. I fear there are dark times ahead.'

Annwyn thought back to the evil that emanated from those tendrils. 'That connection was powerful and dark and it must have twisted him horribly, made him do terrible things, things he would not have normally done.'

Rafael nodded but his expression was full of sadness. 'I wish you had come to us earlier or at a better time. I fear we have not shown you our best this night. Yet on behalf of the collegium, I convey my thanks to you.'

'Now can only be the best time, Rafael. It's best that this evil was exposed. I'm grateful my gift was useful even though the consequences are far-reaching. Are you taking me back to Dane now?'

He gripped her elbow to steer her down the corridor. 'Yes, my dear. Technically, you could take yourself but I feel it is my duty to return you to him. Alas, I have much to say to him and none of it good.'

Rafael found a place that was empty, a dingy section of the corridor. The headquarters of the collegium faded out of sight. Very soon she was back in Dane's empty lounge. There was no sign of him. Rafael had not given notice of their arrival. It occurred to Annwyn rather quickly that Dane had left her to investigate a breach of his wards and that she hadn't had the opportunity to ask what had happened, what the damage had been.

Rafael sent out a mental signal. 'We will await his return. He shouldn't be long.'

As they were still dressed in their robes, Annwyn hurried off to take a shower, certain that Dane wouldn't mind her making herself at home. Her clothes were exactly where she left them, hanging next to Dane's in the wardrobe.

# Chapter Nineteen

It was odd being back in the black-tiled bathroom with the hot water sluicing down her body, caressing her moist folds. It was here that she had first explored the body she had inherited. How different were her feelings now? No longer afraid or feeling displaced, she had come full circle. She was at peace with herself and confident about what was coming next.

She took her time in the shower, even though she knew Dane had returned to the house. Rafael needed time to talk about what they had learned and Dane needed time to digest it before they met again. She wanted their reunion to be perfect. Flicking off the shower control, she grabbed one of the thick, black towels from the cupboard and dried herself vigorously. She wanted to be clean, wanted nothing to get in the way of making love with Dane. He would need and want her. He would need to bury his troubles, his grief, and she was prepared for that.

Wiping the mist from the mirror, she stared at her reflection. So much had changed and yet the face she was looking at was still the same, although the blonde hair was darkened with water and a bit dishevelled. Her skin was damp and dewy. 'Come on, you've stalled long enough,' she said to herself.

With the towel wrapped around her body she left the bathroom, only to be seized by a pair of strong arms. The towel fell away leaving her naked and damp in Dane's embrace. He was already naked and ready.

He didn't speak and before she could say anything his hot mouth stole her breath and his silken lips filled her with passion. His hands reached down and grasped her buttocks, lifting her so his engorged cock rubbed against her sex. Her knees trembled as the electricity between them snapped and crackled.

She ran her hands down his muscled back and cupped his smooth butt and squeezed. The pleasure in touching him sent shivers through her body. Already she was moist and ready and wanted to be ridden hard and fast by her powerful lover.

Dane was equally enthusiastic. He never stopped kissing her, guiding her back against the wall. He was inside her and pumping before she could catch her breath. With his help she wrapped her legs around his waist, not even disturbing the rhythm. He was desperate and hard and passionate, and she couldn't help but be caught up in it. She rode the moment as he rode her, taking everything that he could give her and giving back everything she could.

He bit her neck gently, enough to increase her excitement. It was hot and fast and over way too quickly. Yet Annwyn was satisfied. She was back and she was no longer worrying about their attraction. Although they hadn't discussed it, she sensed that he no longer had qualms about making love to her.

Dane eased himself out of her and let her feet touch the floor for a moment before he scooped her up in his arms and carried her back into the shower. 'Let me do the honours,' he said, his voice hoarse. He detached the shower head and began to soap her, then sluice off the suds. Still they didn't speak, but shared long moments of looking deep into each other's eyes. The connection she'd experienced in Scotland was still there. She wondered if it was as strong for him.

Dane rinsed himself off, then picked her up again. He placed her on the bed and grabbed some towels to dry her. She lay there and let him do as he pleased, aware that this was a special intimacy between them, a real reflection of the trust they now shared.

One day she would love to bathe and dress him too. They had nearly a week of this before the next moon rose. They had time to be together and to think of some way to deal with what was to come. Rafael knew the members of the collegium better than she ever would. Hopefully, he had seen enough to be able to trace the sorcerer behind it.

Dane climbed into the bed, cradling her so that she lay half on him and half on the mattress and, in that position, he caressed her and touched her slowly and carefully until they both drifted off to sleep.

The days passed too quickly for Annwyn—an idyllic existence which preceded a looming demise. The end was coming. The time was borrowed and could never be repaid.

Rolf stayed close to them, and she was grateful for his company. He was there but he did not intrude. He made coffee, cooked food and did work around the house while she and Dane kept close together.

'Thank you,' Dane said one morning as they lay together in bed. 'You uncovered the truth about my father. Although it hurts, it's good to finally have it out and acknowledged by the collegium. It makes going forward, if there is a future for me, easier. I am less guilty taking my place amongst them.'

'I would not have this gift if it wasn't for you, wasn't for...you know. I could have lived my whole life never knowing about this world, about you.' The tears came then because whenever she thought about her love and the potential loss of it, she couldn't help getting emotional.

His forefinger traced the curve of her brow, and he kissed the tip of her nose. 'You are a gift. I'm grateful for this time we shared.' He pushed up out of the bed. 'However, today you're getting out of the house. I've kept you here too long, and I need a little more time with those texts. Rafael sent a message last night giving me another clue.'

Annwyn lifted herself up on her elbows, a smile playing around her mouth. 'And where am I going?'

'Anywhere you like. You can take my car unless you want to conjure yourself somewhere. Just make sure you don't materialise in a cave or in water or somewhere dangerous like that.'

'I see. I think I'll take the car. Rolf tells me we need more groceries. I'd rather he stay here with you.'

He nipped the tip of her nose. 'I'd rather he went with you. I can manage quite well without him.'

She pouted and then said, 'I'm sorry but you can only be rid of one of us. You didn't say what happened about the wards that day. Was it her?'

'No, it wasn't her. Rolf couldn't detect her scent. Whoever it was tried to burn the house down.'

'Really? I was wondering at that burnt smell. Did they do a lot of damage?'

'Not much. They broke one of the wards and stole one of the texts. However, it wasn't an important one and the others remain untouched.'

Annwyn considered what a violation it must have been. Rafael had said that when wards, personal wards, are broken, it can be painful.

'And you…'

He smiled at her, brushing the hair from her face. 'Yes, the breaking of a ward hurts. Nothing too serious, though. Rolf was there and managed.'

She gave him a peck on the lips. 'I'm glad you're okay.'

If it wasn't Nira then who, she thought to herself, and why had Nira been so quiet? Either Annwyn had grown stronger and was able to resist the connection or Nira just wasn't interested any more. Nira had been so focused on getting her body back and on destroying Dane, why would she suddenly stop? Annwyn wondered whether she could still contact the sorceress and whether she needed to be thinking of very kinky sex in order to do so.

As Annwyn dressed she smelled coffee and breakfast cooking. Dane needed some time out and she was prepared to have some herself. As well as shopping, she thought she would drive past her old house and see how things were. She wondered what her workmates thought about her disappearance. With her parents dead and no siblings, she had no one else to worry about her in that way. Thomas's family had forgotten about her a few months after the funeral.

Rolf presented her with a lengthy list of all the things he wished her to purchase. Annwyn ran her eye down the list, lifting her eyebrows at a few of the items, particularly the quantity of meat. When she gawped at him he shoved a large wad of cash into her hand. 'Thanks,' she said. 'I forgot I have no credit cards.'

The journey into Canberra was fraught with traffic due to road works. The trip past the house was emotional. There was a For Sale sign out front and the garden was overgrown and neglected. It seemed that her life there had been someone else's. Her past was as ethereal as a dream. It was as if another person had lived that sad and lonely life, caught in a web of a dark spell without even knowing about it and waiting for the day when things would change. 'I needed to have my life ripped away', Annwyn said to herself. She wiped away a tear, despite being certain that she regretted nothing. She hoped she would continue to regret nothing.

***

Nira's injuries were slowly healing. Naked, she lay against a pile of cushions, legs splayed, arms outstretched. It was hot in the little room, but she enjoyed the oppressive atmosphere. It would be a waste of power to condition the room magically. She couldn't believe she had infiltrated the collegium and escaped. There were to be no more empty promises, no more communication from a master who left her reeling from the touch of his rancid mind. She still did not understand why Annwyn had been there at the gathering. There were too many sorcerers, too much confusion to understand.

The most amazing thing was the surge of power she had received. She was whole again. She was ready to take on the world and be dammed with the lot of them. Yet there was still those two. Dane, the arch prick, and that insipid creature inhabiting her body. She'd always hated Annwyn and the way her husband had fawned all over her, singing her praises. Hypocrite that he was. He was ready to fuck anyone with a willing orifice. Dumb old Annwyn never suspected his affairs. With an ego like his, he'd been easy to subvert. One *compliment on the size of his cock and one expert blow job and he had been hers. Easy* prey. *Too easy.*

Pawing through her carry bag, she rummaged around for Dane's picture. Her fingers brushed the gilded frame and she caught his thoughts of contentment and love. 'Damn him! He thinks he's going to have a life with Annwyn and my body.'

She threw the picture frame and it smashed against the wall. Her power coiled within her belly. She had the strength now to end it. Dane Archwright was going to pay. He had no right to be happy while she, Nira, suffered. Her hope of a place in the collegium had gone. She would have to begin again. She shook her head. No way was Dane going to remain unscathed. Not while she suffered. Not by a long shot.

Tilting her head back, she began to chant, spinning a dark tendril, refining it until it was razor sharp, then she sent it straight to Dane. That should fix them both. That should sow the seeds of misery. Laughing, she nestled back against the cushions and began to pleasure herself.

# Chapter Twenty

Annwyn pulled up at the house in Dane's Lexus and flipped the boot open before sliding out of the car. Two of the dogs came up to greet her. Rolf had released them from their run. The other ones, the wolves, were no longer hanging around. They were members of Rolf's pack and had gone back to their lives. She patted one of the dogs and tossed the other a stick. It was easier to get the groceries out without dogs underfoot determined to trip her up.

She thought Rolf would have come out to help her, knowing his sensitive ears would have heard the car pull up.

Suddenly, an eerie howl filled the air around her, sending her heart racing. In a panic, she dropped the shopping bags. 'Dane?'

Dread infused her. She ran to the house and flung open the sliding door, nearly sending it crashing off its rails. Rolf was there next to Dane who writhed in agony on the floor.

'What's happening?'

'He's turning.'

'But it's too soon. It's nowhere near the full moon.'

'Nevertheless, it's happening.' Rolf's expression was haggard and his voice fearful. 'Can't you help him?'

Annwyn rushed over. Dane rolled over until he was hunched on his knees. The expression on his face was one of torture. 'Dane, can you hear me?'

Dane didn't respond. His eyes were bloodshot and unfocused. Sweat dripped from his forehead and upper lip. 'Fight it,' she urged.

Annwyn looked up desperately at Rolf. He growled at her, not with menace but with frustration. This was it. If Dane turned now, it would be the end of it. She stood back, cast her gaze into him, looking for the curse. It was there, but it was so much a part of him she could not see how to unravel or remove it. There was only one way to deal with this.

'Rolf, I need your help. I need to lure Nira here, but I'm so afraid that I can't think a single erotic thought.' She began to kick off her shoes and undo her dress.

'What do you mean?'

'We have to fuck. Like now.' She lifted her top over her head and kicked off her shoes.

He shook his head, refusing to get naked. 'Dane said no sharing. He won't like it.'

'He'd rather not be a werewolf forever. You know the risk. She's doing this to him right now.' Annwyn remembered the picture. Nira had a connection to him, could skim his thoughts. They'd been so tranquil and happy lately. That must be it. Nira was back and pissed.

'I can't,'

'Yes, you can. You've got to take me and make it as kinky as possible. I need to get her attention and this is the only way I know how.'

Annwyn unzipped her jeans and slid them down over her hips. Rolf stood there, his eyes staring at the wall behind her. *Not very helpful*. She tugged down her undies and then unclipped her bra. Nervous as all hell, she had no stirrings of lust. A whine from Dane. She knelt down and stroked his forehead.

'Fight it, Dane. Please.'

Dane panted as he fought the change. He didn't react to her nakedness.

Rolf was really focused on her now, but he stood still. She stepped up to him. 'Come on, I'll help.' Annwyn began unbuttoning his jeans and sliding the zip down. He did not resist her. When she looked up at his face, his expression was neutral. He shrugged helplessly. He wasn't very turned on by her nakedness either.

His jeans were halfway down his hips when she sprung him from his underpants. He was limp, not ready. This was impossible. Neither of them wanted to have sex, but she was desperate. They had no choice. Her power alone couldn't stop the curse.

Kneeling down, Annwyn took the head of his cock into her mouth, caressing the silk of it with her tongue and gently sucked. Rolf moaned, not with desire but utter futility. He didn't want to make love with Annwyn, but he did want to help Dane. The sound of Dane fighting the change made Rolf growl loudly. Annwyn hesitated, but then felt some reaction from Rolf. He was a long way from being horny.

Annwyn let her mind go free. She shoved all the images of sex with Dane into her head, replaying them until she moistened. It was a start. She yanked Rolf's jeans further down his legs until he could step out of them, desperately sucking on his burgeoning erection. *God,* she thought, *this man is built*. His cock continued to grow the more she slid her tongue up and down the shaft.

She channelled the images of Nira in the sex club, images of her sucking the black cock and being taken from behind. Picturing that cock penetrating Nira's anus, the large scrotum brushing against her buttocks, her own arousal grew. *What an image*! She let it grow, picturing the long shaft withdrawing almost to the tip before thrusting back in. Sliding her own hand between her moist folds she began to rub, hoping that this was sufficient to get Nira's attention.

Yet there was nothing. Nira was a no-show. Another fierce howl from Dane and Annwyn worked harder. Rolf growled low in his throat as she teased his erection with her tongue. Her tongue slid along the silky glans and she cupped her mouth over the tip, creating suction until he gasped. Releasing him, she curled her hand around his shaft working him while sliding her tongue up and down in time to her manipulations. A groan escaped him. His cock hardened further. Letting her head drop, she lathered his balls with her tongue. Rolf jerked and then shuddered. Satisfied her attempts at arousal were finally working, she took one of his balls in her mouth, gently caressing the vulnerable flesh. His hands gripped her hair and tightened. Slowly releasing him, she ran her tongue from the base to the tip, teasing him again with rapid flicks of her tongue. His control was weakening and, unable to hold out against her determined effort to arouse him, he let out a full-throated growl as his erection stood proud before her face.

Annwyn climbed to her feet and wrapped her nakedness around Rolf. He didn't hold her, but he didn't repulse her. She nuzzled his neck, tasting the salty tang of his sweat and then biting his chin playfully. Leaning back, she angled his head, bringing his mouth down for a searing kiss. Dane let out an eerie howl, full of rage and anguish. They both jumped as if he had caught them doing something they shouldn't.

Annwyn turned toward him and sent a direct thought. *I love you, Dane. This is for you. We're doing this for you. Please fight the change and hang on.*

Rolf enveloped her from behind, bringing his strong, sun-tanned arms around her waist and lifting her breasts. He bit the back of her neck. It hurt and she cried out, but there was pleasure too. Nira's kind of pleasure.

His hard cock pressed against the crease of her buttocks as he rubbed himself against her. She tried to remember whether in her last encounter with Rolf they had shared anal sex. Dane had taken her once that way and it nearly drove her crazy. It was like surrendering all of yourself, opening yourself up to be filled, to be conquered. It hadn't hurt as much as she had expected it to. Given that she was in Nira's body and what Nira habitually did with it, the lack of pain made sense. She remembered experiencing Nira's thoughts as she was penetrated from behind. Annwyn's body was not used to it and it had hurt Nira, hurt her more than she expected.

*Come on*, Nira, Annwyn thought. *Connect with me.*

Time was running out. She could see the hair along Dane's hairline lengthening, see the shape of his brow extending.

Rolf must have seen it too because he lifted her and bent her over the back of the couch, face first. Holding her in place, he bent down and began licking her. Facedown, she was helpless. His firm hold kept her from squirming. It wasn't going to be enough. Not nearly enough or fast enough. She needed to connect now.

'Fuck me, dammit, Rolf. Nira likes pain.'

Rolf stood up and thwacked her across the arse, once, twice, and then three slaps in rapid succession. It smarted something terrible, and Annwyn couldn't help but cry out.

Rolf gripped her butt checks with hands bent in claws. It hurt, but it also sent shivers up her spine and expelled the breath out of her body.

Rolf opened her up, exposing her anus and her moist slit. The tip of his cock nudged against her. She was caught on a precipice, wondering where he would go, whether he would try anal or vaginal sex.

She opened herself to him, using muscles she did not know she had, inviting him in. As he impaled her with his hard cock, she cried out. 'God!' He was so hard, so big. She didn't think there was any room for error. One wrong move and he'd split her.

Taking her moan as a signal that all was okay, Rolf began to fuck her. He wasn't gentle. He rammed himself to the hilt. Annwyn was too shocked to even cry out. He pulled back and then impaled her again. The pain was such that it was all she could do to remain open to him, using those muscles that Nira had carefully trained. Every thrust stretched her, pushed her along the path of pain and excitement. There she found a tiny thread that seemed familiar and foreign. 'More,' she said, breathing through the pain. It hurt and yet it was strangely fulfilling. Amazingly, Rolf thrust harder, faster and Annwyn thought she would break apart. The noises she made weren't even grunts, but visceral, incoherent wails.

The connection to Nira snapped open. Annwyn gasped at the strength of it. Her arse was being pummelled. *Come on!* (Grunt!) *I dare you!* (Groan!) She thought at Nira. *Come here and face me now, you bitch. I'm getting it how you like* it.

She could tell that Nira was curious, but not sufficiently curious to appear. She called out to Rolf. 'Stop! Stop that now.' Rolf extracted himself from her.

'We have to try something else,' she said with a shaky voice. That was some fuck. When she climbed off the back of the couch and faced him she was at a bit of a loss seeing his distress. He was still aroused, obviously so. They both turned towards Dane. He was still fighting the change, but it was progressing inexorably.

'Hit me.'

Rolf shook his head. 'I don't hit women.'

'Don't think of me as a woman. Slap me. She is connected to me. I need more to bring her in.'

Again he shook his head, denying her the only thing she could think of to save Dane.

'You slack, cowardly bastard,' she said. She raised her hand and slapped him across the cheek.

His head jerked to the left. His eyes glittered with anger. 'Don't make me. I don't want to hurt you.'

She slapped him again and again until her hand smarted. His eyes glowed with yellow fire. He growled at her, his lips drawing back in a snarl.

She could tell she had Nira's interest now. Nira was there, crouched behind Annwyn's eyes, waiting.

Rolf retaliated. Annwyn wasn't quite ready for it so quickly did he move. An open-handed slap landed on her cheek. She flew backwards and her body flipped over the couch.

When she climbed to her feet, Nira was there. She'd transported to them.

'Is that the best you can do?' Nira said from across the room. The dogs were barking madly outside. They knew her scent, knew what she had done.

'Hit her again,' she said to Rolf. Rolf stiffened and when he faced Annwyn she could see that his eyes were glazed. When she looked behind him, she could see a thin cord spreading out from the sorceress had latched onto him. It was a smaller version of the black tendrils she'd seen at the collegium. It was similar magic. Didn't Rafael say that sorcerers taught their apprentices special tricks, known only to them?

Annwyn didn't have a chance to urge Rolf to shake her off. He slapped her, and she reeled. Blood filled her mouth where lips cut against teeth.

'Snap out of it, Rolf,' she said as she used the back of her hand to wipe the blood away. The charm was missing from his neck. Searching the floor, she saw it there amongst their clothes.

Rolf shook his head and hesitated. 'Grab the charm,' she

hissed, using her eyes to indicate where it was.

He dropped to the floor, pretending to shove their clothes away and surreptitiously hid it in his fist. When Rolf stood up he wasn't quite free of Nira's control, but was more aware.

Annwyn backed up as Nira stepped closer to Rolf. The sorcereress reached down and cupped Rolf's balls in her hand and stroked his erection. 'You are impressive wolf boy. I'd fuck you if I had the time.' Still groping Rolf, she said to Annwyn, 'I want my body back.'

'I know.'

'I'm going to take it. I need blood. His will do.'

"Release Dane from the curse. Can't you see what it's doing to him?"

'I can't release—don't know how.'

Annwyn moved toward her. Covertly, she sent a fine thread of a spell into Nira. One that would track her if she chose to disappear. Nira didn't react to it so it must have anchored without being detected. 'That's bullshit. You made it, Nira. You can undo it.'

'He told me how to make it, but not how to undo it.'

'He?'

'My master. Vollos. I can say his name now. He's dead. I felt him pass. You were there. Why?'

Annwyn blinked. Vollos had murdered Dane's father and now was responsible for ruining Dane's life, taking away all that he was. This woman was his tool, his blunt instrument. What purpose could Vollos having in betraying them and the collegium? Perhaps they would never know. Nira wasn't an ordinary sorceress. She wasn't registered so that meant Vollos was conspiring with the malcontents.

'Grab her,' Nira said to Rolf. Annwyn didn't put up a fight as Rolf wrapped his muscled arms around her neck and held her to him. She could barely breathe and couldn't move.

Another piercing howl from Dane made her desperate. Her gaze riveted itself on his tortured frame. His hands were bent like claws and hair had sprouted on the smooth skin of his back. She had to act.

'Take my blood.'

Nira shook her head. 'That's my body you are bargaining with. No deal. Choose.'

Her gaze flicked between Dane and Rolf. No, she wouldn't let her take their blood, their lives. Silently, she begged Rolf to ease his grip. She tried to call to him, but her words were muffled by his powerful grip that restricted her chin. Finally she got the words out. 'Rolf, Rolf, loosen your grip.'

'Do it,' Nira commanded.

Annwyn felt herself flipped over, face down on the back of the couch. This time she fought back as Rolf tried to penetrate her. Nira was getting energy off this and she had to put the kibosh on that. She'd been happy enough to couple with Rolf to lure the woman here, but she was not about to get raped for her fun.

Rolf scored her back with his fingernails. Pain snaked through her body, momentarily paralysing her. Nira drew that the pain into herself. This wasn't good. This wasn't how it was meant to be. Annwyn had to sever the connection or at least distance herself for what she needed to do.

Rolf pushed himself inside her. Panic welled as he began to thrust, as she tried to fight him, but he held her firm with his hand in the middle of her back and his strong thighs wedged her legs apart. She could have used her power but she wasn't ready to reveal it yet. Nira had seen her at the collegium but she didn't suspect her power yet. She needed Nira to be physically there to end the curse. She also needed to temper the connection between them.

Nira stood face to the ceiling, arms loose at her side, soaking up Annwyn's pain. 'Yes, I love your fear,' she exulted, her voice languorous. 'I love your pain.' She shivered as if drinking it in.

Annwyn despaired for Dane. If he could sense her distress, he couldn't act on it as all his energy seemed to be taken up with holding off the change. It was a battle he was losing.

Turning her head, she could see more hair sprouting on his back and the muscles across his scapula bulging as his body started to change. She couldn't even risk a mind-to-mind message to him in case Nira sensed it.

Rolf withdrew from her and Annwyn sighed loudly as the pressure of him eased. Her body ached now because she had fought him. Her legs shook as she tried to stand up, and she had to use her hands to steady her. Before she stood up fully, a sharp pain flared across her thoracic vertebrae. The sound of a whip cutting through the air warned her of the next strike. Was that Rolf or Nira?

That question was soon answered. 'Give it to me, you stupid mutt.' There was a yelp from Rolf. Annwyn turned to see Rolf on his hands and knees, writhing, with heat coming off him waves. Face to the ceiling, he let out a chilling howl from his tortured mouth

'What are you doing?' She couldn't hide the panic in her voice.

'Forcing his change. Useless cur that he is.'

Annwyn gaped at Rolf. She couldn't see Nira's magic at work. 'How?'

Nira's eyebrow lifted. 'What's it to you? His wolf blood will serve my purpose.' She raised the whip with a swirl and lashed Annwyn across her tender breasts. Air became painful to breathe and she held herself still, hoping the sting would ease before Nira could land another blow. At the same time, frustration rose. She had to act before things got out of hand.

Annwyn crept along the invisible connection to Nira. She wasn't one hundred per cent certain but she thought Nira had flinched after that last lash. So the evil bitch had sudden limitations to what pain she could bear. If that was the case, Annwyn could bear it too, so she raised her chin, daring the other woman silently to hit her again.

Nira accepted the invitation and swiped the lash across Annwyn's naked belly. The tip of the lash cut into her tender flesh leaving five tracks of bloody welts. Annwyn rode the pain, fighting to keep her mind clear. Nira had withdrawn further back into herself. Excellent.

'Satisfied with yourself now?' Annwyn hissed through her teeth. 'I'm giving you one more chance to stop this.'

Nira laughed at her. 'You're pathetic. You think he loves you, but it's just his stupid spell. And you think he likes fucking that body. But it's my body he likes fucking, and he always will. I'm his nemesis. I beat him at his own game, and he will never, ever forget.'

Nira's verbal dart cut into Annwyn like the tip of the lash. It sliced into her vulnerability and left her bereft. But her own feelings didn't matter anymore. Dane's life was at stake. She had nothing to give him except herself. Annwyn built up her power. She didn't need any pain to artificially enhance it. She had lots more.

Nira's eyes widened as she detected the change in Annwyn. Her brow creased, her mouth drew into a thin line. 'What are you doing?'

Instinctively, the other woman reacted to the threat Annwyn posed. A ball of power suffused with all the pain that Annwyn had suffered billowed out and struck her. Annwyn somersaulted over the back of the couch and rolled to her feet, ready to retaliate. Shaking her head, she tried to focus, ignoring her pain. She didn't have a second to lose. Nira might choose to conjure herself away. While she could track her they could not afford the time. This had to end now for Dane's sake.

Annwyn's strike was strong and deadly.

Nira screamed, and screamed as Annwyn's deadly spell drove into her chest, opening her up and ripping out her essence. Tears slowly trickled down Annwyn's face. She didn't want to take another life, but Dane's was in the balance and Nira would not give him a chance, would not help him. The stubborn woman. Then she had chosen to make Rolf another of her victims. Annwyn wasn't giving in to that.

While Nira struggled with the deathly magic, she struck out, sending a dark tendril of power that groped for something, anything. It reached for Annwyn and, instinctively, Annwyn threw out another defensive thrust that shattered the tendril into tiny atoms of harmless power.

Nira's eyes widened when she saw it. The distraction caused Nira to cease struggling against the spell. That brief moment of surprise allowed Annwyn's spell to take hold and shred Nira's flesh to tiny pieces.

Annwyn couldn't believe her eyes. She had torn someone from life. As she looked on, Nira's flesh sizzled and evaporated. The Nira that was in Annwyn's body. There was no going back for Annwyn, no quiet retreat to her life. Her body was dead. She was in Nira's body forever now. Rafael had told her that her power would go with her if she gained her body back again. It was part of her, rather than the physical matter that made up the body. Still it was a shock. She'd ended a life, killed her old existence. There was no turning back now.

Her heart was full of sorrow for what Nira had lost. To the end she had been twisted and evil. That last black tendril was familiar to her. It was the same as the one that was connected to Vollos. There was no doubt that Vollos had been her master. Even though Nira had said as much, she was an adept liar and would have done anything to deflect unwanted attention.

Nira's screams would surely live in Annwyn's memory forever. She fell to the floor and wept as the last vestiges of Nira fizzled out and it grew quiet. Because they were connected, Annwyn had tasted all her fear and pain. She had to fight to maintain her own sense of self as Nira crawled along the connection, seeking a safe haven within her body. It was Nira's body after all, and she supposed it was natural that some remnant of Nira would seek refuge within it.

Annwyn blinked a few times still struggling to find equilibrium. There was a battle going on inside her as Nira fought to remain alive. Annwyn tied her up and shoved her in a corner of her mind. She had other things to think about.

Annwyn's focus turned to Dane.

Dane was lying on the floor not far from her. For some reason, Annwyn couldn't control her emotions, sobbing as she inched across the floor to where Dane lay. For a horrible gut-wrenching moment she thought he was dead. Her hand hovered above his head, hesitant to touch.

Rolf spoke to her from where he sat on the floor. 'He's alive.' He shook himself, reabsorbing the wolf that Nira had summoned.

With a heave, she turned Dane over. He was still partially transformed, the change into a werewolf halted but not reversed. Anguish almost choked her. She thought that with Nira's end the spell would have dissipated.

She caressed Dane's half-transformed face, ran her fingers along his once straight nose, now flat with flared nostrils. She traced a fingertip along his thickened brow, feeling the coarse dark hairs that grew there. His ears had elongated, and she kissed them tenderly. Even like this he was dear to her. She was conscious of Rolf standing behind her, feet apart and arms folded. He'd found his clothes.

With a quick glance she saw him shaking his head. He had nothing to offer by way of remedy.

Perhaps there was something she could do. A seer should be able to find the trace of a spell and remove it. She had done it unconsciously with the binding spell so why not with this one?

Rolf squatted beside her. 'Can you help him? I saw what you did to the sorceress—I still can't believe it. Dane said you had magic, but until then I didn't believe him. You seemed so ordinary.'

'I'm going to try. I can't leave him like this.'

'What do you need?' Rolf asked.

'I need quiet. We can talk later if you want.' As she touched Dane she sent her power into him so that she could slip beneath his skin, like a ward sinks into the fabric of the structure it protects. There she perceived it, the moon-turning curse. It was weakened but it wasn't dead. She spent her time floating along its weft and warp, accustoming herself to its very fabric. When she finally understood it she dissolved it with fine filaments of power, like little trickles of acid eating up the curse. But there was damage there, permanent damage. Annwyn used the memory of when they first met to shore up the tissues that had been rent, and to smooth over the hurt that the curse had made.

Her fingers ran along the memory of the well-loved contours of his face. She smoothed that proud nose, restored those vivid blue eyes and firmed that strong chin. Her tears dropped silently on his cheeks and ran into his newly re-formed ears. Yet the spell went deep. She had to send healing thrusts into him, taking all the essence she had to give and sending it into his cells to repair the damage.

The exertion took its toll. She had used a lot of power in destroying Nira and nearly as much fighting what was left of her in their connection. Saving Dane had taken all the rest. Her strength gave out before she knew whether she had been successful.

Her mind floated somewhere in a dark space without stimulus. She had no idea how long she had been there or what suddenly brought her to consciousness. Exhaustion made thinking difficult. Yet there was something, a warmth, spreading into her. The more she paid attention, the stronger the feeling became. Smooth hands eased along the tortured muscles of her thighs and fingers of warmth brushed across the wounds on her stomach. Hands moved along her arms and caressed her shoulders, leaving reviving strength in their wake.

She heard a moan and realised it was her.

'Annwyn?' Her eyelids snapped open. The room was darkened, yet she knew it was Dane. The scent of lavender, rose-geranium and patchouli infused the air. Dane was giving her a massage, a healing and sensuous massage and something else. She sat up when she realised.

'What are you doing? You need to conserve your strength.'

'You used your power, nearly spent yourself, nearly died to save me. I'm only giving back what you need to survive.'

Annwyn lay back and let him minister to her. She'd didn't realise her efforts could have cost her life. Desperation made her act on impulse.

***

Dane had woken feeling whole. Something he never thought possible again. There were traces of the beast still within him, but he was himself again. More Dane than anything else. Near the end, he had perceived Annwyn, sensed her love and been awed at her sacrifice and her amazing power. She had meshed herself within his flesh and forced the spell out. She had moulded him, taking out the bits of the beast and sealing up the rents in his flesh.

During the ordeal, when the curse was upon him, pain had made breathing hard, but he had clung to it, clung to life. When he had woken to find her slumped next to him, nearly lifeless, he had wept and grabbed her to him. Rolf had been stroking her hair and weeping softly. The werewolf had blinked back tears when he saw Dane. 'She did it. I couldn't believe my eyes.'

In a weak voice he replied, 'Yes, she did it. Amazing and wonderful Annwyn.' He looked down at her. He cried out at what he saw. 'Annwyn!' He cried out again, almost a howl of despair.

Rolf sat up on his heels. 'What? Tell me.'

'She's nearly gone. Oh, no. I must get a grip. She has spent herself restoring me. I must give some of it back.'

'What about the old wizard? Maybe he can help.' Rolf's suggestion was immediately acted on.

Rafael arrived within five minutes. He swooped down on Annwyn, trying to take her from Dane.

'Here let me.' Dane was reluctant to let her go. 'I'll give her back soon. She needs more than what you can give her. I have some power reserves.'

Dane passed Annwyn's unconscious form over to the old man and watched as Rafael carefully traced a finger along her profile. A faint vibration indicated Rafael was feeding his own essence into her. Rafael was strong, Dane could see that. He was nearly as strong as his own father had been.

Annwyn's breathing grew normal, her chest rising and failing with greater certainty. Her colour, too, improved and her face looked less drawn. It was working. She was no longer as close to death.

Rafael stopped after quarter of an hour and sighed loudly. 'That's the best I can do for now. Wait a short while and then give her healing. You should both be ready for it by then. I must go back. There is much to deal with. I can't leave Brun to do it alone.' He looked at Dane directly in the face. 'You were right to be wary of us. We think we have cut out the rot but we will need you in future. Please don't forget your pledge. Both of you come to us soon.'

Dane nodded. Rafael conjured himself away. Rolf watched on while Dane held Annwyn, strengthening her with each beat of his heart. While Dane held her, his own power stabilised. He nodded to Rolf, who then gathered Annwyn in his arms.

Without another word, he had Rolf carry her to his bed. He wanted to heal her. That healing was going to be intimate. He would take his time with it.

Later, when he'd finished the healing massage, Annwyn opened her eyes he could see that her emotion matched his own. She launched herself off the pillows and into his embrace at the same time as he scooped her into his arms. They said nothing as they were too full of emotion to speak. Dane shuddered as he brushed the tears off her cheeks. He found her mouth and possessed it, sinking into the kiss and into the feeling of belonging that had come to be when he was with her.

He broke off. 'Annwyn?' He stroked her hair away from her face, revelling in the beauty of her eyes—Annwyn's eyes. Not Nira's. These eyes contained the essence of his Annwyn.

'Yes,' she responded dreamily, a smile teasing the edge of her mouth.

'It's not the spell. I love you, and I need you never to leave me.' Dane never thought he'd be speaking these words to her or anyone. He loved her and he owned it and he spoke with honesty. He had been hers all along, but couldn't admit it. The spell must have fallen away within a few days. If he had bothered to check, he would have seen it himself. He was only admitting what he had known for weeks now.

Unashamed, she let the tears flow down her cheeks although she smiled. 'I know it's not the spell. I can't believe I feel this way about you. I never knew such love was possible. You are a part of me.'

Her words entwined themselves around his soul. The impossible was possible. She loved him, had proved it by her actions. Did she not nearly kill herself to save him? To hear the words that he never thought to hear overwhelmed him, completed him.

Their lips met with sizzling heat. Dane couldn't keep his hands from her skin. It passed beneath his fingers like silk.

'I have some wolf left in me. Sometimes he will escape my control.'

A smile lit her face and made her eyes shine. 'I have part of Nira in me. Sometimes she will sneak beneath my guard—demand kinky sex.'

He chuckled. 'It looks like we're going to have some exciting times.'

Despite the fatigue and terror of the past few hours, Dane lifted her into his lap, spearing her ever so slowly and held her there. Annwyn gasped when he invaded her moist sex. She tensed and then her arousal washed over him. He wanted her to scream like she never had before. However, he settled for that wondrous and rapturous look on her face as he moved inside her. His penetration was slow and deliberate, building with a measured pace. She slapped his shoulder, demanding more, but he kept himself in check as she began to moan. The look on her face as her eyes closed and her head leaned back showed her arousal was building and he increased the pace. 'More. Faster,' she demanded.

A smile lit his face as he held her, sunk into her. She was no longer the timid woman who'd first landed in his bed.

'Please,' she begged. 'Faster.'

With his inhuman control, the wolf adding stamina to his heady arousal, he had upped the pace and had her screaming his name as he thrust into her.

He laughed at the joy of it. Changing pace, he stopped. He was close and he wanted it to last. Her disappointed 'Oh?' brought a grin to his face. He lifted her by the waist, raising her up and then, ever so slowly, let her slide down his erection. It was glorious. It was frustrating. He wanted to toss her on the mattress and fuck her senseless, he was so close. Yet he held back.

He found the slow movements drove her crazy and it was tipping him over the edge. If she wriggled one more time, he would come. He dampened down his wolf. He clamped down on his arousal, letting it out slowly and lifted her again.

'Please,' she begged him, grabbing him behind the ears. 'Fuck me. Take me. Don't do this…I can't bear it.'

With their foreheads together, he kissed her brow and let her descend along his shaft once again. 'Please, please.'

Her begging was sweet to his ears. With a quick glance right into her essence, he saw the golden glow of her power, kindled by their intimate connection.

He could bear it no longer. Abruptly, he grabbed her under the arms and tossed her back onto the mattress. His control was spent as he thrust into her again and again, biting her neck, sucking urgently on her breasts.

It was intense. Annwyn met his every thrust. Sucked and bit and scratched at him, sending him further into his arousal. He wished it would never end. She lifted her hips to meet him and called out his name.

He changed positions, kneeling between her legs and lifting her hips as he thrust into her. Whatever was left of Annwyn's control frayed. She was screaming now. Dane let himself go. He had pushed her high and met her there.

He loved her. Thank deities, she had saved him so he could keep on loving her. He filled her with his seed, a roar bursting out of him, surprising him with its intensity.

'I love you, Annwyn. You are mine.'

'I love you too. Mine…' She nestled into his shoulder and drifted off to sleep. He watched her for a while, until he was sure she was well and that he hadn't taxed her too much.

***

Annwyn woke up sometime later, still naked in Dane's bed. She sat up suddenly, frightened by the quiet and the dark. Why had Dane left her? She slipped out of the bed and put on a robe, feeling the rawness there. Her body had taken a bit of a beating, but Dane had healed the welts. He was certainly virile. She could get used to that.

Padding barefoot down the hallway, she went looking for him. Then she remembered that Rolf was there too. The

229

werewolf had been damaged by Nira's manipulation. With a pang of guilt, she thought she had harmed him too by forcing him to have intercourse with her.

Even though it had been to save Dane, she hated herself for it. She reached the lounge room and heard murmuring voices. Rolf and Dane were sitting on the sofa, each with a small bottle of beer in their hand. *Typical*, she thought, when she saw them. All that worry and here they are, sitting and chatting. She let out a slow breath. Obviously, it was their way of coping and winding down after a stressful situation.

Dane looked up. He looked normal. He looked like the Dane she had first met. A tear escaped as she held back the tide of emotion that welled up inside her. It was over. She had saved Dane. He loved her. With a hand over her mouth, she held back a sob. Dane was there in an instant, folding her into his embrace.

'Annwyn?'

He held her face in his hands and kissed her lips quickly, but his questioning gaze ran all over her face. 'You didn't get your body back. I'm sorry. Rolf says you destroyed her. You killed your own body…I…can't imagine how much courage that must have taken.'

He was upset. It touched her deeply that he was upset on her behalf and that he was mourning the loss of her body for her sake. She smoothed the guilt from his brow, knowing that he would take the blame. He had talked of it many times before.

'Shh. Don't fret. Don't feel sad. I made a conscious choice. I'm comfortable with it. I've been in this body for so long now it feels like mine. It was heart-wrenching killing another being. However, there is a part of Nira in me, too. I can't help that. I'll try to keep her in check. And you?'

She searched his face and saw nothing but wholeness and vibrancy. 'I'm hoping to put the beast in me to good use.' He bit at her neck and growled low in his throat. She found it quite sexy. She drew back though. 'And Rolf, is he okay?'

Dane stepped back and drew her forward. 'See for yourself.'

Rolf looked relaxed, his hazel eyes with citrine flecks

passed over her, appraising. He nodded once. 'I'm sorry,' she said quickly. 'I'm sorry I had to use you to bring Nira here.'

Dane twitched at her side. He wouldn't remember. Silently, she thanked the deities for that.

'She hurt you. I'm sorry.'

Rolf looked away and scoffed. 'Hurt me? So she took control of my mind,' he shrugged. 'She's done that before and it's the worst kind of mind-fuck. I remember what I did—I remember how I hurt you. I'm the one who is sorry.'

Annwyn smiled then. The welts were gone, healed by Dane's wonderful gift. That moment they shared, the baring of their souls and the way they made love would stay with her. She grinned at them both. 'I'm fine now.'

A sensation of pure happiness burst out of her. A little prick from the remnant of Nira made her twitch. With a furrowed brow, she sent a thought to the ghostly sorceress who loitered in the cold, dark places of Annwyn's essence.

'Sorry, Nira. You lost.'

In 2018
Look out for The Changeling Curse
The Cursed Ones Book Two